Charles Hargrove

The Life of Robert Rodolph Suffield

Charles Hargrove

The Life of Robert Rodolph Suffield

ISBN/EAN: 9783742861115

Manufactured in Europe, USA, Canada, Australia, Japa

Cover: Foto ©Andreas Hilbeck / pixelio.de

Manufactured and distributed by brebook publishing software
(www.brebook.com)

Charles Hargrove

The Life of Robert Rodolph Suffield

THE LIFE

OF

ROBERT RODOLPH SUFFIELD.

by Charles Hargrove

> annoso famam qui derogat ævo,
> Qui vates ad vera vocat.
>
> *Lucan, Phars, 9, 359.*

LONDON:

WILLIAMS AND NORGATE,

11, HENRIETTA STREET, COVENT GARDEN;

AND 20, SOUTH FREDERICK STREET, EDINBURGH.

1893.

PREFACE.

THIS life is written by one whose acquaintance with Mr. Suffield began in 1864, when he was the popular and much-loved Dominican missioner, and closed—for the present—only within a few days of his death as a veteran in the ranks of the Unitarian ministry. Whatever be its imperfections, or possible mistakes, it has at least one merit, that which the subject of it would have valued the most—it is truthful. It is neither a panegyric nor a criticism, but the story of a fallible man, who sought to speak the truth as he knew it, and at the same time live in charity with all.

" My personal history," he once wrote, " will explain the mixture of opposing feelings with which I touch the Roman Catholic question, viz., tenderness, gratitude, and love towards Roman Catholics I have personally known and heard of, along with a great dislike and dread of the system." The writer of this memoir trusts that he has carried into effect what would have been Mr. Suffield's wish, and that, painful as the story must prove to his former co-religionists, there will be found in it no word which will hurt the feelings of private friendship or insult the religious convictions of those he left.

But the true story of his change of faith, and his motives and troubles at the time, is best told in his correspondence with Dr. Martineau, who in the sorest trouble gave him invaluable help and encouragement. For the letters which he has kindly contributed, and for leave to publish his own in reply, the sincerest thanks are due not only from the writer, but from all interested in the subject of the memoir.

CONTENTS.

CHAPTER I.

Family and Early Training.

There lived, about a hundred years ago, in the neighbourhood of Norwich, two brothers of the name of Suffield; they came of an old Norfolk family who had suffered for their religion, and were both by inheritance and by conviction, members of the Roman Catholic Church, openly and devoutly adhering to it at a time when all kinds of civil and social penalties weighed upon its professors. At their houses many French emigrant priests found, from time to time, refuge and hospitality.

Of the two brothers, Thomas, the younger, died a bachelor. He was, writes his great-nephew, "a man of singular benevolence," and his will, bearing date 1800, is a confirmation of this family tradition about him. It is not so much the amount left in charity, but the number of institutions and individuals to whom he leaves small legacies, which shows the man's kindly heart, and justifies the opinion entertained of him to the third generation.

Robert, the elder brother, was twice married; first to Anna Bayley, by whom he was connected with the well-known Roman Catholic families of Constable and Maxwell, and after her death to Anastasia D'Arcy, of Clifton Castle, Galway. By the first wife he had two

A

sons and a daughter; by the second two daughters and a son. The descendants of all, so far as can be traced, are now Protestants.

George, the second son, and father of our Robert Rodolph Suffield, was educated at a school for the sons of the Roman Catholic gentry, which had been opened at Battersea, in a house lent for the purpose by the Earl of Shrewsbury. This is said to have been the first school of its kind in England, it having been hitherto the custom for all who could afford it to send their sons abroad.

George Suffield, as a young man, ceased to be a communicant, and adopted the liberal philosophic views prevalent in his time in the more cultured society. Later in life he was an avowed Protestant, and many Roman Catholics joined their prayers with his son, trusting and hoping that the father of so fervent and devoted a priest would at the last repent and be reconciled with the Church of his fathers.

A Catholic nobleman, writing in the year 1863, when for some reason—perhaps the approach of death—special efforts were made to this intent, says, " I will do anything in my power to assist in the conversion of your poor aged father. Your account of him is quite a romantic history, and I feel much interest in him as connected with my family, and also that he had not given up the practice of his religion when at our place sixty years ago. I most fervently pray that your good wishes and hopes may be realised, and that Heaven will kindly listen to the many prayers which will be and are poured forth in his behalf. All my young ones will pray for him. Your poor father is another instance of Catholics whose families, after nobly suffering every persecution for their faith, no sooner do they enjoy a little sunshine and worldly prosperity, than they forget the struggle they have gone through, and give up that which before they would gladly have died for." Which means, that as long as their religion was under a disadvantage, they held by it as under an obligation of honour and chivalry, an obligation from which the removal of Catholic disabilities set them free.

While his sons were under his care he seems to have maintained a philosophic impartiality towards all the creeds, and naturally had special regard for the religious traditions of his family, but, perhaps, equal respect for the Established Church of his country. The Savoy Vicar of Rousseau's story was his model priest, a man who accepted the outward forms of faith and worship which custom imposed upon him, but made use of them only so far as they could be made helpful to the better service of humanity.

He married Susan Tulley Bowen, a Protestant lady, by whom he had two sons—George, born about 1816, and Robert, the subject of our memoir.

George, in time, went to Cambridge, where he took his degree in 1842, having seemingly had no scruples on the question of religion. He stood twenty-eighth on the list of Wranglers, and on migrating to Clare, was elected a Fellow on the foundation of Mr. Borage, reserved to natives of Norwich. This Fellowship is held on condition of taking Orders within seven years, which being unable to do, he resigned in 1850, and died of small-pox in the spring of 1871, shortly after his younger brother's secession from the Roman Church. He was a man of retiring disposition, a vegetarian, fond of mathematics and music, and held in much account in the very few homes in which he was intimate. In 1863 he published a pamphlet on "Synthetic Division in Arithmetic,"* "an ingenious and independent speculation leading to great simplification of certain cases of division," as the *Athenæum* remarks. It is but a few pages in length, but sufficient to show that the writer was a man of some originality of thought, and specially interested in the cause of education. In his preface he calls attention to the curious anomaly that "at the present moment every student at the University is allowed to complete his academic course and take his degree without being required to undergo any University examination in the 'principles' of arithmetic, whilst the Senior Middle Class candidates, boys under eighteen years of age, are expressly required by a grace of the senate to pass an examination in the *principles* as well as the *practise*." In conclusion he commends the example of one college where lately "a separate and searching paper in the theory and practise of arithmetic" had been introduced, and, "ere long," he adds, "the lecturers in every college of the

---

* Synthetic Division in Arithmetic, with some Introductory Remarks on the Period of Circulating Decimals, by George Suffield, M.A., Clare College, Cambridge: Macmillan & Co., 1863.

University will follow an example fraught with incalculable advantage to the mathematical education of the whole country."

George never professed Romanism, and would no doubt have called himself a lay member of the Church of England, though looked upon as singular in his religious views as in other respects. Evidently, from the little we know of him, he was like his brother, an individual, a man who went his own way of life and thought, and had no care to conform either his habits or opinions to the prevailing fashion.

Our Robert Suffield was born at Vevey, on the Lake of Geneva, on the 5th of October, 1821, in the house now occupied as the club, "Cercle du Leman." His father, though a younger son, was in independent circumstances, and at this time in the habit of travelling in England and abroad, taking a furnished house for a year or six months at any place which suited his fancy or convenience. The little son was baptised in the house by one Sebastian Martinez, a lay relative, who was stopping with them at the time. The ceremony would have consisted simply of the pouring of water on the child while repeating the form, "I baptise thee in the name of the Father, and of the Son, and of the Holy Ghost." Probably neither priest nor Anglican clergyman was to be had at Vevey, otherwise it is not clear why resort was had to the services of a layman. Shortly afterwards the family returned, and he was baptised again for legal purposes in his own parish church, St. Peter's, Mancroft, at Norwich (December 27th, 1821).

It was near to this church that the Jerninghams, Suffields, and Bedingfields purchased a site and erected a chapel when the Duke of Norfolk conformed, and in consequence deprived the Norwich Roman Catholics of the use of his private chapel for their services. But the mother would of course have attended her own parish church when in Norwich, and have taken her sons with her. It was their father's principle that "young people should be quite uninfluenced as to religious belief, and that they should select their religion when they arrived at a ripe age." They were consequently brought up in equal regard for the faith of their mother and that which had been their father's, and it was left to each to decide in after years as to whether he would call himself Catholic, Anglican, or Protestant.

Robert never went to school, but accompanied his parents in their travels in England and on the continent. His youthful experiences must have been varied and unusual, for tourists as yet were few, and the provision for their accommodation and progress often of the roughest. "In 1825 a Continental tour consisted chiefly of troublesome and costly incidents with vetturinos, guides, and hotel keepers, road accidents and brigands, real or imaginary."[*] Nor was his father content that his son should be merely a witness or passive companion of their many adventures. He had decided and peculiar views of education, which he adopted, it would seem, from Rousseau, and wished to train his sons to be self-reliant, and independent

---

[*] Mozley's Reminiscences, vol. I., p. 32.

and observant. He objected to their learning by heart, which in after-life they often regretted, and made it his aim to educate them as much by life as by formal lessons. "In pursuance of this idea he sent Rodolph alone, when about fourteen years of age, to make a tour on the Loire, giving him letters of introduction to families known to him living on the route he had drawn up. The boy felt the honour very much, but it was a fearful joy for so young a lad. At one place he attracted the surprised attention of the gendarmes owing to his having very little luggage besides a pistol. In one town where he stayed a fête was taking place, and the municipality gave a ball, sending tickets of invitation to visitors, and great was the pride of the English boy when one arrived for Monsieur Suffield also." So writes one who had the best opportunities of learning all about his early life, and adds, "At Norwich the Suffields were intimate with various well-known Unitarian families, such as the Taylors, Reeves, and Austins; Lucy Austin, afterwards Lady Duff Gordon, was a playmate of Rodolph's, and about the same age."

"But he had a liking for books and pursuits far beyond his age. Tom Paine's 'Age of Reason,' for example. When the family were on a visit to London he interested himself in the Chartist movement, then at its height" (he would be about sixteen at the time), "and was present at meetings, sometimes in obscure neighbourhoods, at which very fiery speeches were made, and threats of violence uttered against the upper classes. Once he was in some danger, for a

man got up and said he saw a little aristocrat among
those present. Some of the audience became angry,
but he was not dismayed, spoke up and said his heart
was with the people, and so reassured, and judging
by the youth of the intruder that he was not there to
spy upon them, he was left unmolested. He doubted
whether his father knew of these little excursions; if
he had done so he would not have interfered, unless
he had judged it absolutely necessary, as his plan was
to allow his sons the greatest independence."

In 1841 he followed his brother to Cambridge,
where he was admitted a Commoner of Peterhouse.
Cambridge was preferred to Oxford because no signature of articles was required for matriculation, but he
attended regularly the College Chapel, and even when
visiting at Sawston Hall, where a Mr. Huddlestone,
an old friend of the family, resided, and had a private
chapel, he writes that he went rather to see his father's
friend than to attend mass.

There can be no doubt that at this time he was
generally regarded as a member of the Church of
England. The present Lord Kelvin, then William
Thomson, who was his class-mate at college, writes
of him :—

"To the best of my knowledge none of us thought
he was a Roman Catholic. We all, I am sure, believed
him to be an earnest, religious student; and probably
we thought him very 'High Church.' He was quite
out of the run of undergraduates, and did not mix
much in their society. He was undoubtedly, to our
young eyes, very eccentric, but he was thoroughly

respected by all. He had, I believe, a very friendly feeling for myself, which I certainly reciprocated. From all I recollect I think it is probably true that he was a sincere and loyal member of the new High Church party of that time, but that he had strong inclinations towards the Roman Catholic Church, without, however, feeling himself to be a member of that Church, and not of the Church of England."

In accord with these impressions of a friend and contemporary is his own recollection. "At Cambridge I was in constant intercourse with the Tractarians and Ecclesiologists, *sharing all their sympathies*, and my kind friend, Archdeacon Thorp, of Trinity, urged me to take Anglican Orders."

But his time at Cambridge was cut short, partly in consequence of losses his father sustained about this time through the failure of some South American investments, in which he was interested through his brother-in-law, William Gregory, a merchant in that country; partly, also, by reason of his own uncertainty as to his religious position, and he left the University after a residence of less than two years, probably about Easter, 1843.

It was through the Dr. Thorp mentioned above that he was recommended to a gentleman who wanted a private tutor for his son. He soon won the affections of this pupil, as, indeed, he did of all the young people he had to do with as teacher, priest, or minister, and they remained intimate friends to the last. It is thus that this gentleman, now well known in the world as a man of wealth and influence, writes of him after a lapse of nearly fifty years:—"I was a very delicate boy, unable to go to school or to share the games of schoolboys. How happy he made my young life—(and the life of the ailing boy is not generally a happy one);—how he devoted himself, not only to such education as I could receive, but from morning to night to make me interested, occupied, and happy. In 1844, instead of being anxious to get rid of his troublesome charge when he went to see his people, he took me with him, and we stayed some time with his father and mother in Norwich. My remembrance of the former is of the most pleasing kind—of course they are only the impressions of a boy of thirteen— but I think of him as a high-bred gentleman of the old school. He was certainly a Freethinker, and never went to church or chapel in those days. The mother was a very kind and affectionate person of the Evangelical school, devoted to her husband in spite of his religious vagaries, which grieved her much."

CHAPTER II.

SEMINARIST AND PRIEST.

It was in 1846 that, to use his own words, he "became a communicant in the Roman Catholic Church." How the change in his religious position was brought about we have no information; he was used to think of himself as having always been a Roman Catholic, but up to that time, like many others, not faithful either in practice or belief to the requirements of the Church, and he repudiated with some warmth the inclusion of his name in a list of "converts to Rome." On the other hand, there is no doubt that he was looked upon as a High Churchman, both at Cambridge and when engaged as a private tutor, and his friend, Archdeacon Thorp, urged him to take Anglican Orders. Roman Catholics, too, who knew him best, seem to have taken a similar view, and an intimate friend and connection of the family, expostulating with him when his letter on Papal Infallibility appeared, writes, "Surely it must be that you have still a little remnant of the old Protestant feeling left," words which, to a man who had never been a Protestant, would be without meaning. And another correspondent of a few months later date, one who urges his right of appeal as "exceptional, seeing that we are bound by early ties of family and the closest friendship, ever treating each other with the most perfect confidence," writes, " On looking back to the early days of your *conversion*, I remember you wrote to me word that your happiness was perfect, save that your imagination had still ' to pay the penalty of having been polluted with every kind of infidel thought and teaching.'" His case was certainly peculiar, and not to be reckoned among the 'perversions' or 'conversions' which were at that time just beginning, and increased so greatly during the next ten years. Sprung of an old Roman Catholic family, inheriting the traditions of a persecuted faith, and numbering among friends and relations many zealous adhérents to it, he was brought up under the combined influence of a free-thinking father and an evangelical mother, taught to read and think for himself, and sent to a University where Anglicanism was the only religion tolerated among the students. So when after many struggles, of which we have caught but hints in letters and conversation, but which explain both the exceptional fervour of his faith as a priest and his later transition to a free religion, he sought rest and surety in the Old Church of his ifathers, he felt as one returning to a home from which he should never have been separated; and, of course, found in the novel sense of certainty and finality the peace and happiness which is the boast of all sincere converts, and which they accept as assurance of the truth of their new-found faith— an assurance which every church may claim, for there is none which does not from time to time win the waverers from other folds, and make them convinced that itself only is the true church.

He was the guest of Dr. Newsham, then President of Ushaw College, near Durham, when he thus openly severed himself from all connection with Anglicanism or Freethought, and "this remarkable man," he wrote, "continued always my kind guide and father-like friend." Indeed, to the very last he always spoke with affection and regard of Ushaw and its principal and professors, and that the same feelings were fully reciprocated on their part, at least, as long as he remained in their communion, we have ample evidence in the warm invitations which from time to time urged him to come and visit them.

It would seem that immediately on his conversion he resolved to embrace the ecclesiastical state, but instead of staying on at Ushaw, and there entering upon the course of theological study, as one would have expected under the circumstances, he for some reason resolved to enter the famous seminary of St. Sulpice, at Paris, and there he remained until driven out by the revolution of 1848. It may, perhaps, have been due to the desire to free himself from the well-meant importunities of his parents and brother, to whom his determination to enter the Roman priesthood was the occasion of great grief. Certainly from this time onwards there was very little, if any, intercourse between them, a matter of great regret to him afterwards. "He never spoke of his honoured parents," one writes, "in his later years, without tears in his eyes, and regretted bitterly the system which had kept them asunder." It has been the painful experience of many a so-called "convert," who having broken the tenderest ties of home to follow what he believed was the call of God, has discovered his mistake too late, and returned when there was no more a home to welcome him! During his father's last illness, in 1868, there were some who were very anxious that the son should see him, and endeavour to bring him back to the faith of his childhood, but he steadfastly refused to interfere, knowing well that argument and persuasion would be alike useless; perhaps, too, his own convictions were not then so strong that he could have successfully upheld the Roman cause against his father's philosophical faith.

At St. Sulpice he had for a fellow-student Père Hyacinthe Loyson, whom years afterwards he met at Dean Stanley's, and was immediately recognised by him. They met again in Paris in 1878, and continued always on terms of mutual respect, notwithstanding the wide difference of opinion which separated them in matters of religion. Still it may perhaps have needed a little forbearance to receive kindly from one who was a rebel against ecclesiastical authority, and could speak only for his single self, such lofty patronage as is apparent probably to everyone but the writer, in the following sentence from a letter written in 1876 :—" Je vous sais honnête et droit, vous avez cherché la vérité à travers des déchirements cruels, vous pouvez la servir efficacement quand vous l'aurez trouvée pleinment," that is to say, when you have accepted just as much and no more than Père Hyacinthe does. But a large experience had made Mr. Suffield very tolerant, and he always entertained a friendly feeling for one with whom he could have but small intellectual sympathy.

On leaving St. Sulpice he went to Ireland, visited the relations of his father's stepmother in Galway, took a pupil for some months, and mixed freely with priests and people. He could not towards the close of his life recall to mind the reason of this year's stay in Ireland; probably being received with sympathy and warmth such as he could not now look for in his English home, and finding himself among relations and co-religionists he stayed longer than he had first purposed. It was during this year that he made his first intimate acquaintance of the Irish, and all his life, as well in the Roman Church as out of it, he never varied in his warm regard for them and sympathy in their aspirations after self-government. It was a common observation with him that the English people didn't understand the Irish, and that from their incapacity to value rightly the ways and words of neighbours so unlike themselves, arose almost all the bitterness and ill-feeling which cloud our relations.

Whatever may have been the motive of this interruption to his theological studies—and one cannot but suspect that some lingering doubt about the faith or his vocation to the priesthood was at the bottom of it—it came to an end after a year's hesitation, and he returned to Ushaw after the summer vacation of 1849, and on the 21st of September following, committed himself to the ecclesiastical state by the reception of the tonsure and four minor orders. On the following day he received the Sub-Diaconate, which carries with it the irrevocable obligations of the priesthood. On the 25th of May, 1850, he was ordained Deacon, and on the 25th of August Bishop Hogarth made him Priest.

From this time began twenty years of unceasing activity on behalf of the faith to which he had at last definitely committed himself. For ten years, as a secular priest, and another ten as a Dominican, he gave himself soul and body to the service of the Church, seeking nothing in return, and receiving only the profound respect and affectionate confidence of multitudes, high and low, who knew his work, and profited of his holy and sensible counsels.

Records of this, the busiest period of his life, are very few, for he himself kept no diary beyond notes of sermons and services, and his subsequent "apostacy," as they call it, has obscured among Roman Catholics the memory of his services. But one who knew him well in later years, and had often heard him speak of his experiences, which he did only to his most intimate friends, writes, " He had a house at Sedgefield and lodgings in a farm house at Thornby, and rode to and fro to visit the scattered dwellings of his parishioners. He lived a very ascetic life, his diet and surroundings being of the plainest description; at one time he tried to live on foods that required no cooking; he slept on the ground, with a wooden pillow for his head, to which he attributed a slight deafness and a delicacy of the throat which continued all his life. I believe it must have been about this time that his health broke down; those around him thought he was in consumption, and some kind friends took him to stay with them and nursed him till he recovered."

After a year's apprenticeship to the work of a parish priest at Sedgefield and Thornley, he was called by his Bishop to join a community of secular priests at St. Ninian's, near Wooller. He was here with Father Chadwick and Father Consitt, both of whom became in time distinguished dignitaries of their Church. These fathers were not confined to parochial duty, but made it their business to give Missions and Retreats throughout the diocese, and after awhile their labours extended to colleges, convents, and parishes in every part of the United Kingdom.

It was towards the close of 1854 that during one of their frequent absences from home their house and library were burnt to the ground, and there followed upon this check the complete breakdown of the two elder fathers and their retirement to chaplaincies, where they sought rest and health. Mr. Suffield continued alone in the same field of labour as ' Apostolic Missionary,' nor did he give up his frequent journeyings even when, in 1858, he accepted charge of a parish in Newcastle.

As his work and fame during these years was that of a successful Missioner, it may be well to stop here to explain to Protestant readers the peculiarly Roman institutions of missions and retreats.

B

A mission is given to a congregation or parish, and is meant for people living in the world, and unable to put aside their daily occupations. They are asked to give what time they can spare each morning and evening for a fortnight to the solemn consideration of the doctrines of their church and the obligations of their state, and so to bring themselves into a fit state for the worthy reception of the sacraments of confession and communion. Here is, *e.g.*, the copy of an announcement of a mission at Leicester :—

"HOLY CROSS, WELLINGTON STREET. — A Holy Mission will be preached in the above Church by Father Suffield. To be solemnly opened on Sunday morning, June 1st, at 11 o'clock, and continue daily for a fortnight. All persons are invited to attend the services.

ORDER OF DAILY SERVICES.

Holy Mass and Mission Sermon -	8.30 a.m.
Catechism - - - - -	3.0 p.m.
Sermon and Benediction of the	
Blessed Sacrament - - -	8.0 p.m.

Confessions heard daily till 10 o'clock, and from 4 to 7.30, and after Evening Service."

The two Sermons and Instruction or Catechism daily for a fortnight might seem sufficient trial of any man's endurance, for though the substance of discourse would be the same everywhere, a mission to be fruitful would need on every occasion the same earnestness and energy, and entire devotion to the subject as if it were fresh to the speaker. There is no carrying about of written essays from place to place, but the

word must be always quick, and come from the soul
of the speaker. But it is not in the pulpit, after all,
that the great work of a mission is done and the
fatigue incurred. It is in the confessional that the
active and successful missioner spends his time from
early morning to late at night, and there reaps his
harvest. And however legitimate be Protestant
objections to the abuses of auricular confession—
abuses, it is only fair to say, most carefully guarded
against by stringent regulations, binding both on
priest and penitent—there can be no doubt that
this rare and exceptional use of it does act in the
interests of peace, honesty, and morality. Many a
feud is terminated, many an illegitimate gain made
amends for, many an evil habit or connection brought
to an end, by the public exhortations of the missioner
applied to the individual conscience in this private
conference, where the one party can speak all his
life freely, trusting to the pledge of secrecy which
is practically never violated, and the other gives
advice, reproof, command, without fear or favour,
as a stranger, coming and going in brief space, and
having nothing to gain or lose from his penitents.
There are, no doubt, always dangers and temptations
about the confessional, but they are reduced to a
minimum in this case, as they are at a maximum
where a parody of the Roman system is attempted
without special training, or episcopal control, or any
but a self-imposed obligation of secrecy, or check on
abuse other than that of the individual conscience.
We may consistently apologise for the practice in

one case, while we have nothing but reprobation for any weak attempts to introduce it into Protestant communities.

It would probably be within the truth to say that, during his twenty years of priesthood, Mr. Suffield spent more time in hearing confessions than in any other occupation, and certainly while employed in giving a mission, the greater part of his day would be so occupied.

"Retreats" are for the spiritual benefit of persons devoted by their calling to the service of religion, and able to set apart a time more completely to meditation and prayer. A full retreat—such as is enjoined on all religious communities, whether of men or women—lasts eight days, during which time a rigid silence is observed, except, perhaps, for half-an-hour after the midday meal. For the parochial clergy the time is necessarily shortened to four or five days. Here is a programme of a Retreat for the Clergy given at the College at Ushaw :—

    6 0.—Rise.

    6 30.—Meditation (one hour). Mass.

    8 0.—Breviary. Retirement.

    9 0.—Breakfast. Recreation.

    9 45.—Visit to the Blessed Sacrament. Way of the Cross.

  10 30.—Retirement. Spiritual Reading.

  11 30.—Instruction in Chapel.

  12 0.—Retirement. Breviary. Examination of Conscience.

    1 30.—Recreation.

2   0.—Visit to the Blessed Sacrament.   Private
        Meditation.

3   5.—Dinner and Recreation.

5   0.—Matins.   Retirement.   Meditation.

8   0.—Rosary. 8-30, 9-15, Prayers. 10-0, Retire.

In this case "meditation" would be conducted in
the chapel, the priest chosen to conduct the Retreat
suggesting the course of it, and, as it were, thinking
and praying aloud for all to join with him in reflection and aspiration — something in the manner of
extempore prayer, as practised in the more cultured
Nonconformist communities of England.

Of the great benefit to be derived from such occasional retirement from the bustle and distractions of
the world, Mr. Suffield remained convinced, long after
he had abandoned and reprobated what he considered the superstitious practices and obligations connected with retreats in the Roman communion. It
was with more candour and generosity than worldly
wisdom that he advocated the introduction of some
such system in the Protestant community he afterwards joined, and it tended to create in some minds
a doubt of his sincerity, as if a man must needs
denounce as evil every custom of the ancient Church
which he had so long served, or himself be under
suspicion as its agent in disguise.

It was while in charge of the Roman Catholic
parish of St. Andrew's, at Newcastle, that he introduced into England the custom of "Peter's Pence."
It was begun by a great meeting in the Newcastle
Town Hall, which was the first occasion on which

Roman Catholic movements attracted general attention from the public and the press, *The Times*, among others, devoting an article to the subject.

About this time, or perhaps while still at St. Ninian's, he was busy promoting among the secular clergy the "Association of St. Charles," which met with the warm approval of Cardinal Wiseman, the Bishop of Southwark (Dr. Grant), Dr. Newman, and other influential and eminent ecclesiastics. The object of the Association was "to promote among us the Apostolic Spirit, recollection, and prayer; thus securing our own salvation, whilst with unwearied zeal we labour and pray for the sanctification of the Priesthood and for the salvation of our people." The rules were few and simple, and did little more than impress anew upon the members what were really obligations, acknowledged by every pious priest,—each year to join the Clergy Retreat, to observe one day each month as "a day of recollection or retreat, to renew fervour, and to prepare for death," to give daily a half-hour to meditation, and find the time for spiritual reading and the examination of conscience. It is not surprising that only the more fervent priests were disposed to join, but it is remarkable how in this case, as generally, the attempt to quicken zeal and piety, met with dislike and opposition. At least, so we may infer from a letter on the subject from one priest, who writes wishing to become a member:—"An attempt to form an association of a similar character was made here about a year since, but had, for various reasons, to be abandoned. One thing we discovered during the very short time that we entertained the idea of such an association — that the greatest prudence and caution, and even the strictest secresy, were absolutely necessary for its successful starting. I could never have thought it possible for priests to speak of it as I have heard many speak to whom the knowledge of what we were attempting had come."

But priests, though Protestant controversialists are apt to forget it, are simply so many men, of whom the majority are of just average spirituality and morals, and by no means grateful to the troublesome zealots who seek to stir them up to nobler life and fatiguing efforts after perfection.

Although so much taken up with outside work, he was very successful and popular in his own parish, and raised considerable sums of money with an ease which in later years astonished himself. It went as freely as it came, and alms were always to be had at the Presbytery by poor parishioners in distress. He also built a church at Walker, in the suburbs, and at the same time began a work of more durable influence, the "Crown of Jesus," a complete manual of Roman Catholic piety for the people. This book, which secured the approval of English and Irish Bishops, and later of the Pope himself, passed through many editions, and was immensely popular among English-speaking Roman Catholics. Its circulation went on for several years after the author's secession, (it was published anonymously, though there was no kind of secret about the authorship), and it was only after the book had been put in evidence by the High Church Anglican party at the Ridsdale trial at Lambeth Palace, and its authorship was brought into public notice, that it became discredited, and when the publisher, Richardson, of Derby, died, it ceased to be reprinted.

The book did not make its appearance till after the compiler had joined the Dominicans, but it belongs really to this time of his Newcastle work as parish priest, and the authorities of the Order, though allowing him to publish it, took upon themselves no responsibility for it, pecuniary or otherwise. This will, therefore, be the most fitting place for a short notice of it.

The volume is a small octavo of 800 pages, the greater part closely printed in small type, about 40 lines to a page. It was intended to contain everything which the Roman Catholic was bound by his Church to believe and do in the way of devotion, and the much more which the devout might find it of profit to know in the way of doctrine, or to add to their accustomed prayers. The first part begins with "the Sacrament of Penance," how to prepare for, and how to make, "a good confession," and the three essential conditions—contrition, confession, satisfaction—are explained. Of the first of these it may be well to quote the definition, as it is important for all to know what really is implied in the practice common to so large a part of Christendom, and it explains, too, how Mr. Suffield could labour so long and earnestly in this particular work. "Contrition," he writes, "is a great and sincere sorrow for having offended God, accompanied with a firm resolution to avoid for the future all sin and the occasions of sin, to adopt the means necessary for perseverance, and to repair the injury done by your sins." Certainly he will not have lived in vain, however mistaken his creed, who has, by preaching and prayer, brought many of his brethren to such a state of mind. Confession may be needless and perilous, absolution a mere superstition, but this, the necessary disposition for them, is what all who believe in a moral law will approve.

Then follows the "Rule of Life" recommended to those who, by penitence, have entered on the right way; and the rest of this section is taken up with what is to a Roman Catholic the supreme act of religion and sovereign means of grace, namely, the Sacrifice of the Mass and Holy Communion. The "Ordinary of the Mass" is given in Latin and English, and then follow various methods for adults and children to assist at it with profit.

The Second Part consists of a great variety of "devotions" or special prayers and litanies, such as the Stations of the Cross, the Rosary, the Little Office of the Virgin, Litanies of St. Joseph, St. Dominic, St. Patrick, &c., Prayers to St. Benedict, St. Charles, St. Aloysius, and other Saints.

The Third Part contains the Services of Vespers and Compline, Meditations for every day of the month, a selection of passages from the Scriptures, the Epistles and Gospels for all the Sundays of the year, and a Catechism of Christian Doctrine.

There is not in our language so full and complete a manual of Roman piety, and as one turns its pages the words of the greatest of modern converts come forcibly to mind; he is speaking of one who had had some experience of Rome and her ways and thoughts, and was hesitating, as he himself hesitated so long. "He was very strong on the point that Romanism and Anglicanism were two religions; that you could not amalgamate them; that you might be Roman or Anglican, but could not be Anglo-Roman or Anglo-Catholic; *that the whole system of worship in the Romish Church was different from what it is in our own; nay, the very idea of worship, the idea of prayers.*"* They only can know how different who have had some experience of both systems, but an half-hour spent in the study of the "Crown of Jesus" should convince any Anglican, however "High," that the difference between himself and the Methodist was a narrower gulf than that which divided him from Rome.

It would be vain to search in this book for any symptoms of doubt, or even of disposition towards a more or less tolerated liberalism. As long as he was in the Church's livery he was an honest and faithful servant, and if he had as yet any difficulty, and there is reason to suppose that he always felt such, he kept the struggle secret within his own breast.

---

* "Loss and Gain," by J. H. Newman, p. 168.   Ed. 1848.

But how awful a view of life it is if ever a man comes to realise the meaning of words, which these words, just a footnote, describe :—

"It is an ascertained fact, that each day about eighty thousand persons die—eighty thousand souls are judged, and receive their sentence for eternity. Without true contrition none of these can be saved from hell."

And when we turn to the meditation on hell, we read, "How great would be our horror of the shrieks of the damned, if their groans and blasphemies could reach us. The sentence of their condemnation is irrevocable. Hell is the dismal and eternal tomb of souls, the cruel kingdom of Satan." Then follows, "Make an act of faith upon the eternal duration of the pains of hell. *We must believe on God's word what we are not able to conceive.*"

Do these words convey his own difficulty of faith? Certainly they show that he did not find it so easy of explanation as some deem it. "We must believe," that is all that he dare urge, and the shrieks and curses of that kingdom, augmented by its thousands a minute, went to his heart as a real and terrible thing, till at last reason and conscience asserted their lost supremacy, and in God's name he renounced and denied the blasphemy.

CHAPTER III.

Meanwhile this work, on which he must have been busily engaged during the last months of his secular priesthood, was perhaps itself instrumental in drawing him towards what he considered to be a higher and safer life. Hitherto he had been employed far and wide as a preacher, returning to his presbytery only for the rest of somewhat different labour. Now there had lately been revived in England an ancient Order, designed by its founder expressly for this kind of work and life, and so called the Order of Friar Preachers, otherwise Dominicans, or from the black cloak worn by them out of doors over their white habit, the Black Friars. They had convents in all the chief towns of England, but from the time of the dissolution of monasteries had only survived as solitary missionaries in charge of parishes, not distinguished from secular priests except in owing obedience to the General of the Order at Rome, instead of to the bishop, and by some minor peculiarities of ritual. But they shared in the influences of the Catholic revival of the mid-century, and some time in the fifties a convent had been erected for them by a wealthy convert on his estate at Woodchester. Novices had been attracted, and the regular observance had been started in its severest form. No meat was permitted except to the sick; during seven months of the year there was but one full meal a day, the apology for breakfast consisting of two ounces of dry bread with tea, and the supper of eight ounces of some kind of pottage. At midnight all rose to matins, and the day was spent in study, meditation, and frequent attendance at church. The only break in this monotonous round of labour and prayers was the hour's recreation after dinner, and perhaps half-an-hour after supper. Moreover, scrupulous obedience regulated every act of life, and none even of the elders might go out or engage in any occupation without the sanction of the Superior, who was himself in turn bound by vow to submit his will to those in authority over him.

It might seem that such a life would be simply repellant to a man who was his own master, and could take his ease if so inclined. But it would argue ignorance of history and of human nature to so judge. Men and women alike have always been won upon by austerity, and convents have been invariably crowded in their days of strictest observance, and deserted when they grew lax. So it was that many youths and adults entered the noviciate at Woodchester, and among others this well-known priest and missioner, now in his forty-first year, who, it may be well imagined, was received with no little hope and thankfulness as a recruit to the Order. He left Newcastle in July, 1860, and went to reside at Woodchester, but was prevented receiving

immediately the habit of the Order, by the impedi-
ment of a vow made when he joined the Fathers at
St. Ninian's to serve the mission under the Bishop
of the Diocese.

It was on September 21st following that he was
"clothed," as they say, exchanging the black cassock, which he had hitherto worn, for the white
habit which St. Dominick had adopted six hundred
and fifty years before from the Canons of St. Augustine.

It is usual in "entering religion" to take another
name instead of that associated with former life in
the world, and so he chose for himself the name
Rodolph, by which he became generally known henceforth among Roman Catholics, and which he retained,
together with his baptismal name Robert, to the
end of his life. Rodolph of Faenza, after whom he
desired to be called, was one of the first companions
of St. Dominick, and he was attracted to him by the
likeness of their circumstances, the one in the twelfth
century giving up his church at Bologna, the other in
the nineteenth his at Newcastle, both for the foundation of a Dominican convent.

And now began a year which must have been a
singular and grateful contrast to the ten which he
had passed since his ordination in incessant and
exciting labour among the people. By the Constitution of the Council of Trent for the remedy of
abuses which had before prevailed in monasteries,
it is ordered that no one can be admitted as a
member of any Religious Order, nor take the vows
which bind him to it, before he has completed his

sixteenth year, and has, moreover, whatever his age, passed a complete year as a novice on trial, practising all the rules of the Order, and humbling himself in entire obedience to his superiors. During this year he may not sleep one night away from his convent on any pretext however grave, but must persevere in an uninterrupted trial of his patience, perseverance, humility, and bodily capacity of endurance.

The only relaxation made in his favour was the permission given him to continue his work on "The Crown of Jesus," and see it through the press, which no doubt did relieve the monotony of the very regular and quiet life of the simple novitiate, devoted by the rule to exercises of piety, interrupted by no studies except of the Constitutions of the Order and the Plain Chant used in the Offices of the Church.

On September 21st, 1861, having completed his full year of novitiate, he made his vows into the hands of the Prior, Father Gonin, a convert of Lacordaire's, and afterwards Archbishop of Trinidad. The form of vow taken by Dominicans is one of simple obedience to the General of the Order for the time being, and his successors (quod ero obediens tibi tuisque successoribus usque ad mortem), but it is fully understood that this implies and carries with it the obligations of perpetual celibacy and poverty. So that, according to Roman Catholic law, a "professed religious" cannot marry, though he may, of course, go through the form of marriage, and cannot possess anything as his private property, though he may maintain immoral and sacrilegious hold of worldly goods.

As long as he remained a believer in the Church and its doctrine of the higher life, he faithfully observed the obligations he had voluntarily taken upon himself; nor was any charge to the contrary ever made against him. But when later he came to think himself mistaken in so submitting his judgment and conduct to the guidance of an external authority, he had no hesitation in holding that he was absolved from a vow taken under a false impression. He was told, and had believed, that a life of self-abnegation, single, poor, subjected to another's will, was pleasing to God and the way of perfection, and, not content with good, desirous of better and the very best, he had chosen and bound himself to such a life. When it had become to him morally false and impossible, its superiority a mistake, and its observance a folly, then he cast away from him the strait waistcoat which he had sworn to wear all his days, under the delusion that it was a royal robe, and distinctive of the favourites of God.

Indeed, the primary and only explicit vow of obedience became in his new frame of mind almost an absurdity. How was it possible to revolt from the authority of the whole Church as a usurpation of individual rights, and at the same time submit to the orders of one of its chief servants? A man cannot be at the same time a Romanist and a Rationalist, nor could he by any strain of conscience be a Dominican and a Unitarian.

Immediately after taking the vows he was sent back to Newcastle, which he had quitted the year before as the Rev. Robert Suffield, and to which he now returned, in new dress and new name, as Father Rodolph; but presently he was summoned to London, where Cardinal Wiseman was anxious to have a convent of the Order, and there lodged with two other Fathers in a private house in Fortress Terrace, Kentish Town, while the site at present occupied by the fine monastic buildings in Maitland Road, Haverstock Hill, was being negotiated for.

Here he remained for over two years engaged in parochial duties, when not absent, as he very often was, giving missions and retreats throughout the United Kingdom. His life, indeed, was much that of a Preacher, and very little that of a Friar, and when the General of the Order, Father Jandel, a disciple of Lacordaire and a devotee of strict observance, came to England on a visitation of the province in the summer of 1863, he recalled Father Rodolph to Woodchester, the only one of the five or six Dominican communities where there were the means of following out in its entirety the monastic discipline. He accordingly returned there in September, and was, at his own request, made Parish Priest, Master of the Lay Brothers, and Guest Master.

Here he remained for the next four years, but the convent must have been rather his head-quarters than his residence, if his mission engagements were as numerous as they were the latter half of 1866.

Here is the list, copied from a half-sheet of paper, in which they are put down, with alterations and corrections in his own hand:—

C

Teignmouth	...	August 26th to September 2nd.
Llanarth ...	...	Sept. 8th (or 9th) to 13th (or 16th).
Peterborough	...	Sept. (various dates put down and erased) to October 4th.
Tadcaster ...	...	October 7th to October 14th.
Everingham	...	October 21st to November 4th.
Devizes ...	...	November 11th to November 18th.
Great Marlow ...		November 25th to December 9th.
Manchester	...	December 16th to 30th.

It was during these years at Woodchester that he instituted " Our Lady's Guard of Honour," or " Perpetual Rosary," and enrolled many thousands as Associates, all of whom looked to him as their chief. This devotion is one of many, founded on the sentiment which has prevailed so much in recent times among certain Protestant Churches, as well as among Roman Catholics, that the forces of prayer can be economised and made of greater efficacy by skilful organisation. The idea of the " Perpetual Rosary " is to maintain the recitation of the Rosary uninterruptedly, day and night, all the year round. Each Associate selects his own day and hour, and undertakes to devote it to praying, after this ancient form, for the Conversion of Sinners, the Salvation of the Dying, and the Souls in Purgatory. He makes known his choice by letter to the " Father Director " at Woodchester, and his name is enrolled in the register kept for that purpose.*

---

* It may be well to explain that the full Rosary consists of one hundred and fifty beads strung together, and divided into tens by fifteen larger beads. On the large beads the Lord's Prayer is said, and the Angelic Salutation on each of the smaller ones;

In 1867 he was sent to take charge of the Mission Station at Little Hampton, but seems to have had but little more than a nominal appointment, his services being in continually greater request throughout the country.

The following sketch from the pen of a well-known Irish politician will be read with interest as a personal experience of his work at this time. The writer was unknown to Mr. Suffield till several years later, when they met on a political platform, the one being the chief speaker of the evening, and the "Father Bernard" of the article taking the chair.

"FRIAR AND PARSON."

"At a school in Ireland, wherein I spent some of my earliest and most miserable days, the year was begun by what is called among Roman Catholics—and, I believe, of recent times among Anglo-Catholics—a Retreat. The season of Retreat, as the word implies, is a period during which the penitent—to those who believe in Retreats, all human beings are or ought to be penitents—retires into himself from the world without. Accordingly he does not utter a word to any being except his confessor. He reads no books but those of a religious character; he attends several religious services during the day, and his mind is supposed to be wholly absorbed in meditation over

while fingers and lips are thus employed, the devout reciter meditates on the "Mysteries of Redemption," as they are called, beginning with the Annunciation, and ending with the Coronation of the Virgin, devoting the time occupied in repeating ten Hail Marys to each mystery. But generally a string of fifty beads is used for convenience sake, and does service three times over for the entire recitation.

spiritual things—the enormity of his sins, the certainty of death, and, after death, of judgment; the
delights of heaven, but still more the torments of
hell. At this moment the picture of our playground
during times of Retreat is as clear as though I had
seen it but yesterday. I was once much impressed
by a photograph, seen under the stereoscope, of a
street in Paris during the siege. The shops were
open, the cab stood as usual in the thoroughfare,
and there were men and women apparently engaged
in life's ordinary occupations. But the stillness in
those streets where there had been noise, the repose
in that city of pleasure where passions had raged,
and the deathlike lethargy which had succeeded to
the hurried activity of the vivid Frenchman, threw
over the picture an air of unreality. Not unlike this
looked our playground during Retreat. There were
the cricket-ground, and the trapeze, and the long
pole, as usual, stretched mast-like towards the sky;
but unused, untouched, they seemed the memories of
a dead past. There, too, were the eighty boys, still
full of youth's hotly-rushing blood; but, entombed
in silence, and walking each by himself, they could
scarcely pass for the same lads who, a day or two
before, chattered and shouted, ran after the cricket-
ball and mounted the trapeze, hung in affection on
each other's arms, or waged bloody warfare on hostile
noses. There was nothing to relieve the monotony
of the sad time. The Retreat was with us, indeed,
a time of prayer and humiliation, and we felt as
happy when it was past as the released convict on

his first day of freedom. As a rule, too, these days of meditation left little impression behind. Father Chester, the Jesuit, who preached one Retreat, we only remembered as very thin; Father Zerbini, the Italian, was a blank, save that he used strange words; and the Abbé Lemoinne was only remembered by his terrible story of the wicked boy whom the yawning earth one day swallowed.

"But one year a strange change came over the school; and there was a Retreat such as never had been known before. The summons of the church bell was no longer like the toll to a funeral; the visit to chapel ceased to be the hour of darkest misery; the close of the Retreat brought with it some pangs; for this was the occasion when Father Bernard—that wasn't his name—was the preacher. The influence this man gained over the school was wonderful. He could make us at will laugh or weep, or rise to the height of enthusiastic belief; so that after a short time we looked forward to the visit to the gloomy little chapel as the bright break in the dark day. Then, in individual intercourse, he spoke to each boy as though he were his only son; he appealed not so much to dread of hell as hope of heaven, love for an all-good Father, veneration for a Mother that had ever been pure. Those were stirring times, when the Garibaldians were attacking Rome, and how our hearts throbbed as he told us of the Irish Brigade that had gone to do battle for the Pope !

"Father Bernard usually remained seated while he

preached to us, so that we felt as if listening to a
kind friend who wanted to chat to us. But a moment
came when he wouid rise to his feet; his kind eyes
grew bright, his small and slight figure became
majestic, and there rushed out a torrent of picturesque description by which we were swept away
until hearts throbbed and eyes grew dim. To this
day I hear in my ears his parable of the young
man who sailed on over smiling and placid water,
under a blue sky, and, in spite of the loud warnings
from shore, to the all-devouring cataract beyond.
At last came the Sunday on which the Retreat
ended; and even in that small, shabby chapel the
Church of Rome was able to solemnise a service
which could move the heart and awe the imagination. On the altar were tall candelabra, reserved
for great occasions; a score of candles were alight,
and clouds of incense floated in the air. I see before
me now the diminutive figure of Father Bernard
standing out from this brilliant background. Gor-
geous vestments partly hide the plain white flannel
of his friar's habit; his face bears the marks of
fatigue from long fasting and the lengthened service,
and tbe words that restore to us speech and freedom
and joy sound to our ears rather as the sobbing
farewell of parting friends.

"And so Father Bernard left us; but his influence
remained behind. For many a week after he had
gone there was a soberer tone in the minds of the
boys, better thoughts, more frequent confessions.
And his power was far more prolonged than this.

Whenever a boy of St. Mary's met another in after years, one of his first questions was sure to be, 'Where is Father Bernard?' and then his stories were retold and his sermons repreached. To many he was the one oasis fn the desert of spiritual advisers. Amid the long array of cruel clerical taskmasters, or gloomy fanatics, or worldly-minded canters, he was the single priest whose sympathy might soothe sorrow, whose aid might help wrestling faith.

" Some fourteen or fifteen years after Father Bernard's Retreat, one of the boys on whom he had made the deepest impression was passing along the Strand. It was a drear night in October, when the slight fog that precedes the heavier affliction of a later season had spread over the town. Beneath that melancholy pall there are few minds that can preserve a cheerful mood, for it is the warning that the heat, the light, the bright mornings and the long evenings have fled before the approach of gloom and frost and fog. He of whom I speak had nothing to do in shape of work, and pleasure did not attract; and so, listlessly and for want of any other distraction, he sauntered into a chapel. There was little therein to rouse or to cheer. The place was plain, as he thought, to ugliness, and cold to chilliness. For an altar or a pulpit there was an ordinary reading-desk. The seats were painted in a common-place colour; and the place generally looked rather like the lecture-room of a medical school than a spot where men came to worship. The congregation, too, was sparse and mostly feminine, and highly uninteresting. Presently the preacher of the evening appeared, and with a quietness of manner and of language that suited the tranquil surroundings, declared the Bible a myth and the Church of Rome a fraud. It was he whom I had known as Father Bernard that thus spoke. The Roman Catholic friar had been transformed into the Unitarian minister." *

Indeed, to those who knew Mr. Suffield only as the quiet preacher of a rational faith, who appealed to men just to hear and judge for themselves, whether or not what he had to urge approved itself to their judgment and conscience, to those who listened to him, Sunday by Sunday, as their Unitarian minister, it must be inconceivable how powerful and popular and attractive he was as the Dominican missionary, urging in the name of his infallible Church, truths which none might doubt of without peril of his soul. He was everywhere sought after and everywhere successful, if success be judged by the numbers who were drawn to hear him and trusted to him for their guidance in the way of salvation.

"When giving missions he led a most arduous life; so many people flocked to the confessional that he had barely time for rest and food. He generally stayed with the principal Roman Catholic families in the neighbourhood, and if the Church was on their estate, as was often the case, he rarely went outside the grounds. When travelling he always took with him a desk and writing materials, and

---

* C.P.—In *Weekly Despatch* of December 21st, 1879.

utilised his spare moments by writing his letters in the waiting-rooms. The appointments of his houses were the plainest possible, yet he was never without visitors, and good people of wealth and position thought it a favour to be asked to spend two or three days with him to confer on religious matters, and never gave a thought to the bare simplicity of his household arrangements. Presents of game and fruit were frequent, but everything else was of the plainest possible description. He never asked for money, but had large sums often entrusted to him for charitable purposes."

So writes one who often heard him speak in his simple way, without a thought of boasting, of his earlier life, and the witness is fully confirmed by the numerous letters belonging mostly to this time, which he has left behind, many stamped with the coronets of the highest Roman Catholic nobility of England, and many, ill-spelt and scarcely decipherable, from the poorest and most ignorant. Idle schoolboys and young ladies of high family, noble matrons and men eminent by name and office, dignitaries and novices, poor working men and women, all write in the same tone of the most loving confidence. Indeed, those only who have themselves had experience of it can understand how intimate and affectionate is the tie which in the Roman Church unites the "Director" and the soul which has committed to him its guidance. The 'confessor' has to be taken as he is found, and often there is no choice available, but the Director is one selected because believed to be the best adapted to help the soul God-ward, and can be communicated with by letter as if he were on the spot. Mr. Suffield had a great dislike to the system as developed by the Jesuits, but he must have had it forced upon him, as a necessary consequence of preaching obedience, submission of the will and judgment, and self-abnegation, as the highest virtues. It is the perfection of the Jesuit novice to be "as a staff" in the hand of his Superior, and even persons living in the world might aim at some distant approach towards a like merit. Between Jesuit and Dominican the question could be only of degree, for both were bound to the same standard of faith and morals.

To this time, the February of 1868, belongs the lecture, delivered at West Hartlepool, to a mixed audience of English and Irish Protestants and Catholics, and published "permissu superiorum," as is stated on the title page, a permission which does credit to the courage of Superiors, so largely dependent for the support of themselves and their subjects on an aristocracy to many of whom its sentiments were obnoxious. Writing of it in a letter to an intimate correspondent, to whom he sends a copy, he says, "This is the formidable and obnoxious document. I am sorry your uncle and Lord L. are so angry about it. F. got it read to the Queen by, I think, Lady C."*

---

* It will be found reprinted in this volume.

CHAPTER IV.

The Beginnings of Doubt.

But other and graver differences from the views commonly accepted by those among whom he lived, and who looked up to him as an authority in religion and morals, were now pressing upon his mind. The impression made by many passing hints in his correspondence is that he never held the Roman faith with the easy assurance of those who wondered and shuddered at his "apostacy." He had written in "The Crown of Jesus" of "the unbounded faith with which your utmost soul cleaves to those sacred truths which are the heritage of the Church. Out of the Catholic Church an act of faith is impossible; there can be only the glimmering light of human reason speculating with a painful earnestness to put together a body of truth; and when the edifice has been reared, even amidst labour, prayer, time, and anxiety, there is nothing in it of stable, nothing which may not be upset by others working with equal earnestness and sincerity."

But this "unbounded faith" is not unfrequently supported only by "a painful earnestness," more painful far than is the honest seeking after truth, even with a full consciousness of the difficulty of the quest. And during the two or three last years of his priesthood, certainly—if not long before—he was in this most trying position, believing still by force of will, even while his reason revolted under the heavy yoke.

So, perhaps, it might have gone on all his life, the sore trial of his faith remaining unknown and unsuspected of any but those to whom he confided the secrets of his soul for the purpose of spiritual direction; but about this time the question of Papal infallibility began to be mooted throughout the Catholic world, the Ultramontane party in the Church pressing for its definition, so that it should be no longer a pious belief, but a part of that accepted faith of Christendom, which "except a man believe faithfully he cannot be saved." Many there were who had, in a general way, accepted it as long as it was not obligatory, who now began to be anxious and frightened when it was proposed to define its limits, and make it a dogma of the Church. Mr. Suffield himself had expressed the commonly received opinion when he wrote,* "The Pope is 'os Ecclesiæ,' the mouth of the Church. Through him speaks the mystic body of Christ; when the Pope, acting as the Supreme Pontiff of the Universal Church, proclaims to the world doctrine or decisions on faith or morals, he is infallible. Acting in his private capacity he can err in morals or in judgment; but *when summoning around him his doctors, inaugurating solemn prayers, consulting his sacred congregations*, he shows that he acts as the master and teacher of all; then his

---

* "Crown of Jesus," page 499. Italics are ours.

decisions in faith and morals are overruled by Divine Providence to be ever faithful and true." There is no doubt that every word here was carefully considered, and full force was intended to be given to those which limited this claim of infallibility, as well as to the reason given for it. The Pope is infallible, he would say, because he is head and mouthpiece of the infallible Church; but therefore only infallible when by openly associating himself with, and taking advice of, the acknowledged authorities of the Church, he shows that he is acting for and with the Church. This is certainly not identical with the decree of the Vatican Council, in which mention of assistance sought or given is expressly withheld, and the conclusion is added that the definitions of the Pope are " irreformabiles," incapable of amendment, not because the Church gives assent to them, but from their own inherent force, "ex sese, non autem ex consensu Ecclesiæ."

But it will be best to give his own account of the origin of the struggle which ended in his taking a step which he would have himself regarded with horror before the controversy on infallibility arose.

" My Roman Catholic ecclesiastical life was one of great peace and happiness, accepting, as I did, everything on the authority of the Church — an authority which I deemed it wrong to question — I was content. But when the seat and mode of that authority became a moot question during the years previous to the Vatican Council, reading both sides of the question in Roman Catholic works, the gravest doubts arose in my mind, it becoming clear to me that the claim to infallibility was equally false in any of the received theories. Many minds became anxious, some were determinsd not to investigate or think, others were, by the circumstances of their position, more or less reluctantly compelled to investigate and think. I was amongst the latter class; doubts arose, and were again earnestly banished amidst unceasing work in missions, in preaching, and in the confessional; still they kept forcing themselves before my mind. In accordance with the sad teaching of ecclesiastical theology, I regarded these doubts, not as the noble utterances of the intelligence, but as temptations to be suppressed. I tried to remove them by reading, by occupation, and by prayer."

And to these the private and personal remedies always recommended, and so often, it must be confessed, efficacious against doubt, he added what the Church prescribes for all manner of temptations—the full revelation of his state of mind to a wise confessor. Indeed, he consulted three, and, as in duty bound, kept the matter secret from everybody else. One of these told him that his "position was too prominent, that it fostered pride, and from pride came the temptation." His position was prominent, indeed, more so, perhaps, than that of any priest in England. but the temptations of such position are surely rather to insincerity and affectation of belief, and suppression of any thought which might gender distrust, than they are to dig about and undermine the very foundations on which it all rests. So certainly he felt, and his comment on this commonplace of religious teachers is—" It often happens that those accused of pride are, in fact, but the victims of disappointment. What so sad as to give your mind and energy to a service, and to begin to suspect that the service is an illusion ? "

"However," he goes on, "I asked leave to resign all public offices. Worried, anxious, and, in consequence, in bad health, I was glad to be allowed to withdraw to a little mission in a country village, and here I continued two years, only going away when the calls of duty or of friendship rendered absence imperative ; all the time I kept hoping that I might yet be able conscientiously to settle down in peaceful belief. Amidst peasants and village children and country scenes I strove to forget the present, and to fortify my faith by the theologies of the past."

" Many a long evening have I sat in my garden at Bosworth, when a nightingale's song was the only voice to be heard, and prayed that I might die ere the illusion I had lived in and devoted my life to, had utterly passed away."

Husbands Bosworth is a small village on the railway between Leicester and Rugby. The Hall was the seat of Mr. Fortescue Turville, and attached to it was a priest's house and garden, which Mr. Suffield christened "The Hermitage," and a small chapel in a " very wretched " condition, according to the account of the Bishop of the Diocese, the owner delaying the rebuilding of it till his return from Canada, where

he had gone in the suite of Sir John Young, the
Governor-General. There had been great difficulty
experienced in obtaining the services of a resident
priest, and the mission had been served for some
time by the Dominican Fathers from their convent
at Leicester. But this arrangement had for some
reason come to an end, about a year and a half
before this time, and the temporary tenants of the
hall pressing for a resident priest, application was
made to Mr. Suffield, on the chance of his knowing
"some Dominican, an invalid, or requiring rest and
country air, who might be permitted to be there
for a time." This was on the 15th of August, 1868,
just at the critical time when he was feeling the
need of quiet retirement, and it must have come
to him as a special providence opening out the way
for him, when he was straitened both in mind and
health, and knew not where to turn. But he had
certain engagements to fulfil before he might take
time for his own thoughts; and having given promised Retreats to the nuns of Stone and Wigton,
he concluded these years of his active mission-life
with the Cistercian Monks of Mount St. Bernard,
in Leicestershire. The strict observance was maintained at this abbey, as near as possible, on the lines
laid down by the great saint who instituted the Order,
and a letter from the abbot about the details of the
Retreat gives, for the purpose of arranging the hours
for the three daily discourses, a table of "The Winter
Exercises of the Choir," which will be read with
interest. It is strange to reflect how, in the midst

of this railway-traversed England, mid the activity
and advancement and intense life of this nineteenth
century, there survives still the twelfth century, here
and there finding shelter for its faith and ways of
thought and religious observances and dress and manners in secluded convent-homes, among men and women
whose earnestness and consistency all must admire,
however mistaken they deem them. And, after all,
surely it is for the good of the community that there
should be actual experiment made in our age too, of
all plans for the elevation of human life above the
material conditions which ever tend to degrade it.
If the result be failure, that, too, is so much profit,
at least as evidence that in our circumstances this
or that scheme of Saint or Socialist is unavailing,
and no time and means and energy to be wasted
in the effort to restore it. Here, then, is the order
of life observed in winter time by the brethren of
the choir in this Leicestershire monastery :—

2 0 a.m.	—Rise. Little Office. Meditation.
3 0 ,,	—Matins and Lauds. Angelus. Interval.
5 30 ,,	—Prime. Community meet in Chapter. Interval.
8 0 ,,	—Tierce. High Mass. Work.
11 30 ,,	—Sext. Examination of Conscience. Angelus. Work.
2 0 p.m.	—None. Dinner. Interval.
4 15 ,,	—Vespers. Meditation. Interval.
6 0 ,,	—Spiritual Reading.
6 15 ,,	— Compline. Angelus. Examination of Conscience.
7 0 ,,	—Repose.

D

It will be observed that there is provision made for only one meal in the course of the day; in the summer time there would be an hour allotted for supper; but all the monastic orders observe a strict fast from the 15th of September, the feast of "The Exaltation of the Cross," till Easter, and, in addition to the midday meal of fish and vegetables and bread, only a mere pittance is allowed morning and evening.

It was in this austere retreat of mediæval piety that he closed his active life in the Church's service, and hence passed to his secluded country home, where he was for two years to maintain within his own soul an unequal and unsuspected warfare, striving to fortify old faith against modern arguments, and subdue reason to the service of sentiment.

"The illusion" was sublime and sweet, as those only know who have lived under its spell and yielded themselves soul and body to its influence, and to die while yet it lasted seemed to him preferable far to the cold, stern realities of common life—life without angels, without sacraments, without a Queen and Mother in heaven to love and be loyal to, without a Divine Church militant on earth to serve and witness for. And he prayed for death, and lived for many years to thank God that his prayer had been left unheeded, and that he had been spared to learn that the ordinary life of men is better than dreamland, and the service of humanity diviner than service of any church.

May it not be that we shall all, in the clearer vision of a higher life, find like reason to bless God that many a longing desire of our hearts was never gratified, that many a certain seeming good, earnestly sought by us, was always denied?

It was on Saturday, the 10th of October, 1868, that he arrived at Bosworth. He took duty on the following day, and every Sunday in succession for more than a year. Indeed, his diary gives no indication of absence from this quiet home, except for a four days' Retreat in Holy Week given at the Birmingham Oratory, till September 14th, when he preached at the laying of the foundation stone of the new Dominican Church at Newcastle. Thence he went to join the Annual Retreat of the Friars at Woodchester. His last missions were at Chelsea, from January 9th to 25th, and Southport, January 30th to February 15th.

One would suspect that about this time he made a last desperate effort to regain his hold upon the Church; as one learning to swim is frightened, when for the first time he gets out of his depth, and instinctively makes for the shore, and feels with satisfaction the stones beneath him, though they be rough and sharp, so does it often happen when we begin to doubt about a faith we have long held for solid certainty; we dare first to read and think and enquire, all the time believing still, till some day comes the sudden discovery that faith is gone, and frightened we grasp some friendly argument which offers itself, and get back again, and tell ourselves we are still safe—a little while.

Such seems to have been his state of mind during

this little spell of mission work, and a report of the Chelsea Mission from the *Westminster Gazette* confirms this supposition. We see in the light of after events how he was striving with doubt while he preached faith, and conceding the utmost to save what was essential.

"The holy mission, held by the Dominican Fathers at the church of St. Mary, Chelsea, was brought to a close on Sunday last.* . . . . Father Suffield is a preacher of great power, and made a great impression on his hearers. The sight of the striking figure of the preacher, in the black and white robes of his Order, standing on a raised platform in the dim twilight of a winter's afternoon, and exhorting his hearers to listen to the voice of God, and to return to him the joy of their youth, could not fail to impress anyone at all amenable to religious influences. His sermon on Purgatory, on the Friday before the close, was a very able one, and, without being controversial, was likely to influence non-Catholics. Addressing himself to the converts who might be present, he said he had been asked whether it was lawful for them to pray for their deceased Protestant relatives, and explained to them that, although according to the discipline of the Church, the priest could not publicly pray for non-Catholics in the Mass, this by no means implied that we might not do so privately. All they, he continued, who followed Christ in sincerity and truth, and acted according to the lights vouchsafed to them,

* "Westminster Gazette," January 29th, 1870.

we might reckon as belonging to the soul of the Church, although by the misfortune of their education they did not belong to it visibly; *many who spoke against us, ridiculed us, or even persecuted us, would be saved, whom we, in our narrow way of thinking, might be apt to condemn.* The Catholic Church was world-wide, and we must be careful not to confound it with a sect in any way. The royal heart of Jesus would exclude none who were his true followers. In his experience as a priest he had found many such, *some even he felt conscious were by far his superiors in spiritual life, though external as yet to the visible Church.* Such things belong to the mysteries of the Kingdom of Christ. The instructions on Spiritual Direction and Vocation were distinguished by great prudence and wisdom, addressed more especially to ladies, many of whom attended the various services in all weathers, and at great personal inconvenience, and their piety and good example during the mission were very edifying.

"On Sunday evening last this highly successful mission was brought to a close, Father Suffield preaching a sermon of great eloquence; the only fault, if we may be allowed to say so, in his preaching, is that he is apt to be a little discursive. On this occasion his subject was 'Christ our King.' Before entering on it he alluded shortly to a letter of three Protestant gentlemen, sent to him during the mission, on the 'Historic Evidences of Christianity,' and the difficulties they had on this subject. He said the best answer they could have was the sight they witnessed that evening. *He reminded them that Catholics did not profess to answer all the difficulties men might raise.* The proof of Catholic truth, like Christianity itself, was a moral proof. Christ did not set about proving his mission, but he appealed to the heart and conscience of men, leaving it to them to accept or reject them. The Catholic Church did the same, pointing to her wonderful history, how she had spread from small beginnings, not like Mahommedanism, propagated by the sword, or like Protestantism, by the support of kings; but in spite of the dreadful persecutions of the Roman Empire, how she eventually triumphed, and even set up the throne of her Pontiff in the palace of the Cæsars; and when later corruption of morals crept over her, and bad Popes even, and a luxurious clergy were too often to be found, how, in spite of all she had lived on. Then came the Reformation, *in part a just reaction against abuses*, and carried away multitudes from the unity of faith. But she survived it all—and why? Because Christ was with her; and he had promised that the gates of hell should not prevail against her. Whatever the world might say, Christ had said those words; and Christ was Truth itself. And so she had lived on to our days—she alone, as a Church, had succeeded. Let those who reject her try and do likewise! they had not yet done so after three hundred years. In this country there was no unity, even in the essentials of faith, among those separate from the Church. The Catholic Church, then, pointed to her wonderful history, and claimed the obedience of all men. Men might reject her or accept her as they did Christ himself; only he called upon them to examine whether there was not some secret passion which was the cause of their doing so; whatever passion it might be, pride or some more ignoble vice, which made them unwilling to submit to the sweet yoke of Christ. *As to intellectual difficulties, he reminded them of the example of a great man who had said that there were, no doubt, difficulties and objections hard to answer, both as regards the Church and Christianity itself;* but that in spite of it all he accepted the Christian Faith as the word of Christ, the Eternal Truth. *Little minds might say that these difficulties were easily answered; but it was not so* — the true proof of Christianity was a moral one, after all.

"Father Suffield then asked his hearers to join in a solemn act of the renewal of their Baptismal vows, and made a powerful appeal to the men to remain faithful to their allegiance to Christ their King; he knew full well the difficulties and temptations they had to contend against in a great city like London; the example of those they lived among; and so much on every side calculated to lead them astray; he fully sympathised with them, and exhorted them to break for ever with Satan and his works; and then concluded with reading the beautiful passage of St. Augustine, written after his last meeting with his mother, St. Monica, on the joys of Heaven.

"The renewal of Baptismal Vows and the Papal Blessing concluded the service. The church was densely crowded."

CHAPTER V.

THE CONFLICT WITHIN.

Henceforth he seems to have studied rather to keep out of active work, such as he had been so long accustomed to, and to have sought in the peace of "The Hermitage," as he significantly called the priest's house at Bosworth, to regain his old certainty of faith.

It must have been a lonely time—not for want of correspondents, who were numerous, nor of visitors, for so many came out of their way to see him in his solitude and profit of his spiritual counsels, that a farmer of the neighbourhood found it worth while to set up a conveyance to take callers to and fro between the house and the railway station — but lonely, in the secret isolation of his soul from all with whom he had been wont to take counsel and share confidences, and still more so in the anticipation of a severance ever becoming more inevitable, and which could not be long kept secret. For it must have become increasingly clear to him, month by month, that the peace of the country was unavailing to restore peace to his soul; that it was henceforth impossible that he would ever again, as he had fondly hoped, "settle down with quiet conscience in peaceful belief." And all the kindness shown him, the deep regard testified in so many letters, the affectionate enquiries after his health and welfare, added to the secret anguish of his heart. For, spite of doubts about Roman Catholic claims, and scandals which were reported to him from Rome, and disapproval of "the foreign ecclesiastical scheming," which seemed to him in England itself to have supplanted "the old straightforward ways, I still," he writes, "regarded all those with whom I had personal relationship with such tender affection and high esteem that to be severed from them seemed to be an agony." And no wonder, on the one side, where he still lingered, and tried to find firm footing, all was familiar and welcome; before him, life peaceful, happy, honoured, useful, and promise more or less credible, worth the having at any rate, of eternal reward; on the other, all was uncertain and strange — what he should do? how he should live? what verities find to replace the dogmas of the Church? what sphere in that new world of use or honour?

The diary, or rather the notes of his sermons and engagements which he had roughly kept for many years, breaks off with the 8th of April, 1870, when he preached for four days at Devizes. There follows in the thin quarto, which had lasted him for all his notes since 1863, a few pages of extracts or memoranda, in striking contrast, many of them, with the earlier jottings of sermons and discourses, so full of faith, and devotion to the mysteries of the Roman Church. A few of them are here given, as showing how his mind was wrought by thoughts he had tried in vain to suppress :—

"Christianity has been tried and failed; the religion of Christ remains to be tried."

"Catholicism may long remain a verbal creed to millions, a source of spiritual consolation and refreshment, a guide amidst perplexities of conduct and morals—but resting on dogmas which cannot by any amount of compromise be incorporated with knowledge and with facts; assuming as the condition of its existence an hypothesis condemned alike by reason, history, and science; upheld by an organisation which is the assumed enemy of enquiry, of liberty, of the rights of others—it may still delude devout and reverend and high-souled men, but it cannot again regenerate society."

"If we ought, simply because we ought—because the law which we find within us, but did not produce, controls us, haunts us, and claims supremacy over us, then we find in such a fact the revelation of One from whom the law has emanated. As Fenelon says, 'Whence have I obtained this idea, which is so much above me, which infinitely surpasses me, which astonishes me, which renders the infinite present to me? It is in me, it is more than myself; I have not put it there, I have found it there; it does not depend upon me, I depend upon it.'"

"And Dr. John Smith, the Cambridge Platonist, writes, 'God has so copied forth himself into the whole life and energy of man's soul, as that the character of the divinity may be most largely seen and read of all within themselves, and wherever we look upon our souls in a right manner we shall find a Urim and Thummim there.'"

"As Horne Tooke says, 'The London Tavern is open to everyone who can afford to pay the bill,' so the Catholic Church is open to everyone who can recite the Creeds."

"The Bible is the history of the highest religious experiences of the race."

"St. Paul says that five hundred persons saw Jesus after his resurrection—was it once?—all together?—after a stirring appeal?"

"Arguments did not convert to Christianity at the beginning; people *saw* a higher, a purer, a nobler life—and they arose and lived it."

"The Roman Catholic Church satisfies every desire, if only it can induce the mind to accept its credentials unproved."

"Last century what did disbelief end in?—a revulsion to Evangelicalism and Romanism."

"Bowed down beneath internal conflict, Dante wandering across the mountains of Lunigiana, knocked at the gate of the monastery of San Croce del Corvo.* The monk who opened it read at a single glance all the long history of misery on the face of the stranger. 'What do you seek here'? said he. Dante gazed round with one of those looks in which the soul speaks, 'Peace.' The scene leads our thoughts up to the eternal type of all martyrs of genius and

---

* Situated at the extremity of Monte Caprione, which bounds the Gulf of Spezia on the south. The story is told in a letter purporting to be written by Fra Ilario, prior of the monastery

love, praying to his Father, to the Father of all, upon the Mount of Olives, for peace of soul and strength for the sacrifice. Peace! neither monk nor any other creature can bestow it upon Dante. The hand that sends the last* . . can alone take away the crown of thorns."

These and a few similar extracts and memoranda, intended for no eye but his own, and bringing to a close the twenty-years' notes of sermons, missions, engagements of his active life in the Church, are a truthful and effective record of the inner struggle. We see him striving to make safe the natural foundations of religion and morality, while the artificial securities he had so long trusted to are giving way. The old way is wrong, he writes, in effect, but before quitting it, let me make sure where the right way is, lest I wander lost on trackless moors, and exchange what is to me but a poor substitute for truth for what is infinite error.

What especially weighed upon his mind at this time were the scandals in high places, which, from the position he held as trusted friend and counsellor of people of rank and influence, he had more than usual opportunities of becoming acquainted with. It was not that this or that ecclesiastic was a bad man, or even that the church in such a country, or under such circumstances, was corrupt—that he would have accepted as the inevitable result of a ministry which God had confided to the hands, not of angels, but of men. No; what troubled him was that he heard on every side how human infirmity, personal ambi-

---

* Illegible.

tion, underhand devices, were being employed to bring about a new definition of faith—to induce the Holy Spirit to declare His truth to the Church!

In the month of April a private letter, addressed by Dr. Newman to Dr. Ullathorne, Bishop of Birmingham, had somehow made its way into the papers, and writing about it to Father Suffield, its author said, "Of course I never conjectured so unguarded a letter would get into circulation, but now it is done, it is done—and I can't be sorry—and I am glad to hear your judgment confirming me in my impenitence." In this letter Dr. Newman spoke of "an aggressive insolent faction" who were forcing on the definition. "Why cannot we be let alone," he wrote, "when we have pursued peace and thought no evil?" Hitherto Rome had spoken only to inspire the faithful with hope and confidence, "but now we have the greatest meeting which has ever been seen, and that at Rome, infusing into us, by its accredited organs, the *Civilta*, the *Univers*, and the *Tablet*, little else than fear and dismay. When we are all at rest, and have no doubts, and—at least, practically, not to say doctrinally—hold the Holy Father to be infallible, suddenly there is thunder in the clear sky, and we are told to prepare for something we know not what, to try our faith we know not how. No impending danger is to be averted, but a great difficulty is to be created." Then, he added, "As to myself, personally, please God I do not expect any trial at all; but I look with anxiety at the prospect of having to defend decisions which may not be difficult to my own private judgment, *but may be most difficult to maintain logically in the face of historic facts.*" It was here that the two failed in sympathy, and on this that they eventually parted company for life. The one was prepared to believe whatever the Council might decree, no matter what might be the means used to coerce it. The other found insuperable difficulty both in the substance of the proposed definition and in the mode of bringing it about. Did the Holy Spirit act by intrigue and threats? Was the truth of God opposed to 'historic facts?'

And when he wrote of such things to trusted Catholic correspondents, the greater their piety and simplicity of faith, the more entirely did they fail to understand the gravity of what seemed to them so much "gossip." Thus one old friend, who had been his adviser and companion of his labours from the first, and from whom he might have expected a sympathy which he could not look for within his Order, writes under date May 7th:—

"Dearest Brother, — Your letter is simply most painful to me. Why listen to all this wretched gossip about the Holy Father and the Jesuits? Surely you do not fall into the mistake of Dr. N., who, in the words of Dalgairns, in his letter to the *Univers*, 'exaggerates beyond measure the human side, and ascribes the ever-rising and irresistible current which is carrying the Church towards the definition of the Pope's infallibility to a few newspapers.' Is the Church to abstain from teaching a divinely revealed truth because of certain doubts and certain so-called historical difficulties? She would be unfaithful to her commission if she could do so. And as to difficulties, (1) there is a sufficient answer to all that has been stated; (2) if there were not, they are not so good as the difficulties, historic and otherwise, which are brought against the truth of Holy Scripture. What nonsense to talk of historic difficulties against what is admitted to be a truth of revelation! All this intrigue, misrepresentation, abuse, attack upon the Holy Father, which is on the side of the opponents, not of the defenders of the definition, shows the absolute necessity of a definition. To me it is a confirmation of the truth, for it is evidently the work of the Devil."

So wrote one whom he had for years regarded as his nearest and dearest friend; and another, a priest in the Order, who loved him well :—

"You speak of Galileo, &c., but astronomers are now coming round to the Ptolemaic theory again. A recent pamphlet by 'A Wrangler,' discusses the merits of Copernicus and Ptolemy, and the author told me that it may now be regarded as an open question as to whether the sun or the earth moves. As to historical facts, may not history be wrong? It is certainly not infallible. I heard it said that our English history would have to be written again on account of new records coming to light. I believe history is full of mistakes. It seems unreasonable to prefer to rest our souls on such sandy grounds, and to want more than the ' soliditas Petri.' "

It was with such arguments his doubts were met, and the only one which really impressed him was that of which he was himself only too conscious—that the difficulties were not confined to Papal infallibility, but were inherent in the system of a supernatural revelation, whether through a church, a man, or a book.

He had to go through the experience of every convert; his old companions *could* not understand him; it was not love, or sympathy, or respect, or desire to help which was wanting, but the ability to see the real force of the arguments which were undermining his faith. To them it was all a temptation of Satan, they pitied and prayed for him who was undergoing the assault, but to admit that such difficulties were serious, would have seemed to them like an act of homage to the tempter; the utmost respect they could show would be to give attention to discover the latent fallacy which, 'of course,' was in them, It is so always; if we firmly believe, we can ill appreciate objections to our faith; and so we go through life, men of the same abilities and like endowments, each marvelling how it comes to pass that others can be of a different opinion to himself. Those only who to themselves "may seem to have reached a purer air," but have won it not otherwise than "after toil and storm," can fully enter into the difficulties of other minds.

No wonder, then, that at last he turned from friends who all believed, nor knew what it meant to doubt, to strangers who openly professed disbelief of these things about which he was so troubled, questioning incessantly within himself—were they true or false?

CHAPTER VI.

HELP SOUGHT FROM OUTSIDE.

It was in May that he began a letter to the Rev. James Martineau, then Principal of Manchester New College, in London. How serious a step this was, and how great a sin it would be accounted in a Catholic Priest, to consult in matters of faith a schismatic and heretic, those only can understand who have been trained in the certainty that ' the Church ' is the one divine guide and teacher of men. And that the writer fully appreciated the gravity of his act is shewn in the fact that though not a long letter—it might be easily and carefully written in an hour—he took six days over it. "May 19th, 1870," is the date, and below, "finished on May 24th." " I am going to ask of you, " he wrote, " a great favour, and perhaps a rather singular one— trusting to your honour. Will you do me the favour of spending a few days with me in my retired country cottage ? " It was assuredly a 'singular' request to reach a Unitarian Minister from a Dominican Priest, the one known to the world as an avowed advocate of liberty of enquiry, the other known only hitherto as a doughty champion of Roman domination.

" I am very anxious," he continued, " for my own satisfaction, and as affording an additional help to my own mind, to confer with you upon religious

E

questions, which I could not go into by letter so as to be understood, or so as to arrive at any conclusion. I will but make this remark, there are men at the present time who gravely doubt all those portions of religion which rest upon historic (Scriptural or Church) foundations, but who yet having felt in their own minds the terrible danger of removing a system entirely interwoven with faith in God, in the soul, in the conscience, in the soul's future as influenced by the life's habits, question whether they would not better please God by continuing to throw themselves blindfold, and therefore heartily, into a human religion, embodying and successfully carrying into practise those great principles, though accompanied with tremendous exaggeration, rather than to help in shaking in many minds the essentials of all religion, of all virtue, and of all happiness, by setting the example of renouncing the system in which these are embodied.

"Some men are so circumstanced by their antecedents, their character, their position, that they almost necessarily pass from one teaching position into another—and their entire silence would be like teaching that they had lost all faith—and perhaps because they had lost all virtue. Such men, though individually undeserving of anything beyond average influence and consideration, yet from antecedent and existing circumstances unable to get themselves simply ignored, are bound to consider whether, *in a choice of evils*, the shaking virtue and faith in many minds without being able to substitute other grounds for faith and other supports for virtue, may not be more evil and sinful than˙ the consistent ' acting of a part,' by which one would seek to present in exaggerated popular form the hidden truths of God, of conscience, of the soul, and its future.

"Possibly there may be Catholic priests—-perhaps I know such—who may say to themselves thus :—

' I have a great influence—I am in a world-wide society—my Church teaches the great truths of God, goodness, mercy, patience—the influence of God on the soul — the respect for conscience — prayer for the souls' needs—virtue—hope. Now life is short, my own has passed its meridian,—I may destroy in others what I can never replace—I may be able to confer but little happiness. I shall certainly cause to *very many* the deepest sorrow—ancient friendships will be severed — and I shall myself be regarded by thousands and tens of thousands who have loved me, as a Judas who has betrayed his trust, who must have had a bad motive—thus, by a single act, destroying the teaching as well as the holy friendships and sacred confidences and beautiful characters of twenty years — and for what ? Where could such a man, amidst the wildernesses he had created for himself, covered with the ruins of all his hopes, of all his beautiful friendships— where could he stand and say to his fellow-men, ' I still believe in God and love Him, I still hope in Him, though for the simplicity of His truth I have become an outcast—I still believe in the soul, in virtue, in conscience, in charity, and purity and justice, though I may wander forth as an exile from the human heart, every tongue cursing me, every hand raised against me, and even the children and the very poor who have delighted to call me 'Father,' and to trust me as such, turning from me as from a thing of horror and of shame.'

"And unless such a priest were to pass from one insincerity to another, pass over many hearts made sad, and many souls, perchance, made bad—where could he raise his voice and speak to convince both himself and others that truth, and zeal, and love, had not perished in his soul? Where could he tell others to find a home for their soul where they need not 'act a part?'

"Perchance, amidst the unhealed misery of the world they doubt God's *omnipotence*—whilst they believe and bless His *goodness*. They know not where He is or how—or What. Words cannot describe His nature, or His past, or His future, or His mode of government. But still firmly believing there is such a One, and that He is holy, and just, and goodness; and that in answer to prayers He will operate on the soul, though probably not changing at man's behest His physical and natural laws. And supposing such persons do not know any reason why they should pray 'through Christ' or 'to Him,' or practise any rites *as if commanded by Him*—but speak of Him reverently because His name represents to so many millions the highest expression of the beauty of holiness, and His teaching contains so much that is the purest and the most sublime, and yet cannot attribute to the historic form any dogmatic position; still, on the other hand, not wishing ever to shock or wound the feelings or prejudices of others in whom piety is interwoven with some recognition of His name or office.

"There are, perhaps, some priests, who really holding such opinions as these, hardly dare to own it to themselves, because they see nothing outside popular Religion except the desert strewn with ruins, or a few individuals striving to erect a home for the soul and ever failing; whilst the popular Religion seems to succeed just the more that it develops its dogmatic, exclusive of the historic side, and such a priest says to himself: 'Perhaps God intends gross, popular Religion to be the only exponent of his truth, if I were not in it, I would not now embrace it, but perhaps I shall please Him better by continuing in it now, during the short remaining years of life, rather than that I should go forth to seek a shadow—followed by the tears or the execrations of all who have loved me. As I am, I am united in conscious sympathy and intercourse with countless numbers, I am sustained by their example, encouraged by their affection, helped by their prayers—daily I encourage and share their holiest aspirations—I know them to be cruelly maligned, and leaving them, I shall seem to malign them the more, and shall thus wound and wrong old tried friends, loved and revered in the depths of my soul—I love them, and I turn their very love into a sad and bitter regret. And if

I leave my pleasant village home to go forth and literally *starve as a pauper* and obtain the sufferings of a martyr, with nothing around me but unrealised hopes, and a sad fear haunting me that whilst seeking an ideal perfection of truth I have injured souls I shall be powerless to serve, and destroyed happiness I can never restore ! What then? Surely nothing would surround my latter years but despair.'

" If such a man could find a religious home for his own soul, one to which he could point and say : 'If you share my doubts about EVERYTHING taught by historic religions, here you can be received without a misgiving; and if you are a religious teacher, so long as you do not hurt the feelings and honest prejudices of others, *you* can be here and teach here without compromise, and without continuing in a modified degree the assumed dogmatism of your present position',—

"The character of Unitarians and their tone of mind, and high moral standard, and their existing organisation seems to provide an answer satisfactory. Will you, my dear sir, in great confidence, come and confer with me on these matters?

" Be so kind as to be very guarded, for if ever I am compelled to act, my first communication must be with my Provincial,* so that I consult to the utmost the feelings of others, and *protect to the fullest all the trusts reposed in me;* and by some

---

* The Dominican Order is governed by a 'General,' who resides at Rome, under whom is in each Province a 'Provincial,' to whom are in turn subject all the Priors of convents, and all the Friars residing within his district.

printed matter I send, you will perceive somewhat what I mean. If there be no existing religious substitute for the Catholic Church—is it not God's intention that the great religious truths of Theism should be always exaggerated and embodied in a gross popular form, as in ancient times we have the esoteric and exoteric doctrine?

"Somehow, those who have abandoned the Catholic Church, as far as I have heard about them, do not attract me — thoughtful, quiet, earnest men seem almost more to approve those who remain than those who leave—and yet, although I have so sought solitude here, and to withdraw from influence, I am receiving persons (unsought by me) into the Catholic Church; just lately the son of an M.P. has been with me to be received into the Church, and the only two persons of education and intelligence in my village are likely to follow the same example; and a Protestant officer comes to me, and a Protestant lady, to make a Retreat with the same object next month. I am compelled to continue taking a distinct side. Can you help me conscientiously to weigh this grave matter, and to ponder this irretrievable and, to many, perhaps, fatal step?

"Believe me, very faithfully yours,

"ROBERT RODOLPH SUFFIELD."

To this touching letter, in which he laid bare his heart before one who had been hitherto an entire stranger to him, but whose character and judgment he seemed to have read in his published works, and whom he found, as the event proved, fully worthy of the trust he reposed in him, Mr. Martineau replied as follows :—

"LONDON, *May 26th.*

"REV. AND DEAR SIR, — The deep and moving questions raised by your very interesting letter can be freely treated only *viva voce;* so I will not try to say any of the hundred things that crowd upon me, but will simply offer myself to you for Monday evening' next, the 30th inst., if you can receive me for a day, and let me return home on Tuesday evening. A longer time I must not allow myself, having duties, as Principal of a College, requiring my presence at morning prayers and lectures on the following day.

" Notwithstanding the unqualified expressions of faith, which are at times so startling in Dr. Newman's writings, and which are habitual with all my Catholic friends,—Archbishop Manning, Father Dalgairns, and Dr. Ward,—I have always supposed that in the higher minds the hidden strife must be going on between the Divine light and mythologic shadows, which the Church and the Bible have blended, and I have often wondered that the traces were so few of that terrible and pathetic struggle. But now for the first time have I full insight into all which the conflict involves ; still, if it is not ours to manage for God and act as His diplomatists, but to be simply led by Him as children, a clear path may surely be found, often, doubtless, the path of sacrifice.

" The religious life in our set of Protestant communities is not in a satisfactory condition ; and the best that I can say for them is that they offer no hindrance to either thought or conscience, and may be receptacles and vehicles of spiritual reformation.

"Believe me ever, yours faithfully,

"JAMES MARTINEAU."

It would seem as if a reaction followed on this decisive step. His request was granted, yet perhaps he would have been half pleased had it been rudely refused. The sympathy shown him by a stranger to himself and to his Church, must have made him realise more keenly than ever how fast he was approaching the terrible ordeal from which every nerve shrank.

So writing, under date "*May 28th, 1870*," after giving particulars of trains, &c., he continued,—

"I shall not mention your name to any one, thus no curiosity is excited, visitors constantly thus come.

"Might I ask you to see the drift of the line of thought in the 'Crown of Jesus,' which I send you, from pages 64 to 80, and from the latter part of page 81 to the middle of page 91,* the note to page 264,† and pages 498 to 501.‡ I wrote these passages ten years ago, but they represent my entire line of thought for above twenty years.

"The scheme of Catholic Doctrine which I drew up and placed in the 'Table of Contents' will show how, in my teachings, the moral life has been

* This page contains "A Rule of Life," instructions how to live piously and well, most part of which all would approve.
† Quoted below, page 78.   ‡ See page 44.

intimately interwoven with the Catholic dogma and rites.

" Now, though delighted to listen to any observation of a controversial character you might wish to make, I could not say that such is precisely my desideratum.

" I want you first to realise the Catholic interior life—*no one* out of the Catholic Church *ever* seems to understand it even remotely. Thus everything said and written against us is merely like breath upon a mirror, and a child can wipe it away.

" I want you to realise what the system of the Catholic Church affords to every noblest thought, to every purest and holiest aspiration, and how it also gets hold of the lowest and roughest and coarsest, and saves him from being a brute. If ever God breaks the chain of gold that binds me to His Temple—and bids me look around and see that its magnificence is merely a stately vision and a dream of beauty—one memory will ever follow me like the last pleading look of the victim gazing into the eyes of the murderer, and it will be the memory of that love of God, piety, reverence, that tender charity, that chivalry of devotedness, that chastity which has never known a taint, interwoven in the most intimate communications in which every secret of the heart and life has been revealed. I look behind me and around me, at our Priestly and Religious Homes, at our Colleges and Convents, and then at that other large circle of devoted friends in the world whom God's goodness also gave me, and say to myself,—Is there the same elswhere? Truth is not merely in the intellect; it is also in the heart. Better to have moral beauty and credulity combined, like the ivy eating the oak even whilst it beautifies it, than to destroy at once the credulity of mind and the moral beauty of the soul. So I ask,—What is to take the place?

"And I want to learn from you (for I perfectly confide in your high-minded and unbiassed integrity), what is the moral life, the piety, the high devotedness, the unworldly generosity, the spirit of faith and singleness of purpose, of those who are simply Theists? This matter comes almost entirely out of my experience. Yet no one can read the works of Professor Newman and of Miss Cobbe without saying to himself, 'Here is moral beauty and truth combined.'

"But as some are born princes of thought, so there are others who seem to belong by right of birth to a royal dynasty of virtue, and they would have made their worship in the temple of Corinth—chastity; and their pleasure in the garden of Epicurus—fortitude. Are these merely exceptions? and exceptions merely because a high intellect has not wished to stoop into the mire? But amongst the gentry, the young men, the tradespeople, the working classes, what is the effect of the absence of all historic dogmatic belief? Can God and the conscience maintain their empire over the life?

"That is what I want to learn. It is an unknown world to me, but it does not come to me with a good report; but what chiefly makes me shrink from it is this—what they say continually about us; they always impute to us Catholics, evil; if we even do a good thing, it is supposed we must have had a bad motive in doing it; if we affect kindness, it cannot be because we bear no evil, but because we would catch a prose-lyte; if we do a charity, it is to buy ourselves out of Purgatory; the motive must be selfish, and all of us are supposed to be playing a game for power, for money, or for lust. In our communities there must be tyranny, violence, impurity; and amongst Priests and 'Religious' there cannot be chastity, because they are single—so they seem to argue.

" Now, I say to myself, ' Surely they reason from themselves;' and every such attack has made me draw closer to that ancient family wherein, if there be the credulity ef childhood, there certainly is, too, its bright joy of heart, its purity, its tenderness, its devotedness; and these have something to do with God and Truth.

" That profound habit of government of thought produced by the Catholic system would enable me to banish *always*, as I do now, except at formal periods of consideration, all the doubts which arise in my mind; and I should be convinced it was more pleasing to God to do so, and blindfolding my intel-lect to let the old Church, to which I owe so much, lead on another pilgrim through mystic rites and dreams of ancient beauty to the Eternal Home, than it would be to have satisfied the intellect by a nega-tion, and flung myself from a citadel of moral security into a battlefield of doubt, perplexity, uncertainty, without a support, without an example, myself suspected, doubted, an exile from one home, and never obtaining another.

"You see the Catholic system. *What is to take its place ?* It was once all contained in that upper room over the beautiful Gate of the Temple. That room contained the simplest faith, the purest hopes, the grandest charity that had yet combined together in the world. And as the vase of precious ointment broke, and the fragrance unperceived spread far and wide, so the gates of that upper room opened, and one by one they went forth and died, the vase of precious ointment broke, the fragrance possessed the the world.

"Is there such a beginning now? The Unitarian Society, with its high moral tone, its tolerance, its gracious domestic life—does it possess the mysterious gift? Has *it* the germ of a future and most glorious career? or does it merely raise, though more charitably, another protest, as if to afford another witness to that ancient Church which teaches, commands, and is obeyed?

"If so, the heart returns to itself and says, 'God, virtue, noble devotedness, must not be left without a witness; that Society which presents the witness the most perfectly must be the Truth, as far as God yet permits it, to an evil generation.'

"I may as well add, I have read most of the notable works against the Catholic Church and Christianity, as well as all that I knew of a defence.

Thus you see I seek not the controversial, but the *moral* and *existing* evidence of a higher and purer truth, if such exists.

"Ever yours, very faithfully."

One passage of his "Crown of Jesus," to which he drew special attention, is worth quoting, as showing the high ideal he entertained of the priestly office. If Protestants cannot admit the assumption which runs throughout of a distinct privileged caste, with graces all its own, yet none can fail to admire the character portrayed.

"The good priest is always on the side of virtue, of justice, of truth; he is always on the side of Jesus Christ; he is always advancing His interests, defending His cause, tending His flock, announcing His Gospel, administering His Sacraments. From his lips flow words of mercy, pardon, consecration, hope, encouragement, reconciliation, blessing, justice; his heart not limited in its affections by the mere circle of relationship or private interest, dilates and embraces in its charity every form of virtue, of weakness, or of suffering—all in whom sorrow, tears, dereliction, poverty, youth, shame, virtue, piety, or faith renew the image of Jesus Christ. In the midst of an unbelieving age and an unbelieving country, he bears the reproach and the honour of Christ. To how many souls does he, as the ambassador and minister of Christ, bring pardon, virtue, peace, and hope; how many tears dry up; how many good resolutions evoke or strengthen; how many wounded souls heal. Loved, honoured, hated, dreaded, or despised by those who

loved, honoured, hated, dreaded, or despised his
Master; by how many prayers of gratitude is he
borne up amidst his earthly trials; from how many
temptations shielded by the sanctity and reverence
that environ his sacred office. And when at length
the gates of Heaven open to admit those who, having
turned many to justice, shine as the stars in the
firmament for ever, then he, the priest, the minister,
the ambassador, bearing radiant in his soul the august
character of the priesthood, bends before the throne
of Him who commissioned him on earth as the
representative and instrument of His mercy, His
truth, His grace, and from Him he receives the
crown, whilst the souls he has helped to redeem
leap from their thrones of light to hail his approach,
and to raise around their deliverer their sweetest
songs of love and joy."

Such was his "good priest." None knew better
than he did that some were bad, and many very
ordinary men, and that few indeed attained to be
what he pourtrayed. Yet we cannot wonder that
he was loth to abandon claim and effort to be such
a one, and belong to the company of such men to
take a step which would bring upon him the contempt and dread of them all, and to substitute for
this high ideal the very prosaic type of the able
minister of a respectable congregation which he
distantly knew of as accepted by Unitarians. After
all, ideals must be tried by their working power;
what kind of men does such an ideal as this, in
fact, produce? Is the average priest, celibate, sepa-

rate, believing himself gifted with supernatural powers, a man superior to the average minister, husband, father, citizen, bound to set good example, but claiming no superiority to his hearers except special training for his profession and special knowledge of his subject? That is the question which should be determined, and not which ideal is higher; and when he came afterwards to determine it of his own experience, his answer was clear and certain.

CHAPTER VII.

First Intimation to the Public.

Mr. Martineau came according to promise on the Monday evening, and spent Tuesday with his Dominican host at Bosworth. He himself gave a most interesting account of the visit at a public meeting held in the Hope Street School-room, in Liverpool, on the 25th of September of the following year, on occasion of the opening of the new Church in Hamilton Road, Everton. After speaking of the visit to England of Keshub Chunder Sen, "a kind of second John, a soul most congenial to the soul of Jesus," he went on, "an event has taken place recently with which I have had in some degree the privilege of a personal connection.

"A very eminent and remarkable man has given up his adherence to the Catholic religion, and has thrown himself among us as a preacher of pure and spiritual religion. I allude to the Rev. Robert Rodolph Suffield. Now, before Mr. Suffield's name was heard amongst us, at his own request I early paid him a visit at his retreat in the country. I had intimate intercourse with him, and learned precisely his state of thought before he had made up his mind to the step he has now taken, and I was especially struck with the problem which was presented to his religious

F

sense—what is the real essence and nature of Catholicism? Now, I found that the view Mr. Suffield took of Catholicism was this: He said, 'I see in the Catholic religion the only example in the world's history in which the great and fundamental principles of all natural piety and of all natural conscience are made the actuating principles of the life of multitudes and of nations. The great doctrine of the moral government of God, the great truth of the absolute supremacy of conscience, the great hope of a future and better life, these things have imbued the Catholic mind, the mind even of the youngest children of the Catholic Church that have any intelligence at all. They are realities to the Catholic people. They speak of them with the same simplicity and openness with which they would speak of the work of their plough, of their spade, of their shuttle; with which they would speak of concerns of their houses and their homes. There is no shyness concerning them. They are absolute realities to them, and rule their lives. We know that they control the passions of young people, and, if they go astray, by appealing to these images in their hearts, we can recover them again. They are truly a power in life. And now,' said Mr. Suffield, 'what I want to know is, whether outside the Catholic Church those truths have the same power and reality, whether they take their places among the facts of life with the same certainty and with the same efficacy.' He looked upon the Catholic religion simply as an instrumentality for bringing home to men the simple natural convictions of the human heart, and making them live in their consciences and lives. Catholicism thus was to him nothing but a great system of natural religion supported by the most artificial and unnatural of authorities and supports. That is the view he took of it, and he said, ' What I want to know is, if I dare to throw away these artificial supports, shall I find it possible to administer this spiritual theism to mankind, and get hold of the hearts of men? Or am I to believe that it is impossible for the weak mind of humanity to grapple those truths, unless you have a false mythology, and all sorts of pictures and images, connected with them? Does the religion enter by means of the false imagination, or may we fling away the false imagination, and trust to the spiritual power of religion?' That was the problem he had to solve for himself, and he said, ' I fear if I were to profess myself a Protestant I should be propping up these eternal truths with just as false and entangled a machinery as if I were to remain in the Catholic Church. For, if there is no infallibility in the Catholic Church, neither is there in the Protestant Scriptures, and whether I take the one or the other, I throw away natural truths, and fling myself instead on an artificial and unnatural support.' Well, I believe myself that Mr. Suffield here expressed a great truth; and I think the changes which are now taking place in the Protestant Churches are all of this kind. The tendency is to fling away the false dependence upon artificial authority, and go back to the primitive rights of religion in human nature and in human

life. I said to him, I should feel it an impiety, and
infidelity—the only thing I should venture to call
infidelity at all—to doubt that what God has made
true could vindicate and justify itself to the human
heart without any human lies to back it up and support it. If we once found that a thing was a lie, and
was false, or even if it was precarious, it was at the
peril of all veracity and of all fidelity that we dared
to maintain and use it as a means of underpinning,
as it were, and supporting an eternal and all important truth. I believe myself that the Churches are
at last discovering this. This next generation will
be, it appears to me, a great time for the tumbling
down of props. Many are so timid as to believe that,
if such be the case, the things also which have been
propped up will fall. But if we have been building
the supports and constructing all this machinery
under something which is made to stand by itself,
in that case they may crumble to the dust and the
superstructure will not fall. It was once believed
that some old mythological giant was necessary to
bend his back and support the heavens. Atlas has
long ago disappeared among the ghosts of the ancient
world, and the heavens still overreach us and have
not fallen. The old aqueducts of Rome, fitting type
as it seems to me of the artificial channels of grace
which are given by the modern Rome, lie now with
their piers broken and their arches strewed upon the
plain below, but the waters of life have not been spilt
and lost."[*]

---

[*] *"The Unitarian Herald,"* Oct. 6, 1871.

Mr. Martineau left him on Tuesday evening, and the Friday following, he, for the first time, gave public intimation of the difficulties in which his faith had been so long involved; difficulties unsuspected hitherto by any but his most intimate friends, and even by them looked upon as mere temptations which would pass away after a while of trial.

But to explain the occasion of which he availed himself to give this warning to so many devoted friends, and prepare them for the greater shock of his "apostacy," it will be necessary to give a short account of a controversy in which he had been for some time past involved.

A certain Mr. Urquhart, whose name will go down to posterity in connection with the Turkish Bath, which he was the first to introduce in this country, was, in his day, well known as an able but eccentric politician, who had specially made himself conspicuous by his fanatical enmity to Russia, and his determined opposition to Lord Palmerston's policy in China and the East. This gentleman had, in the year 1868, when the General Council was summoned to meet in Rome, made appeal to the Pope, to use the opportunity so afforded to publish a solemn declaration on the subject of unjust wars, and to call the attention of all Christians to the guilt in which those who took any part in them, were, according to the ancient teaching of the Church, involved. Mr. Urquhart was himself a Protestant, but he had appealed in vain to the bishops and clergy of his own Church; "on the occurrence of the first lawless brigandages in Affghanistan and China," he wrote, " I applied myself to the Church of England to obtain a day of fast and humiliation, and I appealed to the Archbishop of Canterbury to excommunicate the Queen; but though some were brought to seriousness and sadness, no priest or bishop was got to move in a Diocesan Assembly for a day of Fast.* "

To the Canon Law, then, Mr. Urquhart turned, and there seemed to find full support for his contention, and indeed many right-minded and zealous Roman Catholics both French and English, were inclined to co-operate with him, or at least work to the same end. So a petition to the Holy Father had appeared in the columns of *The Tablet* as early as the 15th of August, 1868, and had received numerous signatures. " The undersigned," it began, " implore the protection of the Holy See: their concern is aroused upon questions which have to do with their conscience as Catholics, their duties and their rights as citizens, and the interests of all Christendom. They ask from the Holy See and the Council a declaration of the principles which make the distinction of lawful and unlawful war, which guarantee to the armed citizen that he shall not be called upon to exchange his character as defender of right for that of an aggressor and assassin. It is no vain theory that has moved them to this petition ; it is their conscientious anxiety, their apprehensions for themselves and for their children."

* Letter of August 5th, 1869.

This will be sufficient to show how awfully serious the case was for the numerous Roman Catholics who themselves were enlisted in the army or had soldier sons or relations. It was a matter of heaven or hell; for according to the doctrine which some sought to establish, a soldier fighting in what he knew to be an unjust war, if slain on the field of battle, died in mortal sin, beyond hope of salvation ; and moreover the responsibility of determining on the moral aspect of the war rested upon each individual engaged in it.

Now the custom had grown up, whatever may have been the ancient usage, to consider this responsibility incumbent only upon the governing authorities, and it was generally held that the subordinate was excused, in the sight of God as of man, on the plea that he was obeying orders. Against Mr. Urquhart, who openly reprobated this view, and some ecclesiastics who supported him, but had not the courage to give their names to the world, Mr. Suffield maintained that it was the right and duty of the confessor to give absolution and admit to communion every soldier otherwise fitly disposed who went to war when called upon, making no enquiry as to the occasion or justification of it.

He had written in July, 1869, " In this matter I am not accessible to argument, but I am to authority. *All* the bishops, theologians, professors, and confessors, who have as yet written to me, *signing their names*, entirely agree with me, and utterly repudiate the opposite opinions "; and he refers to a passage in a privately printed letter which he addressed to Lord

Denbigh,—"We are told that each soldier should refuse to obey till he has satisfied himself that his government had sufficient reason for going to war, had previously tried fruitlessly in every way to get the grievance redressed, had consulted pious men and ecclesiastics as to the justice of the war, and had proclaimed the war with due formalities. If he is not satisfied on all these points he is to be told that he becomes 'a wholesale murderer' if he goes to battle. If a Confessor should attempt to pacify his conscience by telling him that his oath of allegiance is certain, and his doubt uncertain; that with the slight information at his command he cannot arrive at a conclusion sufficiently certain to justify him in violating his oath; that he may suppose his government to be in possession of information, which if communicated to him, would alter his own judgment; that in the meanwhile his duty is to obey all those commands which are according to the present laws of war, conscientiously abstaining from brigandage, or violence, or crime, to which his passions might prompt him; that he is to dispel his doubts, to form his conscience, and go to battle,—a confessor giving such advice, we are told, becomes 'a participator in murder.'" It was against such teaching that Mr. Suffield felt called upon to protest, and though supported by every authority to whom he appealed, he yet had to endure much abuse and misrepresentation both from Mr. Urquhart, and even from Roman advocates of peace, whose opposition was all the more painful to him, that he largely sympathised with their action, though judging the extremes to which they pushed their opinions, both false in theory and cruel in practise. Not indeed that there were any known to him who did carry out in practise this theory of the confessor's duties, but they condemned the custom which they followed, while he maintained that it was right according to Canon Law as well as expedient.

"During the time of the Crimean War," he wrote, " at another period, and again quite recently, I have been personally blamed with extreme severity, not so much because my practise was like that of other confessors, but because I defended it as being theologically correct, whereas it was imagined that some priests regarded such practise, even though followed by themselves, to be an abuse which ought to be reformed."

And among other authorities he was able to produce the following letter from Cardinal Wiseman to a father who had consulted him at the time of the Chinese war, which seemed to him unjust, as to whether he was right in letting his son join the army.

Talacre, Rhyl, Aug. 7, 1857.

Dear Sir,—I do not see that you have anything to do with your private opinions about the justice of a particular war in deciding your son's going into the army. You may freely let him obtain his commission as soon as possible.

Yours very sincerely in Christ,

N. CARDINAL WISEMAN.

But in spite of the universal practise and the support of the highest dignitaries of the Church, in spite too of the manifest exaggeration by which his opponents gave their cause away, it is still clear that his own mind was not at ease on the question. " I am not accessible to argument," he wrote; and again, "I shall be really glad if you will get the matter formally and publicly settled by authority. Should the bishops declare me to be in error, I shall be the first to submit, and they will remove the obstacle to my co-operating with you," and " should the Holy See decree as you hope, the whole subject will to every Catholic pass out of the range of argument or uncertainty." And in a letter to *The Tablet* of Aug. 28, 1869, "There are those who, like myself, go far along with Mr. Urquhart in his great, noble, and Christian objects, and should the opinions which I have expressed prove to be in any way inaccurate, I can only repeat now what I have said to individual Catholics, that my advice and my practice will be instantly changed at the bidding of ecclesiastical authority, and of course my opinions too at any intimation from the Holy See."

It sounds intensely loyal all this, and yet if any Catholic could have then suspected one so universally esteemed as Father Suffield, the thought might have occurred that, like the Queen in Hamlet,—he " does protest too much." The fact is that he was in a false position, defending on authority what he could not, or dared not argue in support of, and appealing to authority to decide against him. Mr. Urquhart had attacked him with considerable asperity, and concluded his published reply with the words, " a Catholic priest, who has seen your printed letter, wrote these words, ' Father Suffield, whether he wills it or not, is enrolled in the army of evil, and never will you gain him.' " For a whole year he made no answer, and allowed criticism and calumny to have their way, but now at last he was emboldened to speak openly, and reveal in the following letter what had all along been in his mind.

To THE EDITOR OF THE DIPLOMATIC REVIEW.

The Hermitage, H. Bosworth, Leicestershire,
June 3, 1870.

SIR,—Many of your readers and of my friends have expressed surprise that, excepting the occasional correction of an error, I have made no reply to the strictures on my letter to Lord Denbigh.

Will you permit me to explain ? Some of the strictures were personal ; others regarded the public question of the degree of moral responsibility resting on subjects in the event of a war. The personal strictures were quite sufficiently answered by the kind letter Lord Denbigh addressed to me as a public reply, in which he signified not only his hearty concurrence with the opinions I had expressed, but also with the mode in which I had endeavoured to help on the inquiry. This letter he sent round rather extensively. The public question, so far as it regarded Protestants, I did not enter into, beyond a general expression of sincere admiration of those engaged in the pursuit of higher views and practice

of justice. As Catholics had sought my opinion, I
addressed my observations to them. To them and to
myself it was simply a question of the authoritative
application of admitted principles. The question resolved itself to us into whether, under certain speci-
fied circumstances, we could approach the Sacraments,
as that is the clearest test of whether the intended act
or state of mind is mortal sin. I pointed out to Catholics the inconsistent position we should place ourselves in if we denounced as sinful what, under the
authority of the Church, we were under those very
circumstances permitted and even ordered to do.
When Protestants objected that my statements on
this Catholic matter were erroneous and contrary to
episcopal judgments, I printed my statements, and
sent them round to all the bishops for their approval,
approval was given, and in no` instance censure.
When it was stated that Cardinal Wiseman had
taught differently, I obtained an autograph letter of
the Cardinal's going far beyond anything that I had
stated.

But why did not I support these authorities and
the universal practice of the Church with proofs? I
will frankly say why. Because, as a matter of argument, and in my individual conscience, I did not
thoroughly see my way to agreement with the
universal Catholic approved practice and doctrine.
I submitted to it because I knew it to be binding
on us. *There are several other subjects on which, if
I followed my own judgment and conscience, I should
arrive at a conclusion very remote from, and :ome-*

times quite opposed to, the teaching of the Church and of our moral theology. On such subjects I am not disposed to be an enthusiastic defender, but I quietly point out to Catholics, " You cannot take that line without opposing the Church." Or "if you admit such a position, you must necessarily admit such a conclusion, which you know, as Catholics, we are bound to reject." I did not wish Mr. Urquhart to be deceived by the supposition that, on account of strong general sympathies, we, as Catholics, could carry out what he clearly thought we could and ought. The Pope was gratified at Mr. Urquhart's homage ; Catholics were gratified at his recognising a power in our Church and in the Papacy; but in a very few years he will be the most vehement in his declarations that I was right, and he was deceived by the utterance of generalities and un-realised hopes ; and then he, perhaps, will in his passionate devotion to justice, reverse the title of the memoir he published against myself.*

Yours faithfully,

ROBERT RUDOLPH SUFFIELD, O.S.D.

It does not appear that any immediate notice was taken of this letter by his superiors in the Order. It was perhaps judged useless to expostulate, and more prudent to wait in silence for further developments. But we have evidence how seriously it was regarded in a subsequent remonstrance addressed to him by his Provincial, Father Aylward, one of the many who

---

* The Effect on the World of the Restoration of Canon Law ; being *A Vindication of The Catholic Church against a Priest*, by David Urquhart, London, 1869.

loved and revered him. "In that letter," he wrote on the 10th of August following, "which you lately inserted in the *Dip. Rcv.*, there were expressions (quite apart from the theological question of War) which were strangely disturbing to me, and ominously enigmatical. That no man would arrive by the following of his own judgment and conscience at the conclusions which the Church teaches as of divine revelation—this every believer in what is generally called 'revealed religion,' is ready to confess. The saying of St. Augustine, '*Evangelio non crederem nisi me Catholicæ Ecclesiæ commoveret auctoritas*,'* 'I would not accept the gospel if it did not come guaranteed to me by the authority of the Catholic Church,' is a favourite text with Roman controversialists. But the very foundation of a science of supernatural theology is in the belief that truths which reason cannot discover, it will, when rightly exercised, support; and that conscience will approve rules of life it could not itself formulate and sanction. Therefore to write 'If I followed my own judgment and conscience I should arrive at a conclusion quite opposed to the teaching of the Church,' was little short of an avowal of heresy. It was like saying, 'I submit but do not agree.'"

---

* Contra Ep. Fundamenti, cap. v.

CHAPTER VIII.

LAST DIFFICULTIES AND DECISION.

A few days later he wrote the following letter to Mr. Martineau:—

" June 7th.

"REV. AND DEAR SIR,—Your very kind visit helped me in three ways, (1) to realise more my own position and its grounds, by imparting it to another; (2) by perceiving that you deem it, at least, not the most conscientious; (3) by giving me the practical information and hope that piety, virtue, charity, and devotedness are really flourishing amongst those who reject authoritative religious teaching.

"I have now determined distinctly to submit my position to Dr. Newman, in the letter which I enclose, and which you might please return to me with any suggestion.

"I shall not send that letter to him for several days —for I cannot help prognosticating that whatever may be the full result, at least, I shall withdraw from any teaching position in the Catholic Church, and therefore I think I must pave the way so as to save peculiar embarrassments to some who would be very intimately affected, and for whom I must provide that they should be as little as possible affected, by my abandonment of a spiritual trust. Also I must give a private intimation to my Provincial, so that he may be prepared to supply my place without causing any unnecessary injury, or inconvenience, or harm. I have already made an application to Rome to get myself superceded as Head and Director of the Association of the Perpetual Rosary, but without assigning any reason; they knew I never desired office, and will attribute my resignation (which I do not make till my place can be quite filled) to love of quiet and perhaps indolence. Also some other parties, such as my bishop, and some special friends, I must communicate with, so that the position I have occupied in trust from the Church may not be abandoned in a way calculated to injure the Church or them; all this will take about four weeks anyhow.

"Then a great practical difficulty of conscience always arises to my mind,—whether I ought to say to the Provincial, or to the General of my Order, 'I will adopt any course you desire which does not imply belief.' The General would in all probability request me to go to Rome; now without the over-strained fears of many Protestants, I must acknowledge not to desiderate Rome.

"Moreover, as the Catholic theory, the Catholic conviction, is that to 'lose the faith' is a grave and the gravest of sins, the General would say, 'you need not do anything against your conscience, but withdraw to a Religious House in France, and make retreat, and pray and remain in seclusion; you will be maintained there, and can read and pray and think; you will thus bring no scandal on religion, and not wound friends, or betray a trust.'

" This is a subject I had also wished to have gone
into with you. Everything seems such a maze to
me in contemplating this vast change of the whole
habit of my mind, and life, and line of action, that
I do not see with even a proximate guess what is the
highest, most conscientious, and honourable line of
action.

" On the whole I incline to this, after I have done
all in my power to be just, and kind, and considerate
to those I leave, to seek some kind of occupation nearest akin to that of my last twenty years, and therefore connected with some institution of a charitable
or educational character. I have no desire to be the
founder of a sect, or to push myself to the front as
a religious teacher, but if *proprio motu*, and heartily
a Congregation of 'Free Christians' understanding
me to hold the convictions of Theodore Parker,
really confided in me, so as to request me to become
their pastor, it would be according to the habits
of my mind and life.

" Four years in a Catholic Ecclesiastical College,
and twenty years in missionary, pastoral, and confessional duties, and now the peaceful meditative
seclusion of nearly two years, combine with the
pressure of these spiritual anxieties to disqualify me
for the ordinary business of life.

" These are the practical questions which arise
before me, but still there continues a conflict between
my intellect and my conscience. The true religion
should not be opposed to intellect, but it should be
chiefly approved by the conscience. My conscience

G

seems continually saying to me, ' dispel all doubts—whichever is the best and most complete religion must be the true one—if you were as humble, pious, good a man as such a one, or as learned as such other, you would not be thinking of striking off into an eccentric course.'

" I never perform any of my priestly duties without my conscience saying to me, ' that is right—in its mystic signification it is the most complete presentation of the truth.'

" My dear sir, pardon my wearying you with the details of my mental and spiritual agony.

" Accustomed to legislate for others, and authoritatively to teach others and guide them, as an individual (in accord with Catholic theory) I never guided myself : every action, movement, the very horarium of the day, every minutest detail has been prescribed to me, and the perfection set before me was to try to carry it out as the expression of God's will ; belief on authority, practise on authority, have been my law of mind and life. Therefore the mere taking the whole of this gravest matter into my own hands seems, feels, like a grievous imperfection as well as difficulty ; and the harbouring of a doubt is like the dallying with a sin.

" Even as an Anglican I took all on the authority, as it were, of a branch representing the One Church.

" Then I think if two years ago I had hastily acted on a doubt, before I had accustomed my mind to accept some great principles *not on authority*, it would have been the shattering of my whole moral nature, and been more calamitous than the most degraded superstition would be if united with religious and moral life.

"With great gratitude for your kind sympathy, and for certain salient thoughts you suggested in our too brief interview,

"Believe me,

"Yours faithfully,

"ROBERT RODOLPH SUFFIELD."

It will be hard for those who have never had to go through a like trial, to understand this conscientious scruple about an act which would seem to be one of utter abnegation of self for truth's sake. Men may, and do leave the Roman Church, and every Church from motives of self-interest, or pride, or passion, or from mere wantonness and love of change, but his worst enemies could hardly assign such motives as the cause of Mr. Suffield's ' apostacy '; he had everything to lose in leaving the Church,—position, livelihood, friends, honour; his temptation, as has been many a man's, was not against the faith, but towards it,—to interpret, explain, accommodate it so as to be able to profess it and not lie; this was what every selfish motive prompted. And how are we then to explain this contrariness of conscience, whose office it was to approve and support, not reproach and disquiet him? Is it not simply that conscience acquires habits just as do all other faculties of the man, and when it has long been used to condemn a course of action as wrong, it cannot all at once conform to a changed judgment of the intellect, and reverse at its bidding the habits formed by the painful discipline of many years. An instance of the kind, true, though imaginary, occurs in Bret Harte's poem of 'St. Abe and his Seven Wives.' Abe Clewson, a Yankee convert to Mormonism, became an 'apostate' to the faith, and left his wives to sort themselves, as they quickly did, with other partners, while he fled with the one woman of them all whom he loved, married her, and lived faithfully with her far away. But telling his experiences to an old friend whom he meets for the first time since the night of his flight, five years ago, he says :—

> And I did the best I could
> When I ran away for good.
> Yet for many a night, you know,
> (Annie too, would tell you so),
> Could n't sleep a single wink,
> Could n't eat and could n't drink,
> Being kind of conscience-cleft
> For those poor creatures I had left.

Not that they would be deserted, or destitute, or unhappy, that he knew well, but that the old Utah habit of conscience still survived, and he *felt* that to be wrong which he *knew* to be right. Much more must it be the case when the cause which has been rejected, and as it were betrayed, is neither immoral nor absurd, but one which men, at least as wise and good as ourselves, still stand by.

It is this one of the sorest trials of every serious and upright convert, that there is within his own self that which sides with his old friends to reproach and condemn his action; and so his first experiences are of a constant appeal to the judgment of reason to uphold and approve his action.

To this letter Mr. Martineau replied as follows :—

"10, GORDON STREET,

"LONDON, *June 17th*.

"REV. AND DEAR SIR,—The closing days of an Academical Session have brought me occupation too incessant and imperative to allow of my writing sooner. Yet almost hour by hour my thoughts have been with you, since the last kindly grasp of your hand at the railway station. As far as the different habits of my mind permit, I try to think myself into your position, and though I dare not even fancy my sympathy with its difficulties complete, I see too clearly the loneliness, the wounds of affection, the tremblings of conscience which it involves, not to long and pray for the power and privilege of rendering such help in the crisis as brotherly appreciation may make possible. The one difference between the Catholic and the Protestant estimate of duty which your letters bring home to me, and which I find it most difficult to conciliate, has reference to the supposed conflict of claims between the intellect and the conscience. The proposition "The best and most complete Religion must be the true," I can only read conversely—"The true Religion must be the best and most complete"; nor, apart from its truth, could I venture to measure the goodness of a faith. So little can I escape from my Protestant reverence for veracity as the primary and paramount condition of any possible personal religion, and for any reality inwardly given to me as against the fairest fictions recommended to me from without, that I cannot understand the possiblity of invoking the Will against honest doubt and dawning light, without the keenest remorse as for heinous sin. I can enter into any degree of self-distrust : personally, I feel it profoundly, in the face of the collective judgment against me of the Church, or even of any one or two men whom I love and venerate. But this would only drive me to a sorrowful silence in following the little light I have ; and could never justify me in pretending to have theirs. I say this, not in order to argue the question, but simply to indicate my chief difficulty in assuming your point of view and to account for what I fear must seem to you the too great rigour of my judgment on the problem which we discussed.

" The wise and tender consideration with which you are providing for all the interests affected by your mental change, ought to protect you from the reproaches and lamentations of your ecclesiastical superiors and friends, and to secure you reverence as a confessor, instead of reprobations as an infidel. The perversion of the Moral Sense which prevents this is itself enough to condemn the system responsible for it. With regard to any ulterior mode of life, it is difficult to see the possibilities till your decision is so far taken as to render enquiry and consultation practicable. No position, worthy of your antecedents and gifts, is at present visible to me. But I think it probable that some congenial sphere of duty, such as

you indicate, would open to you, and on receiving
your permission, I would do my best to find the way
to it. But your appeal to Dr. Newman can hardly
fail at least to keep the problem in suspense for
awhile; and the marvellous subtlety and power with
which he knows how to speak to just the state of
mind on which you have consulted him, must be
expected to retard, perhaps to arrest, a change which
every influence resists, except the Divine simplicity of
truth.

" I mean still to fulfil my threat of burdening your
shelves with some printed matter that bears my
name. But I have not yet found time to put my
hand on what I want. On Wednesday week I go to
Scotland for three months, and before that day I
hope to send my address and something by book
post."

To this letter Mr. Suffield made no reply for three
weeks, having been, as he writes on July 7th, " in-
extricably involved by friends and others coming on
grave matters from a distance." And all this business made it harder to take the step which yet
seemed inevitable, as he went on to explain ;—

" Perhaps this very confidence, so unbounded, makes
it still more difficult to me to face the terrible alternative. Moreover, there arc three or four families
in which I am so interwoven as to be practically a
sort of guardian, where it might gravely embarrass
the carrying out of certain trusts, supposing my name
appeared as no longer a Catholic."

He then proposes a visit to Mr. Martineau in

London, and in case he should be away, "I thought," he wrote, " I might sustain my hopes of there being a real religious resting place, and a tried successful spiritual foundation outside the Catholic Church, by intercourse with someone earnest, reticent, truthful, and knowing the spiritual life in its other forms. I have thought of Keshub Chunder Sen, and also of Miss Frances Power Cobbe. Will you kindly give me your opinion as to the prudence and benefit of consulting these, and if you think it well, write me a letter of introduction to inspire confidence."

" I thank you for your very kind promise of some of your works, which will be greatly valued by me."

Mr. Martineau had left town for Scotland, and replied to this letter as follows :—

" TALLADH-A-BHEITHE,

" KINLOCH, PITLOCHRIE,

" *July 7.*

" I am full of regret at missing your visit to town, because I find it difficult to refer you by letter to any friend who would avail for confidential conference. Keshub Chunder Sen is travelling in the provinces, and I do not know how to reach him; Miss Cobbe has left town, and will not be back for some months; meanwhile I cannot help dwelling on the possible future, and wondering whether I can in any way smooth its difficulties. I am occasionally consulted about the suitable filling of vacant positions of religious duty, and just now have been asked whether I know of anyone fitted to minister to a Free Christian Church about to organise itself at Croydon. They have already bought a small Church; the leading persons in the Society are cultivated and liberal people, very much in sympathy with Theodore Parker's theology; the constitution of the society will be perfectly open; and, as the organisation is now indeed unformed, there are no habits or usages that may not be moulded to the exigencies of a minister's conscience and reasonable preference. I remember you saying that if such a body of persons were to offer to place themselves under your spiritual guidance the duty would not be uncongenial to you; and, as an opportunity so nearly agreeing with this description is of rare occurrence, I report it to you at once. Of course I have no power in such cases, beyond that of simple advice; and the matter could not be decided without a personal visit and public preaching. If you could throw yourself in faith upon this post of possible duty, I do believe you would find your deliverance in it, and would help to a better spiritual life those who are greatly in need of it."

This communication brought him face to face with the dreaded necessity of a speedy decision. When it seems to one that such a step ought to be taken, often he thinks, and asks, and fears so much beforehand, that this very state of uncertainty comes insensibly to be accepted as if it could continue; and when some suggestion which implies action is made, he is frightened and shrinks back before it. So there are in religion many life-long Hamlets, who are always thinking of doing what they never do, and whose ' conscience,' *i.e.* self-consciousness, ' makes cowards' of them.

> And thus the native hue of resolution
> Is sicklied o'er with the pale cast of thought.
> And enterprises of great pith and moment
> With this regard their currents turn away,
> And lose the name of action.

And thus they abide, Anglicans always leaning to the Roman Church; Roman Catholics always doubting whether they should not be Unitarians; Churchmen who are half sceptics, and so on; never quite sure that they are what they profess to be, hesitating to act till the power of action is lost. Thanks to Mr. Martineau's kind intervention, Mr. Suffield found himself at length at the pass that he must needs decide, and he wrote immediately,—

" July 9, 1870.

" MY DEAR MR. MARTINEAU,

" I have just returned from town and found your kind letter. You cannot but deem me at least partially unworthy of your frank sympathy when you see me still finding excuses (as they must appear to you) to enable me to delay the act by which I am to make myself an outcast from so many pure, and noble, and loving hearts. If ever *one* had wronged me or irritated me, it would have been easier to have acted, for in the impetuosity of anger I might have forgotten a thousand charities.

" However, there is no alternative. My chief immediate difficulty is as to the right course to pursue in regard to Catholics : probably very few would in any case follow my example, but several would be partially affected in their position, and that in different degrees, according to the extent to which I communicated my motives to them. As to my line of action I should therefore be glad to help out my conscience by conferring with Dr. Newman and with yourself.

"For instance Lady · · · simply waits to see what I do; she has told me so, and to prevent complications, is freeing herself from a Catholic governess, and has implored me still to 'guide her children.' It is these kind of questions which I do not as yet see through. I suppose I may make many mistakes, but I must pray God not to make them wilfully.

"And now as to your very kind proposal. I had noticed Croydon in the Unitarian papers, and the very idea you suggest had passed through my own mind, but I determined not to breathe it to anyone. If they felt confidence and sympathy, it would quite meet my ideas and wishes.

"After leaving Bosworth and conferring with Dr. Newman, I suppose the best course would be for me to go to London, to take lodgings, then, quietly and unobserved, to frequent the places of worship with which my future career would be most in sympathy— at least a couple of months should be thus occupied— I could then form my ideas on some practical points, particularly on those which seem to me the least satisfactory, the mode of public worship, and the form of prayer. I cannot but feel that a printed form is needed, which should combine real piety, with absence of historic and ecclesiastical dogmas. There are also some minor points, quite immaterial in themselves, but such as must be determined one way or another in a chapel—*e.g.* whether the young should be attracted by their innate love of the picturesque, surpliced choirs, &c. Regarding these matters I am personally indifferent, but I want to know, 'should anything of the kind be permitted or encouraged?'

" I need not say how I should loathe making a show of myself, or appearing under any circumstances which might seem antagonistic or hostile, but I presume I might after two or three months be asked to take occasional duty under circumstances which would manifest my real intentions, opinions, and feelings.

" In this delay there would be, I think, benefit to myself and delicacy towards the feelings of others; moreover, experience of forms of religious life not known to me except by books, would enable me more effectually to serve others and win their confidence.

" If then your friends at Croydon thought it likely . we should enjoy mutual sympathy and confidence, and if you thought the same, I do not know anything or any neighbourhood I should like so well. It is sufficiently near London to meet those few friends who *might* dare to meet me; and it is not a locality where my residence would look hostile to Catholics, and it is sufficiently unobtrusive.

" As to my religious convictions, in doctrine I agree with Theodore Parker, but in mode I prefer a more scriptural tone; for instance, there is no prayer I like so much as the Psalms, dropping out national aspirations and Oriental craving for revenge. As you said, 'A Theist after the type of Christ,' but not fettered by verbal statements attributed to him. I should like that persons believing in the Atonement (in a sort of way) could attend my Chapel without being shocked, and so families need not be divided; if the husband held 'very advanced' views, and the wife were a sort of half 'Evangelical,' I would rather seek to find the ground on which they could unite, than use the sword to sever.

" I do not think we gain by shocking and wounding the feelings or prejudices of those who have not had time, or have not wished or dared to, think. I should have no objection to perform a ceremony considered pious, if not deemed an obligation or a grace, or to imply on my side belief in its efficacy. I could not use the form 'through Jesus Christ our Lord,' unless incidentally and in a figurative way.

" Ever yours, sincerely and gratefully,

" ROBERT RODOLPH SUFFIELD."

To this Mr. Martineau replied,—

" PITLOCHRIE, *July 13, 1870.*

" MY DEAR FATHER SUFFIELD,

" I have availed myself of your permission to mention, without name, the circumstances of your personal struggle of conscience to my friends at Croydon ; and I have stated that if they wish me to become the medium of an ulterior introduction, it will be necessary for them to arrange meanwhile for temporary services during the next few months. There will be no occasion therefore for any greater haste than your own proposal contemplates. Indeed I was not at all anxious to press you into action faster than your convictions would spontaneously move you. But this Croydon position appeared to me so special, that I should have reproached myself if I had permitted it to lapse by default.

" Your plan of looking around you in London, and gaining insight into the religious life and worship of your probable future associates, seems to me the best possible. Only it is unfortunate that during the autumn months,—till October at all events,—most of the regular ministers are liable to be absent, and the people so dispersed that the usual services are very inadequately represented, and everything is at its very lowest point.

" Your preference for a printed Form of Prayer is now largely shared by our liberal Nonconformist congregations. In my own Chapel, a book is used containing Ten Services; the first two adapted from the morning and evening prayer of the English Church: the last two written by myself: and the intermediate services compiled—(by my friend Dr. Sadler)—from old Liturgies or other books of devotion. I will send you one of our sets of services; but before doing so I wish to have certain alterations made with the pen, which, for ease of conscience, I have found it necessary to introduce. They all of them, or nearly all, have reference to such phrases as ' through Christ our Lord,' which, with yourself, I have a scruple about using. Even with the alterations which I have introduced, there remain expressions in the book which I should not myself have left standing. But our congregations comprise persons of many shades of theological belief, and expressions which speak tenderly to some are almost silent to others; and, on the whole, the volume fairly represents, when corrected, the average tone of religious feeling; more so, perhaps, than if I were to push my own inward wish for alteration further.

"I do not think you would find any desire for enrichments of the service addressed to *the eye*,—such as surpliced choirs, or symbolical acts. The tendency amongst us is to a simplicity too bald and rationalistic, and it is only in the direction of Music and Architecture that this tendency has at all given way. I am often hurt and vexed by the prosaic coldness of our people in these things. But it is connected with one of their highest virtues,—a profound veracity and reality of religion, which will never profess anything but what is rather within than beyond the truth distinctly apprehended.

"What you say about Lady · · · is quite wonderful to me, as showing the extent to which religion may become a matter of personal confidence. Where it *is* so, I do not see the duty of refusing the guidance which is sought, and leaving the dependent minds standing where they are. On the contrary, I should frankly confide to them the grounds of my own change, and leave the result to God. I could not say to another—'I am going whither the light leads; you had better stay where you are'; unless that other found upon the spot an adequate and satisfying light. It is one thing to proselytise; another to help minds spontaneously feeling their way along lines of experience already traced by us.

"I have asked Longmans to send you two vols. of mine: and Trübner to send two, unless they are out of print. And I forward a pamphlet or two which may possibly be readable, though embarrassed with allusions to others which you will not appreciate.

"Believe me ever,

"Yours very faithfully,

"JAMES MARTINEAU."

Mr. Suffield replied the same day on which he received this letter.

"Thank you very much for the books and pamphlets just received, which I shall read with great interest. Could you not publish a small public prayer book, which should contain no expression of doctrine beyond Theism, but which might contain allusions to and expressions about our Lord in such a way as not to imply any dogmatic belief, yet (1) might meet the susceptibilities of those who regard the omission of the name of Jesus to signify the Deism of Revolutionary France, and (2) might awaken those pious associations belonging to all who like ourselves have received religion through the Christian medium?

"When in London last week, a Member of Parliament, nominally Anglican, really nothing, spoke to me of your Chapel; he had been there, was delighted with the sermon, but on account of the prayers determined not to go any more. He said, 'I would rather explain away our beautiful Church of England liturgy than join in a mutilated imitation, implying almost as much which I disbelieve.' This was six years ago before the changes you made.

"Your remarks rather shook me regarding the benefit of a delay after I have taken my position. I am now delayed simply by the delay and embarrassment of my Provincial, to whom I have written confidentially. I wish to comply with his desires and requests as far as practicable. He has evidently kept my application made to him a secret, for to-day's post brought a letter from Lord · · · a novice, at Woodchester, about the most embarrassing I could get. I send it to you that you may realise the difficulties when I want to act honestly without taking advantage of my position.

"As soon as I am free, I see my position and course so clearly, that probably a delay might not be very beneficial. I was influenced in suggesting it by a desire not to give pain to others, and by an almost painful diffidence that I should not be liked or trusted. I am so accustomed to Catholics, and their feelings regarding a priest 'falling away,' (as we always say), that I cannot help attributing the same thought to others.

"I would rather starve and die than be taken through compassion by those who could not trust me.

"The only real difficulty I had, regarded the prayers. I dreaded the idea of initiating a novelty,

H

and I did not hear of any existing forms of worship which I could honestly use, and which those who agreed with me could honestly sympathise with.

"If there be such, or if you would publish one, and thus enable a Christian minister, unfettered by historic dogmas, to conduct a service and have prayers which he could use without inventing something new, my difficulty would be removed.

"My mind has turned upon these matters so much, and is of rather a practical character, that two or three weeks intercourse with others would enable me to catch the great difference of *modus operandi* between priest and minister.

"If, therefore, they had confidence in me, not regarding me merely as a witness against Rome, but as one who has fought a battle and wished to help others before he died—and if they felt honestly able and wishful to receive me as a friend and helper—personally I would rather begin with them their new work, and be thus bound with them in that first bond of sympathy and charity."

CHAPTER IX.

It was a most difficult position in which he now found himself, and which he himself would only have excused on the ground of its essentially temporary character. He was regarded by the world as a priest of the Roman Church and a member of one of its strictest religious Orders, and as such he was performing the daily duties of the priesthood, and his advice was sought by all manner of faithful and doubting Catholics : he was at heart a Unitarian, and only waiting the opportunity to declare himself. But a position of trust once accepted cannot be quitted in a day, there must be some deference shown to those from whom it has been received, and some precautions adopted not to use it to their detriment. No one held more strongly than Mr. Suffield that a man's outward profession should be true to his inward conviction, yet he found himself forced for a few weeks to appear, what he had been in all sincerity but was no longer ; so he continued to wear the habit of a Dominican, while in heart and allegiance he had quitted the Order. The moral embarrassment was painful enough, but it was greatly aggravated by the necessity he was under of giving counsel and direction to others.

Returning the letter which he had enclosed, Mr. Martineau wrote:—·

" PITLOCHRIE,

" *July 17th, 1870.*

" MY DEAR FATHER SUFFIELD,

" I return you the affecting letter of your young friend. It deeply moves my compassion and respect. It is a Divine light of duty which he sees afar, and to which he is drawn by pure and sweet affections ; while he is chained down out of reach of it by invisible but irrefragable bonds of a religion which can no longer be a true and peaceful piety to him. I do hope you will be able to get him dispensed. Surely, at his age, a mistake of his real call, a misinterpretation of the Will of God respecting him, must be recognised as possible by a Church so cognisant of every mood of the spiritual life as the Catholic.

" I am sorry that you have had so unfavourable an impression given to you of the Prayer Book used at my Chapel. If it be well-founded, I fear the slight changes since introduced will not modify it much. But I must say the judgment expressed by your friend appears to me hasty and one-sided : and I shall be surprised if, on examining the book, you find it dwell more than you approve on the historical relations of religion. I think your Member of Parliament must have come in for the *first* service, and been offended by the altered sound of what he was accustomed to at the Parish Church. *That* is the service which I myself like least : but for perhaps the opposite reason, namely, that I never could enter into the admiration constantly expressed for the Church of England Liturgy. The whole structure of the Morning Prayer appears to me framed upon a low type of worship, involving abject conceptions both of human nature and of the Father of spirits. Having joined in the production of this book, by contributing the ninth and tenth services, I could not well desert it to frame another. Indeed the multiplication of such books is an evil which I have always regretted : and I would rather employ an imperfect form which was in general use among those Churches with which I am in fellowship, than the best which was special to one or two places. It is possible for any congregation which prefers it to have from the publisher two, or four, or six of our ten services without the rest. A friend in London will shortly send you the book. I am sorry to find that one of the volumes which I directed to be forwarded to you is out of print, the more so, as it contains the papers which alone, it is probable, would have much interest for you. I meant also to send a volume of miscellanies, containing a paper or two on Catholicism, in particular one, ("The Battle of the Churches,") on the so-called " Papal Aggression," which might at least have amused you with its heresies and perhaps its blunders : but the volume is out of print.

" I have heard from my Croydon correspondent that the Committee of the Society was about to meet, and that the substance of my letter would come before them, evidently with favourable predispositions. I feel sure that if anything comes of this, you will have *no distrust to fear*. No doubt, in the first approaches to one another of minds drawing together from such distant points, there *must* be a temporary awkwardness, and something tentative in method till the communion of spiritual life is matured. But the tact of natural sympathy, and devotion to common objects of human good, will soon wear the first stiffness away. You will have to forgive, I fear, something frigid, some want of graciousness, some prominence of the critical temper in our manners and character. But, believe me, there is a deeper and a tenderer soul behind than this repulsive exterior would lead you to expect.

" Will this vote of the Council and the French War, occurring together, hand over Rome to the Italians ?"

With this letter came " The Ten Services " as it is commonly called, the Book of Prayer in most frequent use in Unitarian congregations, and the perusal of it seems to have set Mr. Suffield's mind at rest as to the difficulty he anticipated in conducting public worship after the Nonconformist type. It was not, however, adopted by either of the congregations to which he afterwards ministered, and he did not feel free to use any of the services, except the ninth and tenth, when asked to preach in Chapels where this book was used.

His reply, dated July 21st, is as follows :—

" The ' Common Prayer for Christian Worship,' which you so very kindly sent me has been a great relief and consolation to me. How strange that writing to three marked places for the best Prayer Book for Unitarian and Free Christian Churches, this was not sent! but instead, books full of orthodoxy and water with very little unction or manly piety. This little book I greatly admire, and if my Member of Parliament friend alluded to this, I do not agree with him. I should feel disposed to use the pen in perhaps ten or a dozen more places, *e.g.*, several of the benedictions at end of service are quite truthful and beautiful, others I do not like.

"This book quite encourages me, for I now see my way to the adoption of a pure and beautiful form of prayer, ready to hand. I have been so accustomed to rest upon authority, that the idea of having to invent something new for myself fills me with additional dread and almost horror.

"I am gradually and one by one cutting the cables, but—pardon my weakness when I say it—each time I have to pierce through my own heart. I understand now that there is an agony in life greater than the agony of death.

"My place will be supplied here by the Provincial on the 12th of August, and a day or two before that I leave for Birmingham. I asked leave from the Provincial to take my books. He wrote very kindly and did not seem surprised, but hoped that the cloud might pass away: he was sure I must have had many mental struggles, and he arranged exactly what I asked.

"He is a good natured and ordinary young man,

without any very deep feelings or thoughts, and takes things easily, thus I am saved the distress of witnessing what would have been the agony of mind of our last Provincial. But letters from dear and intimate friends who partly guess, breathe a tone of pathetic sorrow, so that each post makes me feel what I lose, and what I inflict.

"The Secretary of the Committee of the English Clergy for petitioning the Pope wrote to me for my signature. My reply was sent by some one to the *Westminster Gazette* last Saturday, and this has served to prepare everyone for what they now feel to be likely. It has caused a formal complaint from York Place and other authorities ; perhaps it is just as well.

"On receiving Father Newman's reply kindly inviting me, and the Provincial's leave, I announced in Chapel last Sunday that after August 7th I should be going for several weeks to Birmingham, to confer with Dr. Newman on literary matters in which I was engaged.

"Many now anticipate and fear my intentions, but no one *knows* anything. Here there is not a suspicion.

"Commending myself to your prayers,

"Believe me, &c.

Mr. Martineau's answer was as follows :—

"TALLADH-A-BHEITHE, PITLOCHRIE, *July 28.*
" MY DEAR FATHER SUFFIELD,

" Your narrative of the gradual loosening of the old ties is truly pathetic, and enables me to realise the inner as well as the outer history of this great crisis. I suppose all grand transitions take us into the desert, and have their forty days of anguish. But, through faith and patience, they are the beginning of a diviner life, and their very sadness turns in retrospect to something of a tender glory.

"I am glad you are going to Birmingham, to confer with Dr. Newman,—of all living religious writers the man I perhaps love and honour most, though the more I study him, the more do I wonder at the submission of such a mind to the Roman Catholic theology. Your intercourse with him will have its painful elements mixed with the benefits of his wise and loving counsels. But his large experience will secure a sympathy and appreciation of your recent history which few Catholics could manifest, and which will qualify the estimate of it required by the rule and habit of his Church.

"My Croydon friends having been induced to break off the negotiation for the purchase of a small iron Church, and being obliged to begin worship in a large room, have determined to postpone their services till October, when the summer dispersion is over. They express thankful interest in what they have heard from me, and will beg me, when all is ready with you and with them, to go over and be the medium of a personal introduction. Everything at present is anonymous. I fear the postponement may be rather longer than you would desire. But till October everything is in a state of suspended life with us.

"It is a relief to me to find that you can give so much approval to the Common Prayer. I quite agree with you about the benedictions and some other similar sentences. But in cases where there was an *alternative* given, and *one* of the sentences was such as I could use, I left the other untouched, even though it was objectionable to me. The alterations are not a measure of my personal wish and feeling, but are the least that I could do with. I do not yet despair of getting the book revised in accordance with them."

Before him, Mr. Suffield had written acknowledging the receipt of the books, and expressing the satisfaction their perusal gave him. There was true devotion, he was now convinced, outside the Catholic Church, and independent of all so-called 'supernatural' revelation.

"I must now tell you how greatly your own works have interested me. I have not read yet (at least not to say—read) those of a more philosophical character. I never doubted the existence of *thought* outside the Catholic Church, but if I might give praise, which must seem to you very arrogant and absurd, the *tone* of the moral and spiritual works entirely concurs with whatever is *highest* in Catholic literature; yours is so evidently not a mere protest, or like some publications I obtained, a mere attempt to make sermons without any religion. I was not surprised that such work had emanated from *you*, but it encouraged me to think that it could command the sympathy of others. It seems to me a singular providence that I should, apparently without a motive, certainly without a suggestion, have opened communications with you—for everything you write or say harmonises with my own mind and heart, and I can perceive in it a tone of faith and reverence which would elevate, and also amidst trials and death, sustain. Nor can I tell you what a relief it is to me to find a mind thoroughly honest and independent, and reared in that independence, still holding with a tender reverence the Christian *spirit* and *tone* without the verbal dogmas.

"What amongst other considerations has kept me back so long has been the fear of simply throwing myself into a protest, and amidst people speaking tall-talk about "free thought," &c. It is easy enough for our thoughts to be free—we want them trained by the holiness and fatherly liberty of God.

"The Prayer Book I admire more and more—it, to my mind, only needs the gentle emendations of a second edition from your hands now to make it quite perfect. I like also a little Tract Prayer Book put out by the Hindoo—but he has not caught the pure graphic English, which give additional help to the English mind.

"Some practical details as to myself I really do not see my way through. I, as a Dominican, took a vow of obedience to our General—to my own conscience and feeling (so to speak) this does not seem to me to bind, but the whole is so new a field of conscientious difficulty to me that I really do not see the right, or the reason to give. I see and feel how delicately and thoughtfully I ought to act—and indeed I have given them every advantage over me if they choose to be ungenerous—but I do not see my way clearly ; for instance, they have written to the General ; now suppose the General desires me to go to some House in France or Rome and to remain in seclusion, what he would call in Retreat ?

" *Before God—in conscience and in honour—what strikes you should be my reply ?*

"Probably these difficulties seem to you almost weak and frivolous, but you can hardly realise the minute obedience we have been accustomed to render as of conscientious obligation.

"I feel in my own mind that as they consider that the Pope can dispense the vow—if the conscience of one man can do so, so can the conscience of another. As a matter before God, I really do not feel anxious, but I do not see what would be *the best line* to take —whether to obey and leave the rest.

"In ordinary matters I trust them as good men ; when it touches this kind of matter *I do not*, for the theory obliges them to treat doubt as a crime, and thought as a rebellion. Thus, men ordinarily kind and good, would be quite disposed to order me to an unhealthy foreign Priory, where sickness and the climate would enfeeble mind and body,—it would be done ' to serve the souls of others, and to give me thus a better chance of saving my own, by having less to answer for.'

"I should not like an ordinary Protestant to know this quite so bluntly, for it would encourage the vulgar prejudices which are true only in a certain sense, and under peculiar circumstances.

"How does this strike your own conscience?

"Sincerely and faithfully yours,

"ROBERT RODOLPH SUFFIELD."

"P.S.—I am ashamed to have forgotten to thank you about Croydon. I am not at all sorry for the delay. I think to others it will at least *feel* better, and with a prospect before me, I could easily borrow a few pounds to help me in the interim without being thrown on help which would be meant to compromise me and my independence.

"Besides having made the greater sacrifice—of all friendships—I can bear the rest."

So as the way of truth became more and more clear did the difficulties increase, interest, affection, conscience seemed all allied to stop the path. To become a martyr, yet doubt whether you are not wrong in your very sacrifice, whether the better course would not be to submit is cruel suffering, and through this was he now passing. Happy for him that he had chosen as counsellor one who had the rare gift of sympathy with creeds he had never believed, and states of mind he had never himself experienced.

"KILTGRIE, KILLIN, CRIEF,

"*August 5th.*

"MY DEAR FATHER SUFFIELD,

"I feel already that I owe you a great deal for introducing me to new problems of duty which lie beyond the usual casuistry of our Protestant life. It is only too clear to me how difficult it is to escape from this network of early vows without needless hurt to the conscience of others. The mischief, however, which is inseparable from the collapse of an illusory system has to be encountered; and it is best minimised, as it seems to me, by the simplest and directest action, based upon the true grounds which satisfy the agent's own conscience. You justly feel that a vow or engagement of unconditional obedience for all time to the will of any human being is *ultra vires* for a responsible conscience; being a formal conveyance to another of an accountability which is intrinsically inalienable; and undergoing repeal *ipso facto* the moment the will of the official superior clashes with the immediate inward voice of the Holy and Truth-loving God. This repeal having plainly occurred in your case, I see no legitimate course remaining but to refuse an obedience which has lost its obligation in the presence of higher and incompatible claims. This is only to act on a principle recognised (is it not?) by all Catholic casuists,—viz., that there can be no binding engagement to commit a crime; and that it is less offensive in the sight of God to break a promise or a vow, than, on the strength of it, to commit more heinous or continuous sin. Whoever asks me *to play the hypocrite*, in order to keep my word, makes a demand which, in being uttered, is self-condemned.

"It may indeed be urged that, in being ordered into retreat, you are not asked to commit any sin,— the act being one of mere abstinence and silence.

The proper answer seems to be: "This negative suspense is no complete act of itself, to be judged as an insulated thing. It is an instrumental discipline, with a view to an end, and assumes that that end yet remains to be determined. If that assumption were true, the discipline might be obediently accepted. But I know it to be false. The end in view is already out of reach: the discipline of retreat and devotion has been honestly tried, and to try it again would be a fruitless waste of life, and dallying with the call and appointed term of duty. There must sometime be a moment for decision. I have exhausted the allowable preliminaries. It may be proper for my superior to gain time; if possible my care must now be not to lose it.'

"In short, to take from the General of the Order a medicine on which he rests hopes, but which is foreknown by you to be ineffectual, is to mislead him under the guise of obedience. The ultimate disobedience is not escaped, but only postponed: and the *date* at which it must come cannot be rightly determined, except by the self-knowledge of the personal conscience.

"No doubt, we must always come with a spirit humbled and apologetic into the presence of one to whom we have made promises we cannot keep: and when he charges us with wrong, we cannot deny the fault, only we transpose it, and in answer to his, 'you should not have *broken* your word,' must reply, 'we should not have *given* it.' I must confess, however, that towards a superior who would adopt the sort of policy of banishment at which you hint, I should find it difficult to feel due penitence.

" Your admirable reply to the Papal Committee* delighted me beyond measure ; and I see it has elicited Mr. Oxenham's good word in the *Saturday Review*. I cannot help looking for some large and conspicuous results of the Council,—if not in this country, in Austria and South Germany; except that this dreadful war suspends the working of all ideal interests."

Meanwhile he had been busy severing as firmly and gently as he could the ties which bound him to the Roman Church.

On July 14th he wrote to the editors of *The Rosary Magazine*, with which he had been identified from the beginning, that his connection with it must cease. " It has so happened that correspondents abroad and at home have of late been sending questions which I could not reply to, with what I deemed truth and historic accuracy, without going counter to your feelings and opinions, and to those of a large portion of your readers. Now you will be able to obtain the services of a learned priest, whose ecclesiastical tendencies tally with your own, and I am convinced that the Magazine will gain by my withdrawal."

This letter would have been generally interpreted only as the consequence of his opposition to the proposed definition of Papal Infallibility, which was generally popular amongst English Catholics. He signed himself as of old " Prefect of the Guard of

---

* The letter referred to will be found on pages 129, 130.

Honour and Apostolic Missioner." But the postscript was more ominous, in which he expressed his anxiety 'to resign the Directorship of the Perpetual Rosary as soon as the place can be supplied.' The last of the 'Answers to Correspondents,' which responsible work he had always taken upon himself, and with this August issue was giving up, is also significant of his state of mind: it runs as follows:—

"M.S.—We will pray for you as you desire, but we need your prayers as much."

But before this was in print a much more important and public declaration of his state of mind had appeared in the columns of the *Westminster Gazette*. At this time signatures were being sought to an address to the Pope from English Catholics, praying for the definition in dispute. Not content with a mere refusal to sign, which indeed he was free to do or not, he gave his reasons and sent them to the press. It would be with pain and dismay that many who had been wont to revere him as a teacher, read in their weekly paper on July 16 ;—

"We have been requested to publish the following reply sent to the Secretary for the petition to the Holy Father, which we do without comment:—

"Dear Rev. Sir,—It would not be respectful to your zeal and toil simply to ignore the reception of the proposed address, in which petitioners request the Pope to define his infallibility.

"Knowing with what earnest desire the enemies of our religion, with taunting speech, at once urge us and defy us to proclaim, after 1800 years, the

I

founndation of Christianity; knowing the deep repugnance with which, under the pressure of ecclesiastical opinion and ecclesiastical prospects, canons, priests, and bishops have signed declarations pleasing to ecclesiastical superiors and repugnant to their private opinions; knowing with an intimate and sad knowledge, that the mooting of this question has led to investigations, and then to inquiries, which have paralysed the faith in the minds of numbers of the clergy and of the intellectual laity, and with not a few destroyed it, I must respectfully decline to sign a document in which petitioners ask for a definition, the animus and consequence of which few can be so thoughtless as not to perceive.

"If we get a Pope, vain, obstinate, and in his dotage, shall we ask him to be confirmed in his powers of mischief?

"Do we wish, by exalting the lessons of the encyclical, to render political life impossible to every honest and consistent Catholic, and to render the possession of political and religious equality impossible to any except those sort of Catholics who would use the language of liberty when they beg, and the precepts of the Pope when they refuse?

"Your faithful and obedient servant in Christ,

"ROBERT R. SUFFIELD, O.S.D.

"The Hermitage, H. Bosworth, Leicestershire,
"July 11th, 1870."

CHAPTER X.

REMONSTRANCES AND EXPLANATIONS.

On the Monday following the publication of this letter, the doctrine it impugned was solemnly declared by Pius IX. to be "a dogma divinely revealed," and anathema pronounced upon any who should presume to question it. This made the position he was maintaining all the more impossible, and remonstrances soon began to pour in on him.

On the 19th, a relation and attached friend who held a high position in society, wrote:—

"My Dear Father Suffield,—We were all so distressed and horrified to see your letter in the *Westminster*. I could hardly believe it could be the same Father whom I used to suppose to be so full of devotion to the Church and its head, as one of such an old Order ought to be. What can have changed you so much? Surely *you* are not going the way of Döllinger and the anti-Catholic Liberals. I do hope sincerely that few will read your letter. I really could not help letting you know how astonished and distressed everyone is who has seen it. There must now be an end of these discussions for ever, and, whether people like it or not, they must believe what the Council has decreed; and how delighted Catholics ought to be, and good ones are, to have an opportunity of proving their love for the the successors of St. Peter. Do write soon, something to remove the bad impression your letter has made. I trust you will pray that you may not have caused scandal against your intention."

So some wrote on whose minds had never dawned the idea of "truth," as distinct, or possibly distinct, from the Roman faith; but even more sad were the letters of those who themselves were tried by doubts, and felt the shock of his words as loosening their hard hold on faith. One, unknown to him personally, wrote:—"I am but a young Catholic, having only been three years in the Church, but they have not been happy ones. I have been troubled, almost without cessation, with temptations against the faith, and have been unable to cast away a terrible fear that all may be a mistake and delusion. But I have been more distressed and frightened by a letter of yours, which I read yesterday in *The Westminster Gazette*, than by anything else. If we are to believe that the Holy Ghost is inspiring the Council, how can he dictate that which has 'paralysed the faith in the minds of clergy and laity,' or must I doubt whether he has presided there, and then where is the infallible teaching of the Church, which is to most Catholics the anchor of their faith? And then, Father, that terrible sentence about the Popes! Can it really mean what it seems to express? If you only knew the misery your words have made me suffer, you would forgive me writing this way. Your own 'Crown of Jesus' seems to speak such different language. . . If it looks like disrespect to write this, I entreat you to impute it to ignorance alone, for I am, reverend father, your respectful, but very sad-hearted, servant in our Lord, . . ."

To this letter he seems to have given an answer which revealed his whole position, for a few days after there followed another communication from the same writer, which it must have given him even greater pain to read. " I dearly prize the confidence you place in me, but the pain your letter gives me is very sharp. My own troubles seem lost in thinking of what you must suffer. Oh, I have prayed with all my might that these clouds may be cleared away from your soul. I would be content to go on my own clouded path to the end, if only the Light of Faith might again shine upon you; for I may keep my trouble to myself; no one depends on me for help and direction—but for you, O dear Father, I see and know what your sufferings must be. I have read your letter over and over again, and it makes my heart fail with fear, lest—I hardly dare write the words—lest Faith is gone. Can it be that you believe less than the Protestants? . . . The first day or two after I got your letter the shock almost made me lose all sense of security. I wish I knew what you mean by writing, ' Beware of resting the Eternal Truths of all Religion upon any ecclesiastical foundation.' But I must not presume to argue with you."

Then follows, as in many another letter, pages of pious advice, constantly checked and apologised for; so unnatural to his correspondents seemed the position of advising one who had been the counsellor of them all. It was such a strange reversal of their respective positions, a duty they deemed it, and yet it had an air of presumption and impertinence which they could not forget.

It was not for three weeks that any public notice was taken of the protest, a delay due perhaps to the hope that the efforts made to induce him to withdraw and apologise, in view of the Decree of the Council, might yet prevail; but on the 6th of August there appeared the two following letters in *The Westminster Gazette*, the one from the head of the English Province of Dominicans, the other from the Prior of their house in London.

"To the Editor of 'The Westminster Gazette,'

July 30th, 1870.

" Dear Sir,—I cannot express the grief and surprise that I felt on my attention being called to Father Suffield's letter, which by some means became inserted in your issue of the 16th inst. In my own name, as Provincial of the Dominican Order in England, and in the name of all my *confrères*, I utterly repudiate that letter both as to sentiment and expression. I wish to be all the more energetic in this disclaimer, as I had already been but too glad to accede to a suggestion made by Father Aylward, my predecessor, to the very opposite effect. . . . . Furthermore, I rejoice to say that the pain Father Suffield's letter has occasioned me is very sensibly mitigated by the many communications which have duly reached me from Fathers of the Province since the publication of that deplorable letter, each one for himself protesting against its being supposed to express the views and feelings of our Province; and I am, moreover, happy to state that this is also confirmed by Father Suffield himself, who, in a letter lately received from him by Father Aylward, says, 'Your letter made me recognise one great duty, namely, that of my signifying in a very marked way that such a letter represents in no degree the feelings of the English Fathers.'

"I remain, yours sincerely,

"F. GEO. VINCENT KING."

The Prior wrote: — "I am in no way Father Suffield's Superior, and therefore have no right officially to publish anything condemnatory of his opinions or language as expressed in his letter of July 16th; moreover, it is a great pain to me to be thus at conflict with one whom I not only love as a Brother of the same Order, but whose personal friendship I enjoyed before either of us became Dominicans, and whose zeal and apostolic spirit I have ever held in the greatest admiration. But, lest it might be supposed that the opinions of so prominent a member of our Order are held by other Dominicans, I feel bound [and he goes on to repudiate all sympathy with the opinions expressed].

"F. AUSTIN M. ROOKE, O.P."

His reply was written immediately, and appeared in the next week's issue, August 6th, 1870:—

"Sir,—Our Provincial and the Prior of London

last week wrote to disclaim for themselves and the English Fathers the statements of a letter of mine, which had been elicited by an accidental circumstance. That disclaimer was doubtless a duty on their part, and the duty was discharged with that frankness, delicacy, and tenderness which has always impressed me as the gracious prerogative of the Superiors of our Order.

" The writer of the striking and accurate articles which forms a complete history of the Council, observes, in the *Saturday Review* of July 30th, that ' Father Suffield would not have ventured on so bold and remarkable a letter unless assured of the moral support of his Order,' and strengthens the inference by the example of Cardinal Guidi.

" Will you permit me to give an explanation which is not needed for the protection of those within the Order—who must be revered, loved, and trusted by all who have intimately known them — but which will be a satisfaction to others, as also to relatives of our novices and friends of our Order.

" If it be a consolation to confide to the sympathy of intimate friendship the struggles of the mind and the sorrows of the heart, it is at once a pain and humiliation to reveal to the curious and indifferent the sorrow with which a stranger meddleth not. That sorrow is now mine.

" An incident, not regretted by me, has revealed, almost by accident, the hidden struggle of years ; and now, this, that, and the other will be said against me ; it will be said that I am proud, and

self-willed, and cannot bear restraint. I know not
what might have been the case if I had been fated
to bear the trial of others' faults, but it did not need
much virtue to obey those whom I revered, to carry
out the wishes of those I loved. During the twenty
years of my priestly life I have never been otherwise
circumstanced.

" But first, permit me to defend friends outside the
Order who have been deeply pained by recognising the
position of my own mind; if they were less generous,
they would reproach me and say, ' We leaned upon
you, and you were a reed, and you broke, and you
pierced the hand that trusted you.' I can only reply,
' A heart that loved you was pierced first, but it was
not done by you ; if you suffer, I suffer more : and
your goodness, tenderness, and forbearance have been
the unceasing arguments, making my heart contend
with my intellect.'

" Many known to be intimate and attached friends
will be pained because they will be supposed to sympathise with my views. Their friendships have been
very profound, and cast about my life a joy like the
charity and purity of Heaven ; but it so happens that
very few of these but are intensely loyal to the
Pope, and enthusiastic about everything Catholic
and Roman. Therefore my praise of others must
never imply a censure upon their Catholicity. Those
friendships, interwoven with the honest sympathies
of years, presenting to me in the midst of mental
struggles the gracious influence of the highest virtues,
are in no ways compromised to my opinions.

" Regarding my Order it will be said that the tendencies and influences were un-Catholic, or that laxity permitted such to exist or to assert themselves. Anything more false it would be impossible to utter. At this moment, when I might be supposed most tempted to say the opposite, and to reply to the pathetic appeals of many by throwing the blame elsewhere, the members of other Orders will more than pardon the filial devotion which makes me praise above others an illustrious Order with which they have entered upon a noble rivalry.

" I did not learn my theology in the Dominican school. I have received from the Dominicans no influence except those which inevitably arise from the witnessing of lives utterly blameless, of characters of noble truthfulness and trust, of hearts at once tender and strong, of an authority at once vigilant, considerate, and just; of an obedience rendered the more cheerfully, for it was rendered to those who deserved it.

" Amongst our English and French Fathers and Brothers, I question whether there is one who does not repudiate utterly opinions they understand me to hold. They do not like to speak, for many amongst them have been to me as sons before they were brothers, and whilst censuring me in their conscience and in their mind, they remain silent, lest words uttered should seem like a treason against memories too beautiful to perish. Lest their silence should be imputed to them as a fault, let me still perform for them the familiar office of a friend, and declare that nothing existing in our noviciate, nothing existing in our teaching, nothing existing in our discipline, nothing encouraged amongst us or allowed, would tend in the direction of my opinions.

"Even in the matter of politics, now somewhat interwoven with religion, they mostly have taken a line the reverse of my own; all our Superiors, I think, entirely so.

"Attention has been drawn to one expression in my letter, an expression, I think, comparatively unimportant, wherein, speaking before the definition, I suppose the case of a weak Pope invested with the additional influence that would be conferred on his ordinary acts by a definition which would enable him at any moment to support such acts by an infallible approval.

"As in late years we have not had bad Popes—the endeavour in the election has been to select good men, but not remarkable for sanctity, learning, or strength — I thought it more decorous not to imagine the re-creation of the moral deformities of the days of old; but and unless failure of reason be impossible to an aged Pope, it becomes essential that there should be some means at least of recognising when his decrees are to be regarded as the acts of the *man* as well as of God. A man who centralises all ecclesiastical, political, and scientific authority in himself, and who by an irresistible sentence can destroy the prospects and character of any member of his great religious organisation, must necessarily obtain a vast increase of power when it is defined, that whenever he chooses he can issue a decree more binding than the gospel, because he can overrule by his explanation the very words of the Christ.

" But the passage of my letter, which really was gravest, has elicited the attention only of minds suffering like my own; and, if such thoughts from many anxious minds had been more adverted to, perhaps even those in the highest authority might have awoke from their dreams of power, and asked themselves whether they would rather rule, like the Christ, mildly over the multitude of many minds, and guide the troubled and the weary to the two-fold charity, or, as one lately said, rule over a lessened Church, and almost hail as a deliverance the exodus of minds that desired to believe, and hearts disposed to love and to obey.

" Thus, partly, I unveil the depths of my doubts and of my sorrows, and doing so, I, at least, clear those whom I love. It is not the Dominican Fathers who have created for me this mental struggle, which has been the hidden agony of years. Do not blame them, they had nothing to gain and nothing to lose. With the charity of pure and noble hearts, blindfold they have gone forward, and they have obeyed.

" It is not the aping of humility when I say, perhaps they may have chosen the highest. The great and holy God knows; I do not; but I know this, that they are not compromised by me. No word of theirs has stung me; no impatience of theirs has hurried me; no fault of theirs has scandalised me; no distrust of theirs has aggravated me.

"It is almost my only happiness in the midst of that 'paralysing of the faith,' which the 'mooting of these questions has produced,' to render the homage of my affectionate reverence at the feet of those I love; and I love them not so much because they have been kind to me, as because they have ever been true to what they believed the highest.

"When life advances nothing is sadder than to have to touch the monument of hope, which, day by day, through years of toil, of sadness and of joy, we have been building with painful labour.

"If a passing incident wrings from the mind the expression of difficulties concealed, or in every other act disowned, do not suppose it to be the daring of one who broke to play a part. He only sought first solitude in the cloister, then solitude greater in a country village, amidst simple people and the children of his flock, that he might dispel difficulties and doubts.

"If these difficulties and doubts have been wrong, none but the highest rulers of the Church have been responsible for them; they have not been a pleasure, but an agony; not a pride, but a humiliation.

"And if ever to any readers of these words, one has given joy in the midst of sorrows; hope when all was dark; perchance in the hour of need, you can return the same to him.—[sic.]

"Yours faithfully,

"ROBERT RUDOLPH SUFFIELD, O.S.D."

"P.S.—Might I add some remarks which, after posting the above letter, occurred to my mind as omitted.　At St. Sulpice my chief guide was a strong Ultramontane ; as to Ushaw, and most dear, revered, ecclesiastical friends in the north, amongst whom all my Catholic thoughts were framed, it is needless for me to say how deeply they deplore opinions I have expressed with which they have *no* sympathy, and which represent almost the exact opposite to their own.　If loyalty to the reputation of my Order compels me (unknown to them and unasked) to clear Dominicans from blame, loyalty to the most tender, intimate, and ancient friendships makes me wish to render this tribute to those so unbounded in their devotion to the Pope, and so in harmony with the highest Catholic tone of thought, and who have left on my own heart the example of every virtue, and the memory of a confiding love that never changes. They know how, impelled not by curiosity, but by the questionings of others evoked by the events of later years, I was driven by my very position and circumstances into those enquiries which have at length wrung from me thoughts which trouble compelled me in some way to make known ; not giving reasons, to shake others, but simply stating the facts. They know the anguish I experience in grieving those I love so intimately and whom I had hoped never to have pained, and often I prayed to God I might die before the day should come."

His former Provincial, a man revered by all for his piety and wisdom, and tenderly attached to Mr. Suffield, wrote to him under date August 10th, enclosing a translation of his first letter into French, which he had made by desire of the General of the Order, "that you may bear witness that nothing is extenuated, and nothing is set down in malice." He goes on to say, "I have also sent you a rough copy of my translation of your second letter of August 6th, which I have just finished (with how heavy a heart I will not attempt to say—for—pardon me, if I write it—it looks like a farewell to the Church. I am so sad to be obliged to say so). Others also of your best and dearest friends (for you had many) in the north, seem possessed of the same horrible thought. In the meantime we are all praying for you, both at the altar and in private. God give you grace and humility to make what reparation you can for the scandalising of your Brethren. Truth and love for Christ's Church extort such words from me, for you have brought scandal on the Church, and dreadful ruin on your own soul. The little children have only to take up the 'Crown' and condemn you out of your own mouth.

"Yours, dear Father Rudolph,
"Truly and affectionately,
"J. D. AYLWARD."

And another wrote in the strain of the last sentence of the above letter :—

"*To the Editor of the 'Westminster Gazette.*'

"SIR,—Father Suffield says, in the letter which appeared in your columns last Saturday, that 'his intimate and attached friends,' with very few exceptions, are 'intensely loyal to the Pope, and enthusiastic about everything Catholic and Roman.' Were it otherwise, it would be nothing short of a marvel! Many years of the closest and most valued friendship with Father Suffield have assured me that few indeed could have been much under his influence, whether public or private, without becoming so. I appeal to his public exertions for the Holy Father—to his having been the first to establish the revival of Peter's Pence in this country—to his magnificent open-air meeting of sympathy for the Pope, at New-castle; also to his exertions, as I believe, the first in England, in encouraging the enlistment of Papal Zouaves, among a host of other public instances. Who, indeed, that has heard him give the Papal Benediction at the close of his missions, can forget the burning words of love and reverence, which seemed to carry his hearer straight to the feet of the Holy Father! But were that all, the Prayer Book connected with his name has probably been more instrumental than any other popular manual in spreading faith in the dogmas of infallibility wherever English-speaking Catholics are to be found.

" Faithfully yours,

" T. O. S. D."

The reproach was fully justified, and arose out of the very nature of the case. Converts, such as are thoroughly sincere and compelled by conviction too strong for them, those who go over heart and soul to an alien faith—are men who have, heart and soul, believed what they before professed; and as they have believed they have spoken. They have said strong things against the cause which they felt inwardly to be strongest against their own position; have striven to fortify themselves against 'temptation', and have imparted of their own devotion to all who came under their influence. If the lukewarm and indifferent change their faith, they will do so from some light motion of gain or vanity, or on account of arguments which have come to them with the attraction of novelty. They can never be reproached for past zeal, nor their former protests be adduced to counterbalance their after-denials. But such reproaches are in reality testimonials of character; they should be taken as assurance that he against whom they are directed is truthful and zealous; that his fault is that only to which he himself pleads guilty—that he was mistaken—that he is but a man.

CHAPTER XI

ALONE IN THE WORLD.

In a letter of June the 7th, which will be found in Chapter VIII., Mr. Suffield tells Mr. Martineau of the determination at which he had arrived as one result of their recent conference, to submit his position to Dr. Newman; and he enclosed the letter which he purposed sending after a delay "of several days." He seems to have looked upon it as a decisive step, after which the position of a priest and preacher might be no longer tenable, and he did not care to ask advice until he felt prepared to follow it, whatever might be the consequences. Meanwhile he was trying to do all that was kind and just towards his Superiors to whom he had vowed obedience, and yet more towards the many who looked up to him as the guide of their souls. A sudden rupture would have been cruel to them, and would certainly have been generally attributed to moral or mental indisposition. "The several days" of which he had spoken were lengthened out to several weeks. The first page of the letter is wanting in the copy of it in his own handwriting which has been preserved, but judging from the date of Dr. Newman's reply, it cannot have been sent before the middle of July. For six weeks he had kept it by him, probably rewritten and corrected it, and it represents, as we give it, at least no hasty or angry judgment on a cause so intimately known to him. It is not the outcome of an hour of despondency or a mood of bitterness, but the conclusions of years of trial set down in all calmness of spirit. He begins his story ten years back, at the time when he had given himself more entirely than ever to the Church's service.

"During my noviciate at Woodchester, doubts on the foundations of Catholicity took form in my mind, but I enjoyed it nevertheless. Finding myself in the company of simple-hearted and virtuous young men, I could have gone on with it for years, but at the desire of the Cardinal I was moved to London. I then came across the system of 'Direction,' as pursued by the Jesuits and imitated by others; it filled me with disgust to find pretences of higher spirituality used as means for worldly power, and money, and influence. It was the first great shock. I saw it as a regular system, not like a sin such as a weak or bad Priest might be betrayed into, or abandon himself to irrevocably, but it was the life and system of those specially commended as the spiritual-minded Fathers. Here and there an honest and indignant Jesuit revealed to me his disgust at what he saw. I then looked into books and history and contemporaneous events, and found that, as it seemed to me, all the popular impression regarding the Jesuits was true; I began to find that Bishops and Priests, *those who had experience, when they dared*, said the same. I remembered that the Pope had said to a friend of mine in former years what tended in the same direction ; and then I saw the Pope beginning in later times to use the Jesuits as the tools of his power. Having obtained a moral disgust at the entire system of the Jesuits, and the entire system of ' Direction,' I felt myself becoming critical. Then all I had heard for years from *holy* Priests and Bishops regarding the want of all justice and honesty at Rome among *all* the officials, began to be revived and confirmed by obtaining greater insight into the working of things. It was not a question of gross sins : I began to discover that testimony after testimony of the holiest and noblest men bore witness that all the more subtle sins were dominant there in their fulness. The habitual spiritual pride of those considered good came to me as more loathsome than a gross sin into which a man might have fallen and repented. The most clear and certain information shewed me that the Pope and his *entourage* were using all influence for power. Holy Bishops and Priests assured me that we were governed by some weak-minded and some sharp ambitious flatterers, who, by flattery, governed the flattered. I saw the noblest minds cooling in their enthusiasm towards ecclesiastical authority the more they learned of it, and presently they began to resent it. Never, I think, did I see such minds after *long intimacy* with it impressed with the opposite. I saw it was very human, the tactics of diplomacy, or of an ordinary club, composed of rather selfish, narrow-minded, and ordinary men, not over scrupulous about faults, and *not at all so* about honour. I began to find the same vice more or less pervading all the ecclesiastical organisations. They showed themselves quite as human as anything in the world, but all done in the name of God, so that the managers of these schemes probably deceived themselves into an idea of their own spirituality, as much as they deceived our ordinary lay visitors at Rome.

"Then Ward advanced the fullest claims for this authority, and I read his articles, I might almost say, *intending* to agree with them all.

"I considered we all held Papal Infallibility in a sort of way, though like many truths left somewhat vague. I had always considered myself at liberty to follow the testimony of our Vicars Apostolic and controversialists in denying practically the extravagant claims of Rome. I always believed that the fullest toleration to all sects was consistent with the most faithful and courageous Catholicity. I should have scorned to have petitioned for any favour for ourselves which I was not prepared loyally and honestly to have conceded to every sect if we had been in power.

"The Pope's Encyclical shocked me, it seemed to me that all our line of political and social defence of ourselves was, in spirit, at least, condemned. Sorrowfully I resolved to obey it. A line of action and thought which my conscience disapproved, my conscience also told me to adopt because it came from Rome. Such probably would have continued my state of mind, as I never permitted doubts touching faith to remain at all in my mind. But the investigation started by Ward, when flung as an open question among Catholics, I determined to go into, and the numerous enquiries of others addressed to me, compelled me even the more. Oppressive doubts as to the entire Catholic theory began to possess my mind, but then interwoven with a sort of hopeless scepticism; these made me feel sad, hopeless, desolate. I believed, but without heart and doubtfully; I recognised the same working in other minds; I began to wish that I had never been a Priest; I wished that I had in former years retained my money, so that I could have retired unobserved, and said Mass without doing any other priestly duty, and without being understood to believe the Papal claims; for I saw that if the claims now made mean anything, they mean *a great deal more*, as soon as the power of enforcing the more arrives.

"A general breaking down of health, influenced chiefly by these mental anxieties, gave me an excuse to ask of my Superiors that I might get into some retired place; just then Bosworth was offered, and I came. For a short time I seemed like one still believing in the Catholic Church, and yet hardly believing in God or a future; this cloud passed,—your brother's work* helped me in dispelling that dark cloud of utter scepticism. Then I began, as now, to rejoice again in God, in prayer to God for my own soul's needs, and for the needs of the souls of the living and of the departed, to bless God, to seek God's pardon and guidance, to look forward

* "The Soul, its Sorrows and its Aspirations," by F. W. Newman.

again with an almost more realised *happy* hope *than ever* to a future life, dependent at least for a long time on the habits formed here, but where there would be a state of being probably not so very unlike our present.

" Throughout I always was happy in saying Mass, especially when the cloud of scepticism passed off from my soul; I looked on it as a great and holy sacrifice ; God is in all things, I said, God is in the Holy Host. Even on my saddest, darkest days as to belief, the holy mass has always been offered by me under a mystical explanation, but truly and worthily.

" I am not aware of having ever neglected a single duty which, as a Priest, I owed to others, but in the minutest matters I have, I think, acted, and when so acting, *thought* just as any fervent Priest would.

" But as to the Catholic doctrines, I became quite convinced that the Papal claims were merely a human development. I had *never* any particular belief in the veracity of many narratives in the Scriptures ; I believed the Scriptures because the Church told me to do so, but each question I looked into brought me to the intellectual conviction that it was a *human* development of something never contemplated by Jesus Christ. Then I began to notice that every doctrine has had the same history—that our Lord flung out a few grand truths about God the Father of all, the beauty of goodness and the excellence of charity, and that God so blessed his words and his devotedness, that belief in the unity of God, in his goodness, and a high and pure morality, more or less, was diffused in the world owning Jesus Christ as its founder. Beyond this, everything seemed uncertain. Intellectually, this seemed to me the only conclusion I could come to. I waited until your last work appeared,* to see if you presented any other ground intellectually. For anything beyond the great truths about God, the soul, virtue—it seemed to me that you could only appeal to what had been always my own reply—*the conscience* and the *argument of success*.

"The latter has been my chief argument for Catholicity; the miracles of the Gospel never struck me to be an evidence at all; the manner in which they were wrought, and the manner in which they were recorded, *always* seemed to me to deprive them of any weight. But men have tried to establish sects and schools of thought, and failed, while the Catholic Church has succeeded to a very large extent. It is a great argument; it would be greater if its members *could* enquire logically into its claims and continue its subjects, and if we saw more men of intellect joining it, not merely as the compliment of a previous position reposing on a fallacy.

"The adaptation to the conscience is also a great argument; but there are some doctrines of authorised practice which do not really approve themselves to my conscience, but of which I say 'somehow it must be all right, but I do not know how;' *ex. gr.*, the precise line of sin, whereby a single mortal sin, such as missing Mass, sends the soul to Hell; whereas the entire moral character, lowered by habitual selfishness,

---

* "The Grammar of Assent," dated February 21st, 1870.

petty vanity and caprice, lesser sensualities, habitual but none enough to be a mortal sin, would terminate in Heaven—the broad line, so to speak, between the two states of soul (contrary to our experience and our conscience)—the making disbelief a sin and the greatest sin, so that we have continually to explain away our doctrine when our conscience points out thousands outside better than ourselves—the theocratic position of the Pope, and indulgences, and the contradictory decrees of Popes and the evasion by which we conceal these. The Pope professing to be *practically* inspired, and yet using every precaution not to make a mistake. Spiritual direction, the *frequent* practice of confession, the protection attributed to certain things such as Brown Scapulars, the Agnus Dei, &c. These are amongst matters which I have received thoroughly, and still carry out, and act on thoroughly, and yet which have never commended themselves to my conscience any more than many convent regulations.

"Thus, if I were not now a Priest and religious, but with no previous obligations fettering my conscience, and supposing I were as a teacher in a position like that of the Rev. James Martineau, in London, or else holding a wordly position joining in worship with those who hold the truths revealed to our conscience, and brought home specially to our conscience by Jesus Christ, but without any dogmas resting on an historic ground—(persons who I believe go now under the general name of "Free Christians" or Unitarians),—and supposing that the Catholic system was presented to me as it now seems to me, I should certainly not embrace it.

"Thus I show that the argument to my mind is narrowed to this—considering the obligations which I have willingly taken on my own conscience—that I have with my free will embraced a religion and its obligations—that this religion contains all needed for the spiritual life, and rests on the foundation of all religion—that it commands me to banish from my mind thoughts against its claims, *and that I can do so if it be right to do so,* and practically I only present to myself the consideration of these under a sort of mental reservation and guard—that in itself the life and duties of a Priest are to me of the sweetest happiness, (and my only apprehension is whether I can morally continue such when I know what would be my decision if I had to begin again), that to abandon my priestly life would be the source to me of the most intense misery—this misery intensified by the knowledge not only of the deep pain it would inflict on all I love, but also of moral and religious injury to so many—religious, because it would make many lose all heart; it would be the betrayal of a trust; it presents itself to my mind like a treason, like the act of Judas, but as if I should do for the intellect what he did for money. Then my conscience says, ' and if you, in a dream of romantic integrity, abandoned your priestly and religious obligations and went forth into the world, repudiated, hated, despised, doubted, dreaded, supposed perhaps to have joined yourself to the brutal deriders of all you love and worship with the heart's fondest memories and gratitude—have you moral strength to bear all this ? and then *those* might offer in your abject and abso-lute poverty, destitution, desolation, to serve and help you, whose very help would be an indignity, almost a crime to accept ; because you would know it was meant to make you *seem* to blacken those whom you revere. What complications ! what moral difficulties ! and who else does this ? The two wisest of the ancient philosophers were sceptical about the religious exaggerations and excrescences which formed the popular religion, but they practised these, and advised the same to others. Is it conscientious for you to fancy yourself so very wise that you see through all this, and, by an eccentric act, destroy more than ever you repair ; when men like Dr. New-man remain—do you see clearer than he ? is it not pride ? You are blinded by self-confidence. Do not rush into moral dangers you know not of; consider the obligations you have taken on yourself ; carry them out as well as you can ; do not take an irre-parable step. Beware, form your conscience, remain, dismiss all enquiry, be at peace.'

"Such language I often address to myself, and it is supported by the intense affection I have for so many Catholics and by my almost utter ignorance of every-one outside the Catholic Church ; while everyone and everything in the Catholic Church are to me as part of home. Then the sort of people who have left the Church, and those who attack it, all fill me with loathing. Then the piety, goodness, purity, charity, gentleness of those almost countless whom I know and love. Then the desert as it seems to me without; it is like looking out of a happy home on to a wild moor, or into a street of bustling men of business. Then the thought that in the midst of the agony of such a state of mind, and such a desolation, I must begin life again, and at once think *how* to live, and a fear lest then I should in a sort of despair accept something which would be a compromise.

"I have not gone into any arguments or reason, for all these are familiar enough to you, and one of the strongest arguments affecting my conscience on the Catholic side is your individual example, and my reverence for your great knowledge and lofty conscientiousness. I simply try and describe the results so sad to my own happiness, so sad for the happiness of those who love me.

"Perhaps I might add that, in asking to come here, I anticipated not only a time for calm and continuous thought, study, prayer, consideration unaffected by every influence except the gracious influence of the country and of a few simple poor, but also I expected to have escaped doing anything beyond helping to piety and virtue a little flock of old Catholics; but my difficulty of action has been increased by this, that without leaving my cottage-garden, except for the Chapel, the Protestants have come quite unasked to me, and I have received several into the Church; at the present moment the two most intelligent of the higher class are anxious and enquiring; also Protestants come from distant places. Not a month

passes without Catholics coming from different parts
to confer with me. Then an immense correspondence, in consequence of my being still the Director
of the Perpetual Rosary Association, which I founded
six years ago, and which numbers now thirty-six
thousand, and going out occasionally to give Missions
and Retreats, and as Extraordinary to Convents.
Thus I am still continually compelled to take a
distinct position in the whole of the Catholic movement, and anything I do must grieve and wound
innumerable souls. I have often wished that God
would mercifully, by death, free me from this dreadful
alternative, and I wonder whether others have suffered this. And did not they—do not they—resolve
that they can continue till the end of this short life,
surrounded by this stately dream of the days of old,
inducing themselves to believe that it is true, because
it environs all that exists to them of happiness, of
friendship, of peace.

"My own dear Father, before God, what do you
say? Tell me.

"Your loving son in Christ,

"ROBERT RUDOLPH SUFFIELD."

It was of this letter Mr. Martineau, to whom he
had sent a copy, wrote, after expressing "heartfelt
thanks" for the perusal of it:—"Your confidence
could not be given to anyone more worthy to receive
it, and more skilful to help in moral difficulties than
the venerable and noble-souled Newman. Only there
are crises in life when one has to rise into a truth
higher than the human. But you have laid the

problem with faithful explicitness before one of the most experienced of spiritual counsellors."

Dr. Newman's reply was as follows:—

> "THE ORATORY,
>
> "*July 17th, 1870*

"MY DEAR FATHER SUFFIELD,

"I expect to be here next month, and shall be rejoiced to see you, as you propose. Write me word beforehand.

> "Yours most sincerely,
>
> "JOHN HENRY NEWMAN."

Next month they met as proposed, and for the last time. There was never any ill-feeling between them or a harsh word said on either side, but it was not possible that they could continue on terms of intimacy, and henceforth friendship was transferred from the illustrious convert to Romanism to his scarcely less illustrious brother, the convert to Theism. Of their interview on this occasion Mr. Suffield gave the following account in a letter to Mr. Martineau, under date August 17.

" Dr. Newman fully concurs in what was your own opinion and mine—that in conscience I had no alternative but to act as I am doing, and that my vow does not bind in conscience, and that if the General would desire me to leave the country for a foreign Priory I should refuse. But he also agrees with me that it will be more graceful and considerate toward the Order and towards Catholic feeling to apply for a dispensation." It must, of course, be remembered, in justice to Dr. Newman, that these are not his own words, and that the advice was sought of him by one whose resolve to leave the Church had already been carried out. The question presented to him was not, am I under any obligation still to believe and to obey? but this only. Having ceased to believe, how far am I bound to an obedience which has to a great extent become impossible?

To a faithful Catholic the question scarcely admits of an answer. It is to him as if a man should confess— 'I have committed a great sin, and purpose standing by it; how far am I warranted in a lesser transgression which more or less follows on it?' Faith, entire and steadfast, in all the teachings of the Church, is the fundamental obligation of every Catholic; that broken, it would seem impossible to maintain any which depend upon it. There can remain no recognised obligation but those of the natural law of justice and kindness. So if an English subject were to deny the authority of Parliament to levy taxes of him, or make laws for him, it would be useless to question how far he were bound in conscience by this or that particular law. For good or evil he would be free of any and every obligation consequent upon the Acts of Parliament, and be bound only to the moral law. No doubt he would be constrained by force to obey, and so would the Church constrain or punish if it had power, which it happily has everywhere ceased to possess; but the offence would be, not the special acts of disobedience, but the apostacy which was the quasi-justification of them.

At last the day came on which he had to take the

fatal step which was to cut his life in twain. On Wednesday, the 10th of August, he turned his back upon the faith and friendships, the habits and associations of twenty years, and became of his own deliberate choice an object of pity and horror in the eyes of all who had hitherto loved and revered him as a champion of their faith. Recalling the occasion long after, and when now under the sentence of a fatal disease, he wrote, "as I walked through the quiet straggling village on foot, I passed the old church and the little Roman Catholic school, and listened for a moment to the children's Morning Hymn to our Lady — and left the past for ever behind — the stately, not unpoetic past! and it ranged itself among the grand mythologies of the days of old; like the statue of a goddess in a niche of a colonnade. You admire it, and you leave it behind. The road leads through the images of gods and heroes to the temple of the Universal.

" Roman Catholics naturally regarded my secession as an error, but if they knew the facts they would be obliged to admit that it was a profoundly conscientious act. Every motive, affection, temporal comfort, self-interest, urged me to remain. My personal means had long since been sunk in the Roman Catholic Church. At the age of forty-eight I had to go forth as a pauper among strangers, with no apparent means of livelihood. I had literally no inducement to leave the Church; nothing but sincerity. I again and again considered whether I might not, like the old philosophers, hold an exoteric and an esoteric faith—

publicly conforming to the popular mythology, privately holding a philosophic negation. But I dared not face death in such a state."

On the day after his arrival in Birmingham he wrote the following interesting letter :—

"32, ANN STREET, BIRMINGHAM,
"*August 11th, 1870.*

" MY DEAR MR. MARTINEAU,

"Thank you so very much for your most kind letter. The die is cast. Last Sunday I closed my duties with those dear people. It was a day that I had dreaded, and well I might. I quietly told them that I had some religious difficulties which did not concern any one there; that they had better avoid controversy, and go on as good Catholics. English country people are not very susceptible; but after Benediction in the evening, they, of their own accord, assembled under the trees. I could see them from the Sacristy window. They were all in great sorrow. I believe nothing was said, but they raised a little offering for me, to which even the children gave their mite. I told them I had not courage to wish them singly good-bye, and begged them to look on it as an absence of a short time, and that they must meet me in some excursion; but they felt it was more than that, and outside the Chapel door, young E——, a Christ Church man and convert, threw his arms round my neck, and burst into tears; and dear J——, a young Grenadier Guardsman, whom I had tried to get away on some visit, would not be

K

persuaded, and lost all his spirits ; he never left my side during the next two days, and then accompanied me to Rugby, and when he took leave of me, his grief was so great that one of the men asked whether 'the gentleman was going to emigrate.' The poor fellow said, 'Oh, it is worse—my own dear Father.' All this is very sad—for to the young and to the good it seems like a fall—like a treason. There is now no longer need for secrecy, every friend is saddened, and nothing more can be any matter to them, except that they should see that in no way is anything unnecessary done to wound them. Heretofore all communications addressed to me have been in language of deepest love and sympathy, with a delicacy of feeling almost wonderful. No doubt many will attack me afterwards, and many, no doubt, have done so privately; but as yet the Catholic papers have, I believe, spoken kindly, and, thank God, 'religious blackguards' have saved me the indignity of their praise. I hear one of their organs has attacked me, which I am glad of, and said that my letter in the *Westminster Gazette* would do more harm than my example could do good.

"Two Catholics whom I had formerly served, very good people, wrote apparently without concurrence, in a very nice way, hoping that I would retire into obscurity, and offering to provide the means of my so doing. But though it was done in a thoroughly honourable and beautiful spirit, I felt it implied what I could not certainly always observe, and I gratefully and kindly declined.

"The intensity with which these matters are regarded by Catholics must seem to you quite strange.

"Some letters have, however, amazed me greatly, revealing doubts in quarters I had hardly anticipated, but these persons generally dream of Anglicanism or such like, and when they realise my own opinions they will be shocked.

"I find it better to express my opinions as in sympathy with the Unitarians. 'Christian Theism,' they would suppose, implies 'Deism' in its former irreligious sense, and 'Free Christians' they do not understand, and the name does not suggest religious ideas to those who are unfamiliar with it; whereas they understand Unitarianism to express a rationalistic but religious and moral form of Christianity.

"I have not yet seen Dr. Newman, indeed no one in Birmingham knows that I am here. I feel that I have practically decided all that I had contemplated conferring on with Dr. Newman, excepting what passed with him on former occasions, and now my object would be only the consideration of such questions as those you so kindly and wisely touched in your last letter; also I meant it partly as a conciliatory act towards Catholics, that I might not seem to be throwing myself at once into another camp.

"I have taken lodgings here, close by the Free Library, Library of Reference and Free News Room, and being remote from the Oratory and Catholic Cathedral, my position will not be obnoxious to anyone, and unless some unexpected reason should arise, I shall remain on here until something casts up: I shall remain here quite quiet, but just step in on the Sundays to one or other of the Unitarian Chapels in a quiet unobserved way, as this will be a help for the future, and, except private interviews with Dr. Newman, I shall keep aloof from Catholics, as I know such would *really* be their preference, especially as regarding their Colleges at Edgbaston and Oscot, where I am so well known.

" By the way, the most venerable priest in England wrote to me to congratulate and thank me,—to my surprise—and went on to tell me that at the recent gathering of the Bishops, Dr. Manning had revoked the question of my being formally censured, and that the matter was referred to Rome. Considering that I have resigned every office, and am not saying Mass or exercising any ecclesiastical faculties, I think they might save themselves that trouble.

" Believe me, &c.

" P.S.—Two other proposals from Catholics, apparently without concurrence, have come to me. They are from men of high honour of feeling, and offered, without any expressed or implied condition, but I thought it best to decline them as being hardly fair upon them, and hereafter more fettering to myself than perhaps at present I quite realise."

It must indeed have been a very tempting offer to him every way, for he was all but friendless and nearly penniless. Mr. Martineau was the only person in the world who knew of and sympathised with his position, and precious and faithful as was his friendship in this hour of trial, it was but

of very recent date, and only on one occasion
as yet, had they met face to face. Bound as a
Dominican by the vow of poverty, he possessed
nothing as his own by right, but had a mere use
granted to him of the property which belonged to the
community. Of such moneys as were in his hand he
ventured to carry away with him, the sum of £4,
which he might indeed have regarded as a small
acknowledgment for ten years of devoted service, but
preferred to consider as a loan, which, as soon as he
was able, he returned. Of the unsolicited generosity
which enabled him to meet the necessary expenses of
the first few weeks of his strange life, till he made
friends and found work, it is not permitted here to
speak. That, too, he was desirous to repay when
in a position to do so, but it was not allowed him,
and he was obliged to content himself with appropriating a like sum to certain purposes which would
he deemed helpful to enquirers after truth.

In reply to the above letter, Mr. Martineau wrote
on August 15th, from Scotland, where he was spending his summer vacation.

"KILTGBIE, KILLIN, CRIEF,

"August 15.

"MY DEAR FATHER SUFFIELD,

"My heart bleeds for you in this rending of precious and sacred ties,—the modern counterpart of
martyrdom. Soon, I trust, the anguish will be succeeded by the blessed crown of a lightened and
joyous conscience, clear of human complications, and
bright beneath the approving eye of God.

"H. W.'s letter would be very touching, were not its weakness too obtrusive. Indeed, the insight which I have gained through your recent experience into the working of the Catholic system, deepens my impression of the essential childishness of mind, and untrustful narrowness of piety, which deform the highest graces nurtured by it. To believe that the All-holy God will treat a soul as lost, which, in obedience to Him (or at all events what *means* to be such) performs an act of heroic self-sacrifice, what is this but a debasing superstition, applying the power of religion to the corruption of the moral sense? It is in the highest degree considerate and delicate in you to speak so tenderly as you do *(e.g.* in the *Westminster Gazette)* of the spirit of the associates you leave. But I must confess that with my view of their narrowness of mind, compared with your own large comprehension of things, I cannot but feel your tone of humility excessive. It would not be *self-assertion*, but only homage to the Divine truth which has alighted on you as its organ, to hold your head a little higher. The *Westminster Gazette* letter seemed to me almost to imply a *penitential* feeling, as if you not only desired to release others from responsibility of participation in your acts, but almost looked upon yourself with their eyes. I know you will forgive me for saying this : it is perhaps due to my own defective meekness."

With this gentle criticism of the exaggerated meekness of the letter referred to*, non-Catholic readers

---

*See above, page 140.

will all incline to agree. And indeed at a later date, when he had freed himself from the ties of old associations, and learnt to stand on his feet as a man, instead of making it a virtue to let himself be carried as a child, he would have joined in condemning this excessive humility and self-disparagement. But it is hard to take a step which all whom you reverence, or who have reverenced you, are unanimous in their emphatic condemnation of—nay, which your own self so short a while ago would have been horrified to contemplate the very possibility of—and not feel as if it were somehow matter for humbleness and apology; right, perhaps, and inevitable from the purely intellectual standpoint, and yet on the human and social side, wrong and unkind.

His own view he expressed in this reply :—

"BIRMINGHAM, *August 17*.

"MY DEAR MR. MARTINEAU,

" I thank you for your remarks regarding my letter to the *Westminster Gazette*. If a Catholic renounces the Catholic Church and has neither conscience or gratitude, his course is very clear—for he is embarrassed by no responsibilities. But if he be compelled to the act not, as 'converts' would say, 'to secure his salvation,' but in obedience to a higher law of the conscience, his position, I mean his spiritual and mental position, is more difficult than even you with your lofty conscientiousness and high intellectual gifts and knowledge of life can fully comprehend. I believe that only by degrees could you realise it.

" The transition is a moral and spiritual state,

in which there are no landmarks, or such as attract one's attention only to be avoided.

"To have obtained a certain amount of influence over the consciences and over the happiness of others—to have obtained it by the carrying out of a well-meant mistake—to cause by withdrawing injury and unhappiness to those who gave to me the means of influencing them, does make me feel more penitent than exulting, and I have withdrawn from the Catholic Church like a son from the home of a father who has never wronged him.

"All those entitled to know, are now fully aware that I am no longer acting as a Priest or as a Catholic—they know also my religious opinions and my probable future.

"My letter in the *Westminster Gazette* fulfilled one intention which I had—it has saved me from the ignominy of vulgar and bigoted praise, and made persons understand that I had no protest to offer, excepting the protest of my disbelief.

"On Sunday I went to Mr. Dawson's Chapel. He follows no sect. I was struck by the quiet recollection of the great congregation, and the evident earnestness of a large number of young men of the class of merchants' clerks.

"I have remained quite quiet, and in reality have spoken with none but those few Catholics who, living in the neighbourhood of Birmingham, happened to hear of my being in their neighbourhood, and who, with the delicacy of an unobtrusive reserve, seemed only to wish to shew to me their affection.

"Amongst your many acts of kindness let me thank you for your communications with Croydon. If it takes a little time to prepare itself, so much the better."

To this Mr. Martineau replied :—

"KILTGRIE, *August 21st.*

"MY DEAR FATHER SUFFIELD,

"Without time to write much at length, I return these interesting letters. It is a great relief to me that Dr. Newman's judgment offers no resistance to the course on which your own conscience has decided. I have so great a veneration for his feelings on such matters, that his opposing verdict would have seriously disturbed me. Yet the assumptions from which he starts so often seem to me precarious and misleading, that I felt no security about his judgment on the case.

"Into your sorrowful, almost penitential, feeling in tearing yourself away from so many sacred and tender ties, I believe I can enter. But then, is not the question this :—What is it that justly stirs compunction and regret? Is it the present act of conscience? or is it the mistaken guidance given in the past?—given in good faith, but now found to be illusory. The position you now take no more calls for apology that Paul's repudiation of the Mosaic Law. And I feel jealous of any concession, out of self-accusing humility, to the false Catholic treatment of your present state of mind as criminal. I did not see why you should justify your late associates so much at your own expense, as if releasing them from imputed participation in some *real* offence. I say this, not from any desire to revert to my criticism, but because I doubt whether I made my meaning clear.

"It is curious that you went at once to George Dawson's Chapel. I had been doubting whether to write to him and ask him to call. But though he has noble qualities and much religious power, I did not feel sure that his rough and bold ways might not repel you : so I refrained. But I am glad that you have heard him preach. He is very unequal, some-times verging on the coarse and irreverent, but at others, really great. He was originally a Baptist. I do not think anyone knows his present theology : not perhaps even G. D. himself. He is not a thinker or a student; but he has wonderful skill as an eclectic, in appropriating and distributing the best thoughts of others, with sufficient colouring caught in passing through his own."

By the time this letter reached him he had already had some experience of Unitarian manners and forms of worship, and he expressed himself respecting them in the following reply :—

"BIRMINGHAM,
"*August 26th.*

"MY DEAR MR. MARTINEAU,

"It is too bad to write to you still egotistically, but I know your kindness would make you desire it.

"As soon as the conscientious questions as to Catholicity and my Order were fully decided and acted on, and the matter closed, I could then distinctly throw my thoughts and spiritual life into my altered position. You will be glad to hear that this causes me no difficulty, no void, no pain, *but quite the reverse*. Of course I am grieved, as I ought to be, at the honest grief caused to friends, but no longer with the sense of self-reproach which I experienced in considering the matter before acting (as in that letter written from Bosworth, to which you allude, and which was copied into other papers a fortnight after its appearance in a Catholic paper.)

" Those who oppose through mere anger or spirit of party I am quite indifferent to. But I now distinctly recognise my position, and the genuine pain of others does not in the least degree cause my conscience apprehension, and therefore I sympathise with their sorrow without being sad.

" Also I can already perceive that the *ethos* of the persons and systems (if it can be called so) which will surround me, instead of revolting and offending, and grating something in my mind, exactly conforms with what I have really always preferred. The submission of manner and word to the Priest has never pleased me, and I have always rather tried to adopt a manner calculated to lessen such in others, and the honest kindly independence and equality which I recognise with those whom your kindness has brought me in contact with, makes me feel quite at home ; nor does the system I perceive pursued in the management of Chapel affairs offend me, though doubtless in the hands of vulgar and self-sufficient minds, it might occasionally make me wince.

" Also the witnessing the behaviour, the tone displayed in the public worship, removes from me the sense of shame-facedness and apprehension I had that all would hang on the Minister—I perceive that in reality the instinct of religious reverence keeps things straight.

" On the whole I do not regret the appearance of my letter, as it has, I find, entirely silenced the praise of *Protestants*, who are very angry at my praise of Catholics. They now see that I cease to be a Catholic because I disbelieve, and not because I can gratify them by joining in a factious or controversial opposition.

" This will not gratify the spite of those who specially employ themselves in abusing Catholics, but perhaps to thoughtful minds it makes my *act* the more significant when it is clear that it has resulted solely from the experience of conscience.

" The only point now not quite clear to my mind is my right line towards those who are rather unsettled and write to me; from the dread of helping to destroy spiritual props in minds in which I might not be hopeful of such being replaced, I probably take too much the 'Catholic side,' and 'do not be rash,' 'and you do not feel obliged in conscience to investigate, so you must not, &c.' I do deeply feel the danger if I am hasty or rash in this matter, though I may push this perhaps too far?

" Yours sincerely and gratefully,

" ROBERT RODOLPH SUFFIELD."

CHAPTER XII.

Neither Anglican nor Evangelical.

In Dr. Newman's religious novel, "Loss and Gain," the Story of a Convert from High Anglicanism to Romanism, there is a scene which would be more amusing were it less exaggerated, in which the young man whose dissatisfaction with the Church of his fathers has somehow become known, but who has not yet publicly and definitely declared himself, is visited by representatives of various sects and opinions, who one after another seek to win him to their particular, and to them infallible, form of faith. Mr. Suffield had a somewhat similar experience when making the far journey in an opposite direction, and before yet he had clearly declared himself a Unitarian. One, an Anglican "abbot," wrote, congratulating him "that the true and really infallible head of the Church is leading you to embrace true Catholicity, by which alone we can hope for the reunion of the visible Church. How gratefully and humbly would countless numbers of English Catholics welcome such as you among them. How more than pleased I should be if you would give to me such a visit. The few of us who are here do most earnestly desire to be true Monks, and have learnt to love trials and sufferings in order that we may grow in our Blessed Lord's likeness under our Holy Rule. A visit from you would help us on our road." Nor was this correspondent discouraged by Mr. Suffield's reply:—"My dear reverend brother in Christ," he wrote, " thank you very much for your kind note. I *am* pained by what I hear of your most terrible trial. It is the most intensely agonising one that a Christian soul can know. I myself have endured something of your agony, but I think and trust these fearful failings of the understanding have quickened in me the faith of my heart, and now my understanding is growing stronger also. But all through my struggle I would not have shaken the faith of another for worlds, or given to the enemies of our Lord a triumph in my case. Very dear brother, may not this battle-field even yet see you come off ' more than conqueror.'" It must have seemed strange to him, this fervent appeal in language he was so used to, but coming from one outside of his Catholic Church, and setting up the particular faith of his own choosing as something for which to sacrifice reason and life.

Another well-known Evangelical Nonconformist wrote,—" I have gone over the position you occupy in repeated mental conflicts, and therefore am perhaps qualified better than many to offer a word in season. I earnestly hope and pray that you may not take up your abode in the tents of the Unitarians. I have been a zealous Protestant from my youth, yet of the two I would rather have the Creed of Archbishop Dupanloup than that of Dr. Channing. May I recommend to your notice one of the most interesting books I ever read, "Teachings of Experience," by

Joseph Barker. He passed through Unitarianism on his downward course. I am not anxious to gain you for the Church of England, but for Evangelical Christianity, rightly so called, as I believe I have seen its blessed fruits in living and dying."

Many such well-meant affectionate entreaties reached him, of which one more may be given in full, as a striking illustration of that delusion which is common to men of every religion, making the individual confident that the particular opinions he at present holds are the final truth of God, to which it should be his prayer and effort to lead all his fellows.

" Reverend Sir,—It was with the greatest delight that I read your manly protest against Papal Infallibility. Subsequently, you left, I understand, the Roman Church for the Protestant. Believe me, I am fully able to appreciate this your step, as I too, about thirteen years ago, left Romanism for Protestantism. I was Priest and Professor of Divinity at the University of · · · After I left the Church I went to the British Museum, and devoted myself to Syriac studies. Meanwhile my religious experience had shown to my mind the utter untenableness of Protestantism, which represents not liberty but licence. Among Protestants the most vital points are controverted, so that, to a great many, Christianity is but a loose system of morality. There are, indeed, Evangelicals, Ritualists, Baptists, &c., of a high confessional colour, but is their belief anything else but inconsistency? They cling desperately to certain tenets of their sect, because they feel the cravings of a believing soul. But such stubborn, self-made belief, cannot save. *Where is the Church of Christ and His Apostles?* Our Saviour promised us that the gates of hell should not prevail against her. Thus she, visible, like every other historical institution, must exist somewhere, and, if we open our eyes, we must be able to find her. Where is, then, this One Holy Catholic and Apostolic Church? Up to the Great Schism there was but One Catholic Church, comprising the whole world, east and west. Then Rome and the west separated from the common Catholic ground, which the east preserves *unaltered*—(neither adding nor subtracting anything)—up to this hour; while Romanism, rushing from innovation to innovation, introduced Papism and its tail of new doctrines, shifted the basis of Apostolical Church institution, and led its sectaries to hypocrisy or unbelief.

" After having passed through the Roman domain of false doctrine and papal tyranny, after having wandered through the dreary desert of Protestant individualism, I have reached (some years ago) the safe port of the Holy Orthodox Catholic Church, and I have found *perfect rest for my soul, and a safe prospect in the hour of death!* I cannot tell you how happy I am now, and how much I am satisfied with the impregnable fastness of truth and heavenly comfort, which is the Orthodox Church. I know you will not and cannot take amiss, that I, a perfect stranger to you, beseech you to turn your eyes towards the Holy Orthodox Church. As we were once "confratres" in the same Church, as we passed the same way through Protestantism, so I hope we shall one day meet again in the Orthodox Catholic Church. Yet, though I am a stranger to you, you are not a stranger to me, for many a beautiful song of your "Crown of Jesus" we sing in our household devotions. May the God of Truth lead your steps in the right direction.

"Yours, &c."

It was time for him to speak out and define for the benefit of the religious world his settled position. All these alternatives to Romanism seemed to him at once less reasonable and less attractive, and he had not thrown off the yoke of a world-wide faith to bow his understanding with pain and difficulty under some denominational or local or party dogmatism. He left a Catholic Church for what he believed to be a still more catholic one, whose faith was that common to all religions of civilised men, and one which imposed no sort of penalty on free inquiry ; accordingly there appeared in *Church Opinion*, of August 27th, the following :—

"Through the kindness of a friend we are enabled to publish the following interesting letter from Father Suffield to a clergyman of the Church of England. It will be seen that Father Suffield's ecclesiastical position is not at all what had been anticipated, and will be as little satisfactory to the Anglicans as to "Evangelical and orthodox" Dissenters. It seems to us a sort of Christian Theism with the minimum of dogmatic belief, like what is ably described in the little book of F. Pécant, "Avenir du Théisme Chrétien." A religion edified by Christian experiences,

L

but in reality reposing not on revelation, as such, in the ordinary sense of the term, but on the conscience, and the manifestations of God. Whilst thus entirely differing from him in his conclusions, our readers will be interested in learning what they are :—

"BIRMINGHAM, *August 22nd, 1870.*

"MY DEAR SIR,

"Private communications are so very numerous at present, that I cannot conveniently add to my occupations by contributing the literary help you do me the favour of offering. Moreover, your able periodical partakes somewhat of a controversial character, and is regarded as anti-Catholic in its position. I am peculiarly circumstanced, having resigned all offices in the Catholic Church, and ceased the exercise of priestly and Catholic rites : from the intimate manner in which I have been interwoven in the Catholic body in England, this act causes great pain to those whom the least I should like to wound; and I am anxious to do nothing but what is demanded by the exigences of circumstances or the requirements of conscience, which could in the slightest degree grieve those who have so many claims upon my affection, gratitude, and reverence.

"After long and deep thought, study, prayer, and counsel, I decided that it would be impossible for me honestly to continue to act as a priest. The infallibility of the Pope and of the Scriptures alike, I question, and the dogmas resting solely on either of those authorities, I am not able on that account to admit.

"It is my desire to unite with others, and to assist them in the worship of God and in the practice of the two-fold precepts of charity, unfettered by adhesion on either side to anything beyond those great funda- mental principles as presented to us by Jesus Christ.

"Though relieved from all the obligations of my Order, I do not wish to consider myself as alienated from the Catholic Church, or from other Christian communities, by any personal act. I leave none, and join none: I assume a position hostile to none; if one man hurls an anathema, another man is not com- pelled either to accept it or to retaliate it.

"Having understood that those who are commonly called Unitarians, Free Christians, or Christian Theists, thus agree in the liberty inspired by self- diffidence, humility, and charity, to carry on the worship of God, without sectarian requirements or sectarian opposition; that they possess a simple, but not vulgar, worship, and a high standard of virtue, intelligence, and integrity, and these after the Christian type, moulded by the Christian traditions, and edified by the sacred Scriptures;—holding the spirit taught by Jesus Christ, and the great thoughts by virtue of which he built up the ruins of the moral world; and yet not enforcing the reception of com- plicated dogmas as a necessity, or accounting their rejection a crime;—a communion of Christian wor- shippers, bound loosely together, and yet by the force of great principles enabled quietly to maintain their position to exercise an influence elevating and not unimportant, and to present religion under an aspect which thoughtful men can accept without latent scepticism, and earnest men without the aberrations of superstition, or the abjectness of mental servitude to another—such approved itself to my judgment, and commended itself to my sympathy.

"I intend adhering to the pursuits of the clergyman and of the Christian teacher, and communications are in progress in another part of England which may terminate in my accepting thus a duty conformable to the habits of my life, and which will not throw me into a position of hostility, or embarrassment as to those honoured and loved Catholic friends, with whom so greatly I should prize to maintain kindly intercourse, inasmuch as I am only externally severed from them by my being unable to believe certain dogmas which a Catholic is bound to regard as essential. Thus I hope I have not only thanked you for your obliging offer, but adequately explained my position, and shewed that the future you were commissioned to hold out to me in the Established Church, would not be deemed possible by the authorities who have done me the honour and kindness to communicate in my regard, as soon as they are made aware, that the Articles and the Athanasian Creed would be amongst the insuperable barriers to my entertaining such a proposal.

"Many write to me evidently under a grievous misapprehension. They anticipate from me the denunciations of that vision of beauty, which I have left simply because, like a vision, it had everything but reality. Allied as I am by relationship with several of our ancient Catholic families, allied by the ties of friendship with nearly all of them, I feel it is a shame to myself that any stranger could suppose one word of my lips, one thought of my mind, could cast a reproach on those beautiful and honoured homes where old traditions received a lustre greater even than antiquity and suffering can bestow—crowned with the aureola of charity, nobleness, purity, and devotedness. Such memories print on my heart their everlasting record. To cease to believe and to worship with them was a martyrdom, which none but the Catholic can understand.

"I have ascended now to another stage of my life, to rise to it needed sufferings of the mind and of the heart, the sacrifice of everything in the world I cared for; but I perceive a work to do, and by the blessing of God, I shall strive to perform it. Youth, strength, vigour, and hope return to me with the expectation. Truth obtained by suffering is doubly dear to the possessor.

"Very sincerely yours,

"ROBERT RODOLPH SUFFIELD."

In accordance with the advice of Dr. Newman he made application to the General of the Order for a dispensation from his vow of obedience; it had become impossible for him to be faithful to it any longer, but it seemed "more gracious and considerate" to seek remission of it through the recognised channels. On the other hand it was impossible for his Roman Superiors to enter into his view of the case; to ask dispensation on the ground of loss of faith appeared to them as if a wife were to seek the annulment of her marriage on the ground that she had been unfaithful to her husband. The answers he received from his English Superior and from the General of the Order were as follows :—

"THE MONASTERY, WOODCHESTER,

"*August 15th, 1870.*

"MY VERY DEAR FATHER SUFFIELD,

"My heart is too full of sorrow to say much, although what you confided to me from time to time in past years invariably made me fear some such denouement as the present. Your mind always seemed to me to be struggling with difficulties which were an enigma to me, and several times that you said you would like to die suddenly convinced me that you were in a state of mind few would be able to understand. Still I always hoped that a time of peace and calm would come. For it is anguish itself, my dear Father, to think of you severed from us and from the Church, and that too in the very eventide of your life, and with a future before you which at present, I am sure, cannot look anything but gloomy and dark. The prayers, however, of many fervent hearts will follow you, and I trust support you in what I must call your lonely wanderings. I feel, however, what you say in your letter, 'there is no alternative,' and I will therefore not delay in putting your case before our General, and asking for the dispensation from your vows. Believe me, yours, with all sympathy and affection.

"FR. GEO. VINCENT KING."

To a Roman Catholic sudden death is dreaded, because it implies death without the last sacraments, without absolution, or extreme unction, or the viaticum which sinners trust to for salvation and saints long for as last preparation to meet their Lord. To desire sudden death means, therefore, to have no regard for these solemn rites, and the fact was, as he long after avowed, that he did shrink from a dying avowal of faith when his mind was full of doubt.

The General wrote :—

" ROME, *28th August, 1870.*

" It is under the auspices of St. Augustine, whose rule we profess,* that I write you this letter, inspired alike by my fatherly affection and my profound grief. Your Provincial has written to me that you have commissioned him to apply for a dispensation from your vow of obedience, but you cannot be ignorant that the Sovereign Pontiff alone is able to dispense you from it ; and you ought to know too that he does not grant such dispensations even to those who are allowed to become secular priests.

" And what legitimate motive can you have moreover to justify such a demand? You say you have lost the faith ; it is beyond doubt a tremendous calamity, but not without remedy, and is by remaining in the Order that you will discover that remedy and apply it. Your fall, it seems to me, has been your

---

* The 28th of August is the feast of St. Augustine, whose brief rule of Clerical life is the foundation of " The Constitutions of the Order of St. Dominic."

own fault. You speak in your letter to the papers, of years of strife and anguish and doubt that you have had to go through, and yet not one of your brethren had ever a suspicion of it; you exhausted yourself in your lonely struggles, in which you counted too much upon yourself and your individual reason, passing by the means of assistance which Providence had put at your door, and which you would have found in the counsel of your brethren and the direction of your Superiors. Then when this inner struggle has exhausted your strength and the moment of weakness has come, it is the public of whom you have made a confidant, and by a newspaper that we have the pain to learn it.

"Yours has been a great fault, and at the same time a great misfortune. May your own eyes be at least opened to see it. Think of the great number of souls whom God has given you the grace to lead into the truth and establish in the ways of justice, and do not force upon them the cruel spectacle of the blindness of the guide who had led them into the light. Near to the threshold of eternity do not belie, do not dishonour a life consecrated to the Apostolate by the shame of an apostacy.

"Follow the counsel that my affection for you and my desire for your salvation inspires. Withdraw to one of our convents, or if you prefer it, to one of the Passionists', or of any other Order, and there make a serious retreat, closing the door upon all the noises of the world, and occupying yourself exclusively on the great business of your salvation.

"For the present I ask no more of you, and I beseech it of you rather than command it.

"Adieu, my son, I will unite my prayers to yours to implore our Lord to enlighten and bless you.

"FR. A. V. JANDEL,

"Mag. Ord." (Master of the Order).

It is a type of thousands of like letters written by those who stay to those who go. They mingle reproach, and prayer, and entreaty, and insist upon infallible but impossible means of recovery. "Come back, put yourselves under the old influence, banish the new ones, and if you are earnest and persevering in your efforts, you may yet be as we are." So they cry to us from out the narrow room which they imagine the vault of heaven, but we cannot return till we grow blind; we have seen the real sun and the stars, and cannot again be persuaded that the painted ceiling is the sky. "Why didn't you seek advice?" they say. Because, dear friends, we knew so well all you could and would say to us; why pain you, why expose our trouble and your shame before the time?

It is singular how both of these letters speak of him as an old man drawing near his end, while he was really in mid life. The fact probably was that austerity and anxiety had so worn his frame that he did impress people as aged beyond his years. Certainly many years after those who knew him best would not have thought of him as on "the verge of eternity." Save for one long and serious illness, he enjoyed good health and spirits for twenty years from the time these letters were written.

A short notice of his "fall," which appeared in *The Tablet*, the leading Roman Catholic journal, seemed to many to insinuate that there had been some moral delinquency on his part antecedent to his change of faith, and so had given to many of his old friends, who were in mourning for his loss, just cause of offence. In consequence, his English Superior, who from his official position would be of all others most intimately acquainted with his life, and the first to hear of any breath of scandal against one of his subjects, wrote to the Editor of *The Tablet* :—

"My attention has been called to a short notice in *The Tablet* of the 3rd instant, in which the writer says that F. Suffield ' had for some time been a cause of anxiety to his Superiors.' At the end of the same paragraph it is said, ' We take leave of this unhappy Priest without dwelling on the sad causes which have led to his apostacy, instructive though they might be.' What the writer of that notice really meant to insinuate it is not for me to decide ; but I am sorry to say that those words have been interpreted in a sense highly injurious to F. Suffield's character, and as casting blame upon his late Superiors. In letters sent to me within the last ten days, that notice has been called ' a disgraceful, vulgar, and lying paragraph.' It is said ' that none but one himself infamous could impute to F. Suffield any moral blame ; that the writer in *The Tablet* insinuates what he dares not say, and doesn't perceive that he throws much deeper blame on F. Suffield's Superiors than on F. Suffield himself.' I may add that many and

severe remonstrances have been made to me by
F. Suffield's numerous friends about the 'ambiguous
meaning of the notice in *The Tablet*.' I feel, therefore, that F. Suffield's own request to me that I
should say something on the subject is only just and
fair. However, as I have been Provincial only about
three months, my testimony in this matter may
probably be considered of little weight; I have therefore written to Father Aylward, my predecessor, on
the subject, and, I think I cannot do better than
reproduce his words. Father Aylward, writing to me
in reference to F. Suffield, says :—' Whilst I was his
Provincial, I felt no uneasiness in reference either to
his moral character or to the orthodoxy of his doctrine. His sad defection from the faith came upon us
all, as you know, with the suddenness of a thunder-
clap. None of his *confreres* in the Order knew
anything, nor suspected anything, of those distressing
doubts which he now says harassed his mind for
years (even before he joined our Order). Almost up
to the last his sentiments were most loyal to the
Holy Father; and if ever I had to withhold my
sympathies from his views, it was chiefly on matters
purely political, and on which he never professed to
speak the mind of his brethren. Deplorable as his
fall from the faith is, truth and justice demand that
the charges alluded to which would convey any
impeachment of his moral character, or of the
sincerity of his faith (however much he may have
been *tempted* to doubt), should be met by his Superiors
(and I am one) with a frank and peremptory contra-

188

diction. The affliction which his sad case causes us
would not be alleviated by hearing things said of him
which would simply be against the truth.' I need
hardly add how fully I concur in those sentiments
thus expressed by my predecessor, Father Aylward.
Asking you to insert this letter in your next issue,
believe me, yours sincerely,

"F. Geo. Vincent King,

" Dominican Priory, Haverstock-hill,

" *September 14th.*"

To this the Editor subjoined this note:—

"Our short notice, referred to in somewhat extreme
language by our correspondent, was as follows:—

'Mr. Suffield had been for some time a cause of
anxiety to his Superiors. He has written a letter to
say that he repudiates the Scriptures, the Pope, and
even Christianity, as understood, whether by Catholics
or Protestants, and that he joins the Unitarians, or
free Christians, or Christian Theists. We take leave
of this unhappy Priest without dwelling on the sad
causes which have gradually led up to his apostacy,
instructive though they might be. We simply commend him to the pity and prayers of all.'—We did
not feel justified in mentioning in this notice the
causes which, we had been assured, had led to this
miserable apostacy. They seemed to touch more
closely than a journalist is warranted in doing in the
details of personal and private life. We have now,

however, no alternative but to mention, under reserve, what was actually told us, viz., ' that F. Suffield had been so engrossed in external and active works for many years, that he had become lamentably neglectful of his own spiritual life of prayer, and that this and his want of observance and docility to the directions of his Superiors, had for some time been naturally a cause of anxiety.' A letter from a Priest whose position gave him a means of knowing, confirms this statement from another source, though it does not coincide with the impression conveyed by the F. Provincial, who, of course, speaks with authority. But, granting the correctness of our information, what more instructive or practical lesson could there be for those among us who are tempted to act as though a life of activity in external good works could secure final perseverance without a life of prayer! No apostacy from the Catholic Faith—and we presume our Very Rev. correspondent would not maintain the contrary—can possibly take place without grave moral fault, except, indeed, in case of insanity, and then we should not call it apostacy. For Catholics it can only be a question of in what did the fault consist? Again, there is no axiom more undoubtedly certain, or more salutary to remember than ' *Nemo repente*,' &c. If we have unwittingly injured one whom we would rather pray for than uselessly annoy, we regret having done so. And we particularly regret that any words of ours should have given pain to our correspondent, or to any of his *confreres*, in a matter itself so full of sadness."

The next week appeared this rejoinder :—

"Sir,—In your last number I see a letter from the present Provincial of the Dominican Order in England, stating that the late Father Suffield and some of his numerous friends are complaining of the manner in which this fallen man has been spoken of in your columns. Allow me to assure you that very many Catholics are justly shocked at the maudlin sensitiveness about his character! displayed by one who is an apostate from his Order and his Faith.

"It is a public secret that many Fathers of the Order had been long anxious concerning the fate of a Religious, who, to other delusions, had added the not uncommon one, that the spiritual life can last to the end, if a Priest allow himself to be absorbed in external work. As to the doubts which the late F. Suffield now entertains—or more properly speaking, has thrown off—concerning the Catholic Faith, he himself has published to the world that they have been of very long standing. The thoroughness of the Catholic tone which has been conspicuous in *The Tablet*, will, I trust, not evaporate like the Rev. Mr. Suffield's spirituality.

"I enclose my name because, though I have good reason not to appear prominently in this sad business, I want you to see that I have a right to speak about it.

"I am, Sir, yours faithfully,

"*September 20th, 1870.*"   "Veritas.

CHAPTER XIII

He was quite right, the editor of *The Tablet*, in his statement that according to the generally received belief of Roman Catholics, "no apostacy from the Faith can possibly take place without grave moral fault, except, indeed, in case of insanity." But the hearts of Roman Catholics are as tender and true as are those of Protestants, and the transition from love and reverence to censure and abhorrence is no easy one. It is interesting to note this struggle in the many private letters written to him at this time— some boldly defying the accepted maxim and acquitting him of fault, and others preferring the alternative of believing him insane.

Here are a few extracts from the private correspondence of a family, all the members of which were on very intimate terms with him, and deeply attached to him. They are from letters of August and September, 1870.

"Tell Father Suffield, with our united kind love, that we read with *much* interest the article on the " Infallibility," in the *Saturday Review*, which he was good enough to send us. Tell him how frightful have been the consequences of its proclamation to numbers who were anxious to believe in our Faith and enter our Church."

"I have received several very *triste* letters from Father Suffield, and I am quite sure you have, like me, been most distressed. Would that all men could be satisfied with the pure and simple Catholic Faith, without diving into works written by heretics and infidels. Father Suffield has been in weak health for years, so deep study and great reading have been too much for him."

"As to Father Suffield, I don't like to think about, much less to talk about it. I don't know anything that has shocked me so much. . . . Good-bye, say your prayers as hard as you can, or the Devil is sure to have you. By Jove! I don't know who is safe. Count no man happy till he's dead. 'The grey-haired saint may fail at last.' Father Suffield has taken my breath away."

"I was so glad to get your letter and find you had taken poor Father Suffield's part. I thought, two years ago, that the bad state of his health with the strict duties of his Order would tell upon his brain. I was right it seems. The poor man has a terrible bee in his bonnet, which, however, I am glad has taken the ultra form it has, in leaving the true Church for such utter trash as that which he has embraced. He was so well known and so much respected that he might have done serious harm to our dear Faith. But now people will understand that the mind is weak as well as the body. But you have too many reasons to be grateful to the dear Father to think of anything but his goodness, and pray hard for his return to faith and salvation."

" Never go to stay with Father Suffield, the poor man is gone all wrong. He read and fasted till he hurt his health. Pray God he may be made right again. E. had a nice letter from him."

" *26th October, 1870.*

" Do not be induced to stay with poor Fr. Suffield, nor be with him on the same intimate footing as of yore, not because he has seceded from the true faith so much, as because he must have a screw loose, which may become looser and looser. I have read a letter of his which I think anything but reassuring, and I fear the future for him more than the harm he can do now, which is the reason why I wish you to be prudent."

" *September 12th, 1870.*

" I was so delighted with your dear little paragraph written in defence of so valued a friend as Fr. Suffield, who must be going through a martyrdom of suffering, for no Catholic can feel affection for him now that he has deserted the faith, and no other sect can feel gratified, as he positively declined to belong to any, so he will stay, as he justly says, much alone."

Another, a priest, who, with all his family, had been till now among his most attached friends, writes :—

" My Dearest Friend,

" We have been talking of writing to you, but two things prevented me—(1) The difficulty of knowing how to begin to you. (2) The fear of getting a painful letter back touching on subjects we loved to talk

M

of in happier days, but which now, to hear anything of from you is like a knife to the heart.

"You may fancy the agony we all suffered when you left Bosworth. It has been as yet *the* trial and pain of my life. I think of you constantly, but it is the priestly form of years ago which used to be my support, my comfort, my instruction. How I remember the joys of my meeting with you! Now I would do anything that was right to help you in any way, for soul or body; but what can I do but pray that before your departure into Eternity you may again hear the voice of our Lord and return to him?

"Poor Martineau never knew the truth, and I trust even he may see it.

"To argue with you is a thing I will never do. It would do no good and perhaps engender bitter feelings, or at least give rise to bitter words. But it is an awful thing, and a terrible trial and suffering. For myself I shall never, never forget you and all the love and kindness you have ever shewn me. I would offer myself to pains and death if I could bring you back, and I shall never give up hope. How often I think of words you have uttered and that have borne fruit in me; never to be forgotten words, though now bringing pain. I appeal against your present self, to your old self, to the priest who ever led me on, till your fall came. For myself, by the help of the Infinite God, I will be faithful, and never pry into his mysteries, lest I should be dazzled by their splendour. I submit my poor little intellect to His, and am glad to believe mysteries I cannot understand. Pride may lead me to believe myself rather than the voice of Christ, unless I fear and pray and watch, and may God grant that I may die, if by living I should be unfaithful to Him. This is my determination to live and die in the Communion of God's Holy Church. Your loving friend of days gone by."

This letter is from the same hand which had written to him a while before:—"I think you speak rather strongly about persecution, as I suppose we cannot deny that punishment in this world for wilful and obstinate heresy is right and most just. When, or how much it is expedient, is another thing." But love is stronger than all dogmas and conviction, and "many waters cannot quench love, neither can the floods drown it"; and so the same sad wail of wonder and pity and obstinate affection and abiding gratitude is repeated in letter after letter, from priests and laymen, ladies and nuns. Holding fast to the assumption that it was "God's Holy Church" they were members of,—that not to be for a moment questioned under pain of grievous sin,—all the rest followed; of course what his Church teaches is true, and to question it on the ground of difficulties of understanding is absurd. What those who so argue always fail to see is, that what they assume is the very point in dispute. The pride must border on insanity which leads a man to doubt God's Word or God's Church, and prefer to their testimony his own feeble reason; but his own reason, however feeble, is the light by which he must determine, if indeed the book or the Church be divine; no amount of confident assertion avails in place of proof. So all these remonstrances, numerous and affectionate as they were, were of necessity unavailing.

His successor at Bosworth wrote, telling him all about the parish, and then went on:—"And now, dear Father, permit me to refer to a subject at once painful and distressing, since it brings before the mind one whom I have loved and revered and admired for goodness and holiness and unbounded zeal, who gave joy and consolation to all who crossed his path, but is himself now sunk in a sea of desolation and bitterness. You understand that I mean yourself. And may it not all be a temptation, may not those doubts you spoke to me about in your letter be a trial of your faith? You say in your letter to-day that you have used means for many years, yet the difficulties remain. Does that imply that because you have resisted temptation for years, you must now yield? I am sure you know the Christian's rule of faith, the Christian's guide—submission to the Church—too well to oppose it now without making shipwreck of your soul's salvation.

"You know, and I am sure have often taught, that temptations against faith are not to be met by argument and subtle reasoning, but by a speedy flight and turning away of the mind, and they who argue upon matters supernatural, will, in all probability, reject what they cannot comprehend. I am speaking to one immeasurably my superior in every way, and amongst other things, in intellectual power, and therefore I will not argue, and if I did I could not succeed in proving to you what my own reason can never comprehend. But, I believe because the Church teaches—and, dearest Father and brother, excuse the freedom I take, when in the name of God I implore you to use the same words, notwithstanding all your doubtings and fears and difficulties, and I am sure your reward will be immeasurably greater than that of many who have not had the same trials to contend with. It would seem I were speaking as a child when I give advice so simple to one who is much more capable of advising me than I him; but my heart is full, and I express my feelings in the simplest way. I have said several masses for you, and have to-day offered up the Holy sacrifice, beseeching the Blessed Virgin, for whose honour you have done so much, to help, comfort, and save you. That our prayers may be heard is the earnest wish of your ever affectionate brother."

There were but few exceptions to this manner of loving entreaty, and those from correspondents whose previous acquaintance with him had been less intimate. Two instances may be given as illustrating the feeling commonly entertained by Roman Catholics towards those whom they call "apostate priests," and making the more striking the exceptional regard shown for this one. These extracts are from letters written some months after this, when he had settled down in the Unitarian ministry, but the same remark applies to some of the extracts given above.

It is a Priest, an Oxford convert, who came by chance into his neighbourhood, who writes :—

"I cannot but be overpowered with grief and anxiety on your account. It is as yet impossible for me to believe that you can have lost the faith which you once had, and which carried you through so many glorious works as a Catholic Missioner. I should not write to you now except that, like many others, I sincerely loved you. *Of course, love to one who denies our Blessed Lord cannot be ; and by one who does so heinous a sin against God, cannot be desired. As I know nothing and wish to know** nothing of the grounds upon which you have renounced the Catholic faith, I don't desire to enter into the matter with you. I only wish you to know that I shall pray for you ; my affection for you will oblige me to do this. Many are doing the same. They and I consider you are labouring under a mental delusion, which you have been for mysterious purposes permitted to fall into. With much sorrow and regard I remain," &c.

But indeed this letter is but a weak attempt at being righteously bigoted. Our other extract is from one who represents more correctly what others ought to have felt and some tried to feel : —

"Edified as we were at . . . by your zeal and devotion, we were pained and shocked at your leaving the Church, and are quite aware how intensely miserable you must be and how difficult it must be to retrace your steps. But time is short, &c. How then can you hesitate to throw off the mask you have assumed? only those who have been brought

---

* All these words are underlined in the original.

up as Catholics can feel how impossible, utterly impossible, it is to believe in any other than their own Church; and were you to declare the contrary, you know we would not and could not believe it. When I remember your discourses and devotion in the past, and contrast with it your present life, it is so fearful and appalling that I cannot help sending these few lines to implore of you to stop even now. Think of the numberless souls you will be contributing to lose, think how they will torment you for eternity for causing them to be lost. What are you now but a subject of pity to those you have left, and an object of pity to those you have joined. Forgive me for writing thus plainly. I know my words will reach your heart sincere and true as they leave mine." He could forgive most things, but what always angered him was any doubt thrown upon his sincerity. To give up everything in mid-life, to leave friends, position, provision, and come out into the world friendless, penniless, unknown, had been a bitter trial;—to accuse him of having done it all in pretence and hypocrisy was absurd; but it was nevertheless atrocious. But such letters were rare. The following is more typical of the feeling generally entertained towards him, and especially by those whom he had himself won to the Roman Church. How pitiful the struggle it reveals between the assumed duty of abhorring heresy as mortal sin on the one hand, and gratitude and respect and affection towards a spiritual benefactor on the other. It is from a lady who has since won distinction as an authoress.

" 20th August, 1870.

" DEAR REVEREND FATHER,

" Your letter gave me great pain and has made me very sad, but still what could I have you do more than you have done. If your conscience cannot submit to believe what the Church teaches, why I know you cannot force it. Dear Father, how can I say you have done right in leaving the Church and not believing what it teaches, and yet I could never bring myself to say that the Father and friend I have loved and respected so long could have done what you have done. I never knew that you had been so tormented and agonised about the very questions I so often used to write to you about: I never dreamed I was causing you pain in so doing : not to save my life would I give you pain if I could help it. But now I am coming to the purpose for which I write, namely, that as you said in your letter you had dropped all priestly functions and ceased to be a Catholic, I cannot, much as it costs me, aid myself by writing to you for advice when I want it, and must of necessity choose another director. Do not think I have done this without a stern and resolute struggle, but my sense of duty has gained over the love which I have for you and will ever have. Yet never, never shall anyone be permitted in my hearing to say one word of disrespect against you, and I hope you will continue to look upon me as a friend who never forgets one who was her father, and who continues to pray for happier times. I am often troubled with doubts, and I am continually being told different things by different persons, and it sends me almost wild."

The following, dated August 16th, 1870, is interesting, as a revelation of the sore straits to which at this time many learned Catholics were reduced :—

" The last month I have had to endure the greatest trial of my life, now happily ended. From the unexpected opposition in the Council, I felt sure that there would be no definition, and the vote of a month ago struck me with such a sense of impossibility that I did not know what to do, and for some time I did not feel able to approach the Sacraments. It was not only the Infallibility; in the Bull I saw the formal enactment of that system which I always dreaded. Five years ago I said to a Jesuit Father, if there were a General Council, the majority being all Papal nominees, would, of course, vote for the extremest Roman views; would it then be a free Council? He got angry, though a most amiable man, and told me I should end by being a Protestant. I never could see how the Pope can appoint and depose all Bishops at will, though I have always held the indefectibility of the Roman diocese. But there is a wide difference between the belief that the Pope can never, acting freely, deny the Faith, and holding that he is correct in every moot point of faith and morals. And the apparent cases in which the Pope has ruled wrong, seemed to me insuperable difficulties. Then the number of Latin bishops, as against Teutonic, and of bishops without sees; the tacit compact that none shall be Pope but an Italian, no matter whom God has chosen; the trammels imposed on the Fathers; most of all the epilepsy of the Pope which never leaves the blood, and almost always destroys the mind at last ; those considerations quite shook my respect for the authority which proposes the new constitution to my faith. Then I saw your first letter in the *Westminster Gazette* (the others I have not seen). I admired its bold, certain tone, though I was unable to think the word 'vain' rightly suggested of Pius IX. I have found all the harm in the world done by want of intellect, far more than by vanity or pride. I do not believe that the Pope or Archbishop care a straw for worldly motives; they think they are doing God service.

"I never suffered so much mental distress, aggravated by the brainless crowing of the Faithful, who know nothing of the difficulties, which are so terrible to those who have read history without bias. When I read that we're already bound to believe, I was unable to feel myself still a Catholic. I had a long talk with one of the best Oratorians, which hardly gave me any light. My usual Confessor, a hot Infallibilist (and not very wise), knowing my mind and hearing all my great difficulties, said he would still give me absolution, which I did not expect; but I seemed to be unable to attempt confession.

"I had, while expecting to be refused absolution, considered what would become of me. I could not dream for a moment of wilfully leaving the Communion of Rome, no matter what the Centre of Unity does. But, I said, suppose I can't believe and can't

be shriven, am I to live as a heathen, without sacraments? And I had thoughts about the Greek schism,
for I never could think for a moment of being an
Anglican, or of any other sect.

"After I left my confessor's room, though I had
been offered absolution, I began to feel that I was
wrong in spite of all difficulties. True, the system I
don't like has been authorised as the correct one.
True, it has been done by means not pleasant to see.
But it *may* be right in spite of my sense and my fear;
and as to the means, there are ways of God as to
our own private lives which are as unintelligible as
anything of this kind. And, in spite of all that may
be said against the freedom of the Council, God cannot have so deserted the Church as to let a clear
majority of all the bishops in the world betray their
trust and vote a lie. It is impossible, this dogma; be
it so: but so is the Resurrection, for which I see not
one shred of evidence in Scripture, or anything else.
Without the authority of the Church, I should certainly not believe that St. Paul teaches the same
belief that we have about it. I should, treating the
matter as a Deist, conclude that he had invented a
theory to reconcile an old superstition with common
sense, without quite breaking with the former. Nay,
my whole nature protests (or would protest) against,
not Christianity absolutely, but against its being
imposed upon me as an essential thing. So if I
refuse what the Church now proposes, can I logically
stop there?

"All this occurred to me for the hundredth time at

least; but in a moment I was freed from further difficulties. I saw, and still see, all the contradictory things which trouble so many. I knew that I was not threatened, as yet, with deprivation of the Sacraments, and also that some of our bishops say no one is bound to believe till the end of the Council; yet I felt that God gave me a word, exactly as when I became certain, in a moment of time fifteen years ago, that I must join the Roman Communion to be within the pale of salvation. And since this I have been not only at peace, but in fulness of joy, as if I had received the faith for the first time. I have, I believe, been in great danger. I am not sure of having grievously sinned; but I neither thought of wilfully jumping out of Peter's barque, nor of staying on board (as some are doing) while in secret mutiny. I asked for more faith, and have got it. It may be possible indeed that they are excused by their good faith, or their implicit belief in anything proposed by the Church; but, while I feel I have no right to judge others, I am clear that I have no business to set myself up to judge either Council or Pope. As I said to my mother when I left the Establishment, 'If I am deceived, God has deceived me.' You will smile, I fear, when I say that I have more trust in Rome now than I have had for years. It is rather like 'amantium iræ.'—But Talleyrand was right in saying 'Les affaires de Rome ont porté malheur à tous ceux qui y ont touché.'

"I have just received a letter from F. B. which may interest you. I cannot agree with him. He is quite mistaken in attributing any errors of mine to any desire to think for myself. I have never wished anything so much as the dominion of just authority. I *feel* with the crushed opposition, but, I am certain, I *believe* with the majority.

"P.S.—August 17th. I have now read your letter in the *W. G.* of August 6th. At that time I could have expressed, and certainly felt, all that you say. I am deeply pained to see how far your difficulties have gone. I have heard you a good deal abused lately, and have snubbed diverse who talked sneeringly about 'the verge of apostacy, &c.,' and having been tempted so much myself, I am very anxious to see what you will do.

"One thing I should like to say, because it may be, perchance, of some little use. I have heard you preach and speak, and read your writing, and I have always admired the clearness, calm, and purity of your style, 'qu' on y voit.' Well, in your letter of August 6th I see faults which can hardly be all misprints, and a general excitement which makes me feel sure your mind has been exercised past its power of thinking calmly. In that case I can only pray that you may not feel bound to take any further step towards widening the gulf already existing between yourself and orthodox thought."

This last remark will have been made by other readers of the letters of Mr. Suffield's here reprinted, and it has been a constant temptation to the editor to amend the solecisms and make the meaning clear. It has been thought best, however, to leave them untouched ; their defects bear witness, which cannot be gainsaid, to the sincerity of the writer. He did not, as a sophist, sit down to justify by the best arguments he could discover conclusions to which he had been led by self-interest, or worldliness, or pride. He wrote as out of the fulness of a soul in which reason and affection were contending for the mastery, so that he was being forced to a course he inwardly revolted from. He knew that every word he wrote went as a knife into the hearts of those whom, alone in all the world, he called friends, loved, and was loved by ; and he could not stay to correct the grammar of his utterances and mould the sentences.

After all, there is no fault in these letters which the grammarian will not find equalled and exceeded in some which are, nevertheless, accounted to be inspired.

For the rest, this correspondent reveals in his letter the secret which so much puzzles Protestants ; how can Roman Catholics believe such impossible things ? —they ask ; and often they assert that educated men only pretend to believe in them, forgetting, indeed, that they themselves believe in much which seems to the outsider quite as impossible.

Habit, indeed, is for the most part the reason of faith to one and the other, they believe because they always have done so. But the Roman Catholic who is instructed and thoughtful, believes because he *ought*, because it is his duty and salvation, because he firmly makes up his mind to it, and resists any suggestion against the faith as a temptation of the Devil.

Hence the difficulty for any good man to free himself from the system ; he must *begin* by what he believes to be the grave sin of doubting; and probably Mr. Suffield would all his life have remained in the Church, forcing down his doubts, but for the quasi authorisation to doubt and to inquire which was afforded by the vexed question of Papal Infallibility.

Two other letters he received at this time from men both eminent in the Roman Communion. The one, an ecclesiastic, whose orthodoxy has never been called in question, " wrote to the effect that, as he believed it possible for a person to leave the Church without incurring guilt in the sight of Almighty God, so he gave him credit for sincerity, and for following his conscientious convictions in the step he had taken."* The other, a layman, well known in the Church and outside, wrote on the 8th of August :—

"The slight knowledge that I have of you, personally, hardly justifies my thus intruding upon you. Nevertheless, having read your letter in the *West minster Gazette*, I cannot refrain from offering you the respectful assurance of my sincere and deep sympathy. These are times of trial indeed to the best and noblest among us, as well as to some whose imperfect faith is supplemented by still more imperfect works ; and the trial is increased by the utter inability of many good men to enter into, or understand the difficulties of some who are but sincere seekers after truth."

On the 30th of August he wrote again :—

---

* The writer's own words.

"Your kind letter has been forwarded to me. I earnestly hope and pray that time may assuage the bitter pain you are now enduring. How often what seems to us the greatest of misfortunes turns out to have been our very salvation. Confiding in the good providence of God, I feel sure that the recent definition will be ultimately a blessing to the world in one way or another, and not only to the world but to the Christian Church also. My occupations, however, and my line of thought are so remote from theology, that it is comparatively easy for me to be silent and wait. This does not, however, prevent me from having the *keenest sympathy* with anxious loving souls, whose position and feelings do not allow them to assume a similarly passive attitude. With every best wish for your happiness, and with sincerest sympathy and esteem, believe me, yours very truly."

It was a few months later, when he had settled down at Croydon as a Unitarian minister, that he received a gratifying proof of the kindly remembrance in which he was held by his late parishioners, in the shape of a handsome silver-plated inkstand, with the inscription, "To the Rev. Father Suffield, from his friends at Bosworth." He sent the following letter in acknowledgment :-·

"93, TAMWORTH ROAD, WEST CROYDON,

"*February 2nd, 1871.*

"MY VERY DEAR FRIENDS,

"I thank you sincerely for the beautiful token of your affectionate remembrance. I quite understand that you do not thereby signify agreement with me in my religious position, but simply wish to testify that you love me as a friend who loved and will always love you.

"Unable to believe certain opinions fundamental to all Catholics, I shall never cease to love tenderly all of those who, like yourself, like the Fathers and and Brothers of my late Order, like my many dear devoted friends, were my chief argument inducing me to consider myself enabled conscientiously to banish the intellectual difficulties I felt.

"What you used to hear from me last year, is what I now address to my little flock here—what previously I addressed to you, was the full teaching of the Catholic Church;—in late times I spoke to you chiefly of God, His providence, virtue, charity. Then I had begun to think it possible that the counsels I was taking with three holy and learned ecclesiastics of the Catholic Church might result in my being compelled to resolve to sever so many precious and beautiful ties of sympathy, communication, and affection.

"Always shall I recommend to God those at Bosworth and elsewhere, who so numerously have been my kind and sympathising friends.

"May every blessing attend you and your children whom I have loved so well, and when this short life is closed may a unity be obtained hereafter which here seems to be attainable.

"I beg a perpetual share in your prayers, and to remain always

"Your loving, grateful, and devoted friend,

"ROBERT RODOLPH SUFFIELD."

N

And so he took leave of his Catholic friends; however kindly the feelings they cherished towards him, it was impossible that any degree of intimacy could be maintained between them. A close friendship may, and often does, exist between persons of different religions, but it must be on the terms that neither party regards the other's faith or unfaith as a sin and outrage on his own. Old love may survive, and pity keep back blame, but it must be at a distance. So he had little or nothing to say to Catholics till the approach of death renewed their vain but loving importunities. He had arrived now into a new world, and soon found himself surrounded by new friends less demonstrative and less reverential, but as many and as genuine.

CHAPTER XIV.

MINISTRY AMONG UNITARIANS.

It was indeed a new world into which he had
entered, and he set to work at once to make himself
at home in it. On August 14th, his first free Sunday
for 20 years past, he attended morning and evening
at George Dawson's Chapel, the next Sunday found
him a worshipper at the " Church of the Messiah,"
and the next at the " Old Meeting House." He made
friends rapidly among Birmingham Unitarians, and
at the beginning of the next month accepted invitations to Manchester and Liverpool. His stay, however, was very short, for on the 7th instant he returned
to Birmingham, where, on the morning of the 11th,
he conducted service and preached at the Church of
the Messiah. It was but six weeks before that he
had celebrated Mass in the morning, and given "The
Benediction of the Blessed Sacrament " in the evening to his little flock at Bosworth : but great as the
outward change was, he had been so long preparing
for it, and was, moreover, so naturally inclined to
simplicity of ritual, that he took readily to the Puri-
tan bareness which then, even more than now, was
characteristic of Unitarian services. Indeed, so far
as can be ascertained from his diary and correspondence of the time, he does not seem to have given
attention to the contrast, but to have been absorbed

rather in the thought of the great truths common to all systems of religion, and anxious, above all, to say nothing which would wound his old friends, or gratify what he knew to be unreasonable prejudice. So his first two sermons were a candid examination of what had long been his great argument for Catholicism—its success. And he asked, the first time he spoke in a Unitarian pulpit, the success of Jesus Christ, to what was it due? He showed that it was not due to belief in his Divinity, for that was slowly apprehended—nor to his miracles, for he was at pains to conceal them—nor to a Church system organised by him—nor to prestige or success while living—" it arose out of failure, spread like fragrance of the broken vase, and silently possessed the world."

On the Sunday following, he preached at Upper Brook Street Free Church, in Manchester, where then the pulpit was vacant, and they were anxious to obtain his services as their minister. He repeated in the morning his sermon of the previous Sunday, and in the evening returned to the same subject, but regarding it from a more positive aspect. His brief notes of this discourse are as follows :—

" Cause of his success—his personal character, human, and therefore imitable, and our encouragement—chiefly his simplicity (he aimed at no effect), neither all hero nor all gentleness—tender and strong—severe and considerate—unostentatious—attractiveness of simplicity, repulsiveness of pretentiousness—his devotedness—self-sacrifice."

He left Birmingham on the 22nd, and went to

Croydon as the guest of Mr. Mallison, who at that time was actively interested in the proposal to commence free religious services in the town. On the Sunday following he preached at the Stamford. Street Chapel, in Blackfriars. It was the time when day by day news was coming of siege and battle and slaughter in France, and he took his text from the *Book of Lamentations*, i, 20. "I am in distress; my heart is turned within me : abroad the sword bereaveth, at home there is death." He spoke of the compassion which the English people should feel for the dead and wounded on either side, and how death was the lot, not of soldiers only, but of mankind. "May our compassion go beyond death, and follow the pilgrims as they travel forward?" Yes, he answered, all religions recognise the kinship of living and dead, and the yearning of the bereaved is the sanction of the doctrine of the Churches. The sermon was probably disappointing to those who had gone to hear a distinguished convert from Romanism, and was not wise from a worldly point of view; militant Protestants, and good and useful men some of them are, are suspicious and intolerant of anything which smacks of Roman doctrine, and ask of a convert, not that he should palliate, but protest, and from his own experience, furnish matter to make their protest the more effective. His own comment in his reminiscences, dictated to a shorthand writer shortly before his death, is, "my first Unitarian sermon was on quite a neutral subject. I adopted a similar course for a long time when asked to preach on special occasions, causing disappointment to Unitarians, who naturally looked for some expression of my motives and reasons for renouncing Romanism and embracing the Unitarian position. This was owing to a morbid dread I had of wounding the feelings of my old friends, who had always been very kind and good to me. But it was a mistake; especially when on an early occasion I preached in favour of a Roman Catholic religious belief, which I hold on broad grounds, but which is identified with the Roman system. To this, perhaps, was due the absurd impression which arose in some quarters that I was still a Roman Catholic under a Unitarian garb."

But, indeed, he never had the art to hold back the expression of convictions which were likely to be unwelcome to his hearers or injurious to his own prospects. While yet a Roman Catholic, and under the obligation to entertain no thoughts on matters of religion but such as his Church approved, he was far too outspoken on political subjects to suit his Superiors. Now, that at a great price he had obtained freedom, he was not minded to adopt any kind of compromise, but spoke publicly his beliefs and disbeliefs without regard to what might be said of him. There were some who accused him of insincerity—had they known him better, imprudence and want of reticence would have been their changes. He had never to reproach himself with having said what he did not believe; there were times when perhaps he might have repented of having spoken too frankly and to no good purpose.

He seems by this to have made up his mind to
settle for a time at least at Croydon, where it seemed
as if a Church had been gathering for his ministry,
while he was being prepared at Bosworth for their
service. So our lives fit into one another, and men
and women far apart, in place, and thought, and way
of life, are adjusted, themselves all unconscious of it,
each for the other, for,—

> There's a Divinity that shapes our ends,
> Rough-hew them how we will.

It was on the 2nd of October that he conducted
the first free religious service held at Croydon. The
temporary place of meeting was a Nonconformist
Chapel in London Road, which had been hired for a
couple of months. They began together, congregation and minister; it was an experiment on either
side, and the success must have appeared doubtful
to both. Could he accommodate himself to the ways
and faith of such a congregation? Could they, few as
they were, succeed in establishing a Church?

It was the day observed among Roman Catholics,
and more especially by the Dominicans, as " Rosary
Sunday"; and the new Unitarian minister had been
long distinguished among English Roman Catholics
by his ardent propagation of the devotion of the
Rosary. Year after year he had preached on it and
explained it this first Sunday of October, and had
always attracted crowds to hear him. Now, to a
mere handful of liberal religious thinkers, he ex-
pounded his own views of "Free Christian Worship."
What they were will best be told in his own state-

ment, written to the *Norwood News*, in reply to an assertion made in that paper, " that the members of the Free Christian Church repudiate nearly all the doctrines most dear to Christians."

" We believe profoundly in the Great and Good God our Father, the universal and all present Spirit ; that His providence, His power, and His mercy never fail; that He should be adored both in public and private worship ; that we should earnestly pray and strive to keep those laws of piety and virtue planted in the human heart, recognised by the experience of mankind, and presented with singular majesty in the Hebrew and Christian Scriptures— these Scriptures we continually use and reverently read. We believe that our immortal soul is for good or for evil, day by day building up here the monument of its own eternity. We believe that God has the will and the power to pardon our sins. We believe that no single soul has been created for eternal wretchedness. We believe the words in which Jesus and St. James describe the end and essence of religion. Regarding all men as the sons of God, we believe Jesus to be the Son of God, and amongst his brethren the greatest in the wonderful influence of his life, his teaching, and his death. We pray in the mode and with the very words he taught. We believe that every man must truthfully act according to his conscience, and, therefore, if unfortunately he hold a superstition, he must practice it. We would rather for his sake that he could be freed from such spiritual bondage, and, with holy and virtuous joy, advance into the liberty of the children of God : depending not on priests, sacraments, ministers, churches, sects, bibles, atonements, expiations, rites, but on the living God. Him we find sufficient. I have been accustomed for years to have intercourse with characters beautiful, and pure, and kind, who conscientiously held a superstition. I now enjoy intimate intercourse with those whose faith, and hope, and virtue rest on what is universal to all religion—God and the conscience. They do not deem my ministrations or those of any other man necessary for salvation. They place their confidence and their hope in Him, to whom alone Jesus directed the aspirations of his disciples ; I find them as devoted, as holy, as spiritual, as earnest, as noble, as truthful, as Christian in their tone of thought and life, as the best of those I have left. They differ from many Christians on points of Jewish history and Biblical criticism, and they do not feel enabled to believe in the everlasting torture of millions of souls ; but surely they hold the greatest of the truths, which are dear to all Christians."

So far as to what he retained of the doctrines usually associated with the Christian name, but among his own few fellow-believers who desired his ministry, his anxiety was that there should be no misunderstanding, and no subsequent trouble because he believed perhaps less, perhaps more than some of them. He was the free minister of a free congregation, and on neither side was any obligation imposed or accepted, yet he felt it desirable to have a quite clear understanding. He had to decide at this time between remaining at Croydon, which he had only bound himself to till Christmas, and accepting the tempting invitation which came to him from the ancient and influential congregation at Upper Brook Street, Manchester.

On November 6th he laid the matter plainly before the congregation, and read to them the communication he had received from Manchester, where, at a meeting of the congregation, held on October 9th, it was resolved unanimously, "That the Rev. R. Rodolph Suffield be earnestly invited to become the minister of this congregation from Christmas next, and that Dr. Marcus and Mr. Aspden do wait upon Mr. Suffield, in London, to induce him to accept the office."

His own notes of what he said from the pulpit ran, —" ask for prayer—express my opinion on the two places—interest, edification, gratitude in connection with present work—remarkable agreement of opinion and sympathy." Then written, apparently as spoken, " When your kindly confidence induced you to ask me to become the minister of this congregation, I was advised by many men of experience in the Unitarian body not to mention my opinions on religious matters. This advice did not commend itself to my judgment, and therefore I took means of making known my line of thought without committing myself to any pledge. If your numbers were as large as at the Chapel at Manchester I should consider that I had sufficiently manifested my opinions, because in a large town those who disagree can easily separate and go elsewhere, and their absence leaves no gap. Our numbers here are so small that it is specially desirable that the minister should be in harmony with the pervading tone of thought in the congregation as to the object, and character, and method of his ministry. On all these matters my opinions are quite formed. Compelled entirely to disbelieve in the supernatural powers claimed by the Catholic Church, the truths not exclusively Catholic that remain to me I believe as distinctly as heretofore, but upon a wider and stronger evidence,—evidence which my Catholic training weakened but did not destroy. It will be satisfactory to my own sense of justice and respect for yourselves, to let you understand such part of the history of my own mind as will explain to you the spirit in which I should embrace any ministerial duty, and the objects which I should propose to myself. Heretofore I have in no way alluded to my antecedents; I wished to speak to those who had a right to hear what I believed, but I did not wish to indulge a vulgar curiosity, or even to appear to pander to vulgar prejudices and hostilities with which I have no sympathy.

"I should regret declining a position of influence and importance at Manchester if it should appear that my idea as to our objects differs from that of any considerable section of yourselves. Therefore, next Sunday and the following, I shall endeavour to unfold to you briefly the prolonged process of investigation which, from a Catholic priest, has made me a Unitarian minister."

This was probably the only occasion that he spoke from the pulpit, except by way of allusion, of his past life. It is the kind of subject which attracts but does not edify, or even if it may do so, only at the cost of the modesty which a true gentleman will not sacrifice without certain call of duty.

Controversy too he avoided from the first. Thus, on November 20th, we find in his handwriting,— " Notice.—Three or four persons, strangers to me, have written to request that I would treat publicly and controversially certain questions at issue between Catholics, Anglicans, and Dissenters. They must pardon my not obliging them. I do not contemplate introducing allusions to the different Churches, except just so far as is necessary to explain certain conclusions bearing on and elucidating what I believe to be fundamental, moral, and religious truths. I shall be very glad indeed to arrange with any persons to go into such questions privately, and any one of any class in society, or any religious position or any age, will be equally welcome."

On December 4th he held his last service under a hired roof, the congregation having purchased for their use an iron Chapel in Wellesley Road, which has since been superseded by a handsome stone building, but is still retained by the congregation, and used as a hall for social meetings and lectures. When giving notice at evening service that they were meeting on that spot for the last time, and passing as it were out of their brief nursery period as a congregation, he said, " the Sundays we have met here together have proved the most marked epoch of my life. Mr. Martineau, who will preach next Sunday, is the friend who came to see me at Bosworth, when I wanted to learn whether in the ranks of free thought and of intellectual faith I should find the same earnestness, zeal, and virtue which I had witnessed elsewhere. The united interest I have witnessed among yourselves in inaugurating this religious work forms a striking reply to my inquiry."

On the 29th of December the congregation unanimously agreed to a resolution inviting him to become their permanent minister, an invitation which he had already resolved to accept in preference to that from Manchester. Mr. Maurice Grant, the Honorary Secretary of the congregation, in conveying to him the message, wrote, " I may indeed congratulate you on the warm interest you have been able to create on your behalf in so short a time, and hail it as a happy augury for the future of our little community. I heartily hope you may be with us for many years, and direct our efforts to establishing a really ' free ' Christian brotherhood, devoted to the one true God, and earnest and zealous for him." It is significant of the tone prevailing among its members, and much encouraged by himself, that there was added to the formal invitation,—" And the congregation are prepared to co-operate heartily with him in carrying out such objects as may tend to promote the prosperity of the Church and benefit the neighbourhood generally."

This active interest in the world's welfare is characteristic of a denomination which makes no claim to be " *The* Church," as distinguished from the world, and does not, therefore, set itself with a single eye to seek its own good as if it were God's cause. While yet a priest Mr. Suffield had been inclined to take a wider survey than was considered good for ' a religious' devoted to the Church; now that he was free he busied himself—not only as a citizen but professionally, and esteeming it part of his duty as a minister of religion—in everything which was for the good of his neighbours.

It was in response to a letter announcing to Mr. Martineau his final decision in favour of the Croydon congregation that he received the following reply:—

" LONDON, *January 5th, 1871.*

" MY DEAR MR. SUFFIELD,

" Your letter touches me deeply. I thank God if I have been in any way associated, even by an illusion of your kindly thought, with your emergence into higher light.

" I am convinced that your decision is the right one; and I look with great hope to the enlarging life of the Croydon Society under your spiritual care. I like the idea of your ' conference ' of young people. Only, I should think it important that *you* should keep firmly the lead and direction of it, so that it should be essentially an occasion of instruction emanating from you, and not incur the risk of passing into a debating class on terms of democratic equality. Under the latter conditions the boldest and most voluble work their way to the front, and suppress the more reverent and spiritual minded. You will gradually discover how great a power is *impudence* in our Protestant culture : and you must help us to gain more of the Catholic reverence and tenderness."

He took an immediate active part in all the philanthropic and educational movements of the town to which he was admitted as a worker. Yet amid it all, he writes, "I felt like a boy beginning amongst men," —for the first time for so many years allowed to think and act for himself,—"everything around me seemed strange and new"; and again, he repeats "the seven years at Croydon were full of interest, and interest of a permanent kind, moreover securing to me many and dear friends. But everything seemed strange and new to me, and I have felt more calmly in later years."

He had great need of someone who should be a constant companion and partner of his new life, its cares, and joys, and varied moods, and such a one he found in the elder daughter of Mr. Edward Bramley, the first Town Clerk of Sheffield, who was able also to bring to him that which he lacked, experience of Unitarians and their ways.

"Some persons suppose," he wrote, when now in view of death, "that such a momentous step as secession from the Roman Catholic Church is influenced by a desire of marriage. It may be with some. In my case it most certainly was not. I do not think I had adverted to marriage. The lady who became my wife, and the joy and companion of twenty happy years was not known to me until I was established in a position of independence at Croydon."

He was married on the 7th of December, 1871, by the Rev. John Lettis Short, at the Upper Chapel, in Sheffield, of which his wife's father was an influential supporter, and for a long time honorary secretary, an office since held by his son, and now by his grandson.

The marriage of a priest is looked upon with horror by Catholics, who deny indeed that it is a real marriage, any more than going through the form makes a couple wife and husband, one or other of whom has a partner still living. And there are not a few Protestants even to be found who regard the step with disfavour, and would at least honour more highly the priest who, breaking his other vows, still remains celibate. But the feeling is unreasonable on any ground, except that which Protestants reject, the superiority, namely, of celibacy to the married state. A vow, according to the definition accepted among theologians, is a promise made to God respecting something which is not only good, but more than ordinary and obligatory good, "*promissio Deo facta de bono meliore.*"

Now if a person, believing that it is pleasing to God that he should remain single all his life, and that by so doing he will serve God better and live nearer to Him, makes *on this account* a vow of perpetual chastity, it would seem clear that he is bound by it only so long as he sincerely believes in the hypothesis on which he acted. To conclude that he was mistaken, that God has no pleasure in witnessing those whom He has made male and female, living apart, and as

if wedded love took from love of Him, this may be,—
Catholics think it is—a dreadful heresy, but it certainly looses the bond of the vow taken upon the
opposite belief. So if one should, out of gratitude to
a benefactor, solemnly promise to do certain things
for him, and should subsequently discover that these
things were not desired by him or were indifferent, it
would be weak and foolish, out of mere scruple, to
keep the promise. So thought Mr. Suffield; and
when once he had given up his faith in the Church's
teaching about this and greater matters than this, he
never doubted that it was lawful and right, and for
him in his position the better thing to marry, nor did
he ever in after years express a moment's hesitation
or regret about the step he had taken.

During the few years he spent at Croydon he was
very actively employed both there and in London in
all manner of work; for his own congregation—for
the British and Foreign Unitarian Association, of
the Council of which he was a member,—for the
liberal party in general, and in every movement,
social, political, and religious, which he could assist.

There is no need to enumerate the many societies
in whose work he was so associated, but it may be
well to give some particulars of " The Liberal Social
Union" which he was the means of starting in London,
and which long after he ceased to be able to take an
active part in it, continued to bring together thinkers
and enquirers of many schools. His own idea, which
was mainly carried out, is thus expressed in a letter,
printed for circulation among persons likely to join:—

o

226

"CROYDON, *October 9th, 1873.*

" DEAR MR. HUTTON,

"I quite concur with you that it would be very desirable for London Theists and Unitarians to be brought into closer cohesion. We need a society in which, moreover, could be combined some of those Liberal Churchmen, Liberal Nonconformists, Jews, Hindoos, Mahomedans, Buddhists, Parsees, Confucians, Comtists, Inquirers, and Sceptics, who, conscious of the difficulty of theoretic abstract theological speculations, yet earnestly desire the promotion of the spiritual and moral life, as well as the duty of thought and reverent inquiry brought to bear upon such. There are many now who believe in the religious life without feeling able to assert any religious dogma. Others who consider they can rationally affirm certain dogmas, but deem such subordinate to life and subject to inquiry. We desire from amongst some of such persons to form a ' Circle' of friends who could pleasantly co-operate and who would like to unite at Conversaziones, Discussions, Lectures, and even perhaps at Excursions. As Socrates maintained the duty of a practical religious moral life, refused to dogmatise, questioned everything, and encouraged the friendly gatherings of those who sympathised, we might call such a society the ' London Socratic Circle.' The following suggestions might arise for our consideration.

"It should meet on neutral ground. Perhaps the Trustees would permit Dr. Williams' Library to be used. It should have no President or Vice-Presidents, so that no influence should seem to predominate. It must have a spirit, but no creed. The Committee ought of necessity to embrace men and women, foreigners and natives, students and professional men; also various schools of religious thought. The Committee would appoint Secretaries and Treasurer; a Monthly Chairman for public occasions; also Stewards and Stewardesses.

"Those who are being invited to form the Provisional Committee summoned to secure *one* Conversazione, are persons likely to desire the formation of some such society. Should we find that an adequate number of ladies and gentlemen of various schools of thought and various nationalities can agree thus to combine, we should ourselves form a 'Circle,' and then give a Conversazione to friends, for the sake of making known what we had accomplished, and asking the adhesion of those present as being already known to us and trusted. After that evening, no new member could be received without due notice to the Committee and vote by ballot.

"Such a 'Circle' would in reality be an extension of the Student's Union, from which it is now emanating. When we had set the example, 'Socratic Circles' might get formed in all the provincial towns.

"The publication of this letter, according to your request, will afford in a crude form the sort of object which will, I suppose, engage the consideration of the Provisional Committee."

"P.S.—For three years I have had an 'Alfred Circle' for friendly intercourse at my house, alternate

Tuesdays, 7.30 to 11. I hope those who receive this invitation will, when possible, come."

In March, 1877, after more than six years of incessant activity, his health broke down, and he left Croydon for some months' holiday, which, by the kind consideration of the congregation, was prolonged to February of the next year, when he resigned the pulpit, and was succeeded by the Rev. E. M. Geldart, of Balliol, a convert from the Anglican Church. In giving to the secretary notice of his resignation, he wrote :—" Whilst expressing my great regret at parting with friends from whom both myself and my wife have invariably experienced the greatest kindness, I have the satisfaction of feeling that the period of my ministry among you has been marked by the greatest harmony, and that in all my efforts for the spread of our religious cause, I have ever met with hearty, thoughtful, and zealous co-operation." That this kindly feeling was reciprocated was proved by the testimonial, accompanied by the sum of £340, subscribed by the members of a congregation which was neither numerous nor wealthy. Writing in acknowledgment of the generous gift, he used the significant words, " I thank you, one and all, for the delicate, I would almost say the compassionate, consideration wherewith you encouraged me during those first years of my emancipated life, succeeding by an almost too rapid transition the specialities of my past." Indeed, neither he nor they realised at the time how difficult and trying his position was, and how admirably he succeeded, on the whole, in the task he had undertaken. An old established congregation with traditions and organisation would have been able to guide and support a minister coming to them new to the work; but there was no such thing at Croydon, there were only individuals who had to be made into a Church, and all his natural talents for organisation were called into full exercise. He did all that was required of him and more; what was wanting, and caused him to look back upon his Croydon ministry with mixed feelings, was experience of the free ministry. He had been a priest all the years of his active life, and more a priest than others, inasmuch as he had given himself heart and soul to his office; now he knew as well as any one the difference between the functions of priest and minister, was scrupulous beyond others in insisting on the independence of each member of his flock, but it was impossible that he could rid himself at once and completely of the habits of a lifetime; and if, in trying circumstances, he may have once or again forgotten that he was no longer a " confessor " or " director of souls," it surely was what was almost inevitable to one in his position in the first years of his changed life. To others who had exercised priestly functions for but a short time, or who had never been in positions of authority and trust in their Church, the transition would be comparatively easy; to him it was the more difficult, just because he had been so eminent in the esteem of his co-religionists, so habituated to share all their confidences, and be consulted in their most intimate affairs.

He was long prostrated both in mind and body, but kept looking forward, to use his own words, to a time when he might, "in restored health and renewed strength, serve again those causes, religious, political, social, dear to all" with whom he had been working. At length, in February, 1879, he felt capable of undertaing temporary charge of the "Unitarian Free Church" at Reading, and observing the interest taken in the cause, was prevailed upon to accept the pulpit. Here he remained till his death, though in June, 1888, he resigned the pulpit, wishing to be free for the future from permanent engagements.

As minister of Reading he had the great advantage of the experience gained at Croydon, and looking back upon it from his death-bed, he wrote,—"My life has not been an unhappy one anywhere, but I regard the last twelve years as the happiest period." He was actively interested, as at Croydon, in all the unsectarian work for the welfare of the town, but had not the additional distraction of London affairs to contend with. "In Reading," he writes, "it has been my privilege to have been a working member on committees of the Junior Liberal Club, of the Liberal Association, the Temperance and General Philanthropic Society, the Charity Organisation Society, the Dispensary, and the University Extension Movement, as well having been chiefly instrumental in founding the Literary and Scientific Society."

He was anxious that it should be known that his resignation in 1888 was due neither to dissatisfaction nor doubts. "My ministerial office amongst you," he wrote in a circular addressed to the congregation, "has been one of quite special happiness ; no word, no act has ever marred our unbroken harmony. To the last moment of life, my wife and I shall retain in grateful memory your affection, your thoughtful zeal, and your loving earnestness for the great principles of which our Church stands as the local representative. May our holy cause still, as ever, prosper in your hands." The congregation in response to this communication presented him with an address, in which they wrote,—"It would be impossible for us to acknowledge in adequate terms the services which you have rendered to the Church at Reading during your ministry here. We have all learned to esteem you as a friend, and to value the thought, earnestness, culture, and thoroughness which have characterised your teaching, and we owe it in a special manner to you that so much success has attended the effort to promote the extension of our cause in this town." They accompanied this address with a substantial testimonial, a witness to the unbroken friendship and esteem in which they held him till death.

He continued to show the reality of his interest in that cause by frequent services in all parts of the country where he was invited for special occasions, or could help in the absence of a minister. At Northampton he preached regularly for three months in the autumn of 1888, and won the enthusiastic praise of the congregation, who, in their annual report, speak of his services in terms which his modesty would not have consented to put in print.

He had adopted the office of a Unitarian Minister after long deliberation and at great cost. He never repented of his choice. The last words he dictated to the reporter who took from his lips a brief account of his life, were these :—

"With unceasing joy and gratitude I have always adverted to my secession from the Roman Catholic Church, and my having found so happy a religious home in our Liberal and Unitarian Churches."

An ideal life it certainly is not, that of a Unitarian Minister, nor did he pretend to find it such. It has its seamy side, its discouragements, its worries, its humiliations, and he had his experience of all. But these things are incidents of human life in every position, and the man who in spite of them finds work, and help, and thanks, and appreciation, and friendship, and freedom, has made himself indeed 'a happy home' on earth.

CHAPTER XV.

His Last Days and Death.

Mr. Suffield was leading a very peaceful and, at the same time, active life for more than eighteen months after his retirement from the regular ministry. The following account of the last few weeks before he was laid aside with the disease which ended his life, will be read with interest :—

" March 29th, 1891, which was Easter Sunday, he preached in the evening at Wood Green.

" April 5th he preached at Cardiff, and lectured the next evening on Savonarola.

" April 21st, 22nd, 23rd, and 24th, he attended the Triennial Conference in London. He was the guest of Mr. Mackenzie, at Croydon, so had an opportunity of seeing many old friends. He was not present at all the meetings, as he was suffering very much, and found difficulty in walking. At the Conversazione he remained seated nearly all the time.

" April 30th he went to Oxford to meet Count Gobelet d'Alviella, who was delivering the Hibbert Lectures that year. They had corresponded for several years, but never met. He lunched at Dr. Drummond's, attended the lecture, and dined with the Count and Countess at the Randolph.

" May 3rd he preached for the last time. It was at Sale, near Manchester, and he delivered his lecture on Savonarola the next day. One of the sermons was his farewell sermon at Reading. He was very unwell, and I have sometimes wondered whether he chose it purposely, thinking it might be the last time he should ever preach. He stayed at Leamington two days on his way home; he was really ill there, and awoke to the fact that he could not be suffering from rheumatism merely, so decided to see a doctor on his return to Reading.

" He got home Friday, May 8th, was at a committee of the Literary Society that evening, at Church the following Sunday morning, at a committee of the University Extension on the Monday evening, and at a meeting of the executive of the Liberal Association on Tuesday evening, May 12th. That was the last time he was out to walk. It took him more than an hour to get to the office, and it is not a mile. He was to have taken the Chair, but he had to go into a shop and send on to say they were to begin without him."

On May the 14th he called in his own doctor, Mr. May, who attended him with great care and kindness to the end. By his advice he went to London, accompanied by his wife and her sister, to consult Dr. Allingham, but by that time was so much worse that he had difficulty in walking the few steps across the station platform. He returned home at once, and was presently informed, by Mr. May, of the character of the illness from which he was suffering—a malignant tumour of the bowels. He doubtless must have feared something serious, but expressed no apprehension before, and the communication came upon him as a terrible surprise. Writing shortly after to his oldest friend, who had been a Dominican with him, and was now, like him, a Unitarian minister, he said :—

" My journeyings from home are at an end. My local doctor and the London specialist have pronounced my death warrant—incurable cancer in the bowels. This came as a great surprise to me, and a terrible shock to my dear good wife. I do only hope that she may not have the trial of witnessing very excruciating sufferings, which I really should dread more on her account than my own—though I don't profess indifference to pain! We have had a very happy twenty years (next December), of married life, and I wish that our last months together should be such as to leave a tranquil and even happy memory."

It was to the same friend that he wrote, in pencil, when now too weak to use pen and ink, signing himself "your ever loving friend, R. R. S.;" and then recalling his correspondent's last letter, with its conclusion—"yours for ever,"—he added, as a postscript, " as you to my mind truly say, '*Always in God.*' " They were almost the last words he wrote.

He received from friends of all Churches numerous kind letters which consoled him in his trial with the assurance of wide and deep sympathy. He was in the habit of keeping such letters in a small bag, which he took backwards and forwards with him as long as he was able to change from room to room, and had continually by his side from the time he was confined to bed.

Père Hyacinthe Loyson wrote, recalling how long ago he had "served Mass" for him at Issy, and how, later, they had met at Neuilly, the one a Unitarian, the other a "reformed Catholic." He went on to express regret that in giving up "the false divinity of the Pope you have ceased to believe in the true divinity of Christ," and concluded with the touching words :—

"Nous reverrons—nous sur cette terre? Je l'ignore èn tout cas, j'espère vous revoir de l'autre côté de la mort, là ou Dieu saura bien réunir les âmes droit es qui l'ont cherché sincêrement, même par des sentiers trés differents.

"Tuus in Christo,

"HYACINTHE LOYSON."

Anglican clergymen, Quakers, Congregational ministers, members of Parliament, as well, of course, as those of his own faith, all wrote in the same tone of respect and affection and sorrow, even if tempered, in some cases, by expressions of regret for his opinions. One letter may be quoted as a sample of what many are like. The writer, a clergyman, said ;—

"To myself the news of your illness has caused a profound and personal sorrow. I could fain that we were more at one in accepting the faith of the Divine Incarnation and Atonement of the Son of God; but since I have known you, I have always recognised in you not only one of pre-eminent gifts and culture, but one who had the purest and noblest aims, and was indeed a seeker after God. I have learnt much from you, and wish I had known you longer and seen you more."

From Dr. Martineau, the first friend of his new life, he received the following :—

" THE POLCHAR, ROTHIEMURCHUS,

" *June 28th, 1891.*

" DEAR MR. SUFFIELD,

" Deeply as the tidings in your letter of the 25th inst. grieve me, I thank you from my heart for allowing me to receive them from your own report; and still more for the generous spirit in which you review our relations to each other since the first memorable interview in 1870. If we are about to be parted,—and that by my too obstinate survivorship,— I pray that it may be in mutual benediction. It is consolatory to know that the great transition to which you were led by the call of conscience in 1870, has, on the whole, not failed to bring the promised peace of mind and heart. Our ministry is far from offering an ideal life; but, measured by the present standards of attainable spiritual value, it may well content a humble and dutiful soul.

If indeed you have to expect the graver sufferings of your fatal disease, may God uphold you in the faith and patience which have sustained so many through the *via dolorosa !* But I do not despair of hearing that, by aid of modern alleviations, the path from world to world may prove less formidable than shrinking nature is apt to imagine. In any case, it is not a lonely path to one who remembers the words, ' I am not alone, but my Father is with me.'

"With kindest and warmest sympathy with Mrs. Suffield, from my daughter and myself,

"Believe me, always,

"Yours with faithful affection,

"JAMES MARTINEAU."

He had for some years been honoured with the friendship of Mr. Gladstone, who had sought acquaintance with him in 1874, and continued it ever since. From him, too, he received a very kind letter of sympathy, written the same day as that of Dr. Martineau. "All that I have seen and known of you," he wrote, "has tended to cause interest, respect, and regard. Most earnestly do I wish that we could stand on the altar steps together." The letter was in reply to Mr. Suffield's, in which, telling of his approaching death, he had declared his persistence in "rejection of miraculous Christianity, and satisfaction in pure natural Theism." Mr. Gladstone, in reply, expressed his inability to understand "how a man of upright mind,—and I am better convinced of your uprightness than my own," he added,—"could make his halt in spiritual Theism a thin and pale reflection of the Gospel of Christ." He went on to speak of the inability of man to maintain "the great and glorious dogma, the truth of one God," without the aid of revelation, and concluded:—"But God lays His own foundations in His own way, shapes and seals His children as He will. You are, I think, essentially a man of peace. In writing, as I have written, I do not desire to forego that character; and my hearty desire is, that by whatever path into the heart of the Eternal Peace you may be led.

"Believe me, with unimpaired regard,

"Most faithfully yours,

"W. E. GLADSTONE."

It was their parting, as at the grave side, for Mr. Gladstone had not the opportunity he hoped for, of calling to see him. The difference between them was wide and deep, and each had felt impelled even to the last to insist upon it, but immense as it was, it had not impaired their friendship and regard for one another. Would to God that the example of this eminent Statesman and Churchman were followed by some who share his sturdy orthodoxy, but have none of his Christian charity!

But probably more gratifying than even these letters, were such as the following from a young lady, a chance acquaintance made at the sea-side :—

"Although it is four years since we met, the memory of your kindness to me is very distinct, and when I look at my album I stop at your photograph and think over things you said to me about the duty of being kind, and making those around me happy, and I feel stronger to meet the little daily trials and worries, and more anxious not to put my own interests first. When I think that even in so short a time your character left its mark on mine, I see what a great influence you must have had over so many people, always for good, and the knowledge that it is so must be good for you to have, and I know that I am only one of many who would thank you from their hearts.

You will not care to be troubled with any letters, but I must write to tell you how sorry I am for your illness, and also express a little of the gratitude I shall always feel towards you."

His old friends in the Roman Church were also much moved when they came to hear of his approaching death. Many had continued all through the years of his alienation to love and pray and hope for his return, and now their efforts were intensified, and pressing appeals were made to him to consider his position and repent before it was too late. Nothing could be more touching and tender than these appeals, but they were marred, all of them, by the curious presumption that he must really know himself to be in the wrong, and that it was only courage he needed to enable him to abjure what for twenty years he had professed. He couldn't be sincere, they argued, he must be convinced that in the Roman Church only was salvation for his soul; to them it was so evident, how could it be less so to a man who had so long believed and taught as they did still? And rather than give him credit for uprightness and honesty in leaving their Church, they professed to believe that he was now deliberately choosing eternal damnation as a preferable alternative to provoking the censures of his Protestant friends—censures which could not reach the chamber where now he lay dying, and which would have amounted to no more than expressions of pity that he should have been prevailed upon in the hour of bodily and mental prostration to recant the convictions of long years of intellectual vigour.

On the 18th of September he received a visit, of which he dictated an account and sent it the next day to a near friend, with a few words in pencil,—"I am in extreme pain," he wrote, "but I must gather up power to send you enclosed interesting overture. It is *not* private, but it would not be in good taste for me to publish it *as yet*. In course of time it will be another matter, and I place it in your hands therefore." The memorandum is as follows :—

"OVERTURES FROM CARDINAL MANNING.

"Friday, September 18th.—To-day the Rev. Kenelm Vaughan (head of the South American Missions), now staying with Cardinal Manning, called on me, and in the most gentlemanly, considerate, and graceful way communicated verbally the following messages from the Cardinal : —

"1st. Affectionate and sympathetic interest and greeting.

"2nd. Earnest entreaty to rejoice people all over the world by my return to the Church.

"3rd. That the Holy See is prepared to concede the fullest powers of absolution and dispensation to the Bishop of Portsmouth, so that the conditions required would be adapted to render any reconciliation to the Church as easy to myself and as little trying as possible.

"4th. The Bishop wishes me to know that he will gladly come to me on any day I may propose.

"The whole conversation was conducted with the finest courtesy. Of course I begged His Eminence to

P

accept my sincere appreciation of his kindness, his motives, and his communications, but at the same time I expressed in the most emphatic language possible that return to the Roman Catholic Church is to me an utter impossibility."

Father Vaughan wrote the day following from the Archbishop's House, Westminster :—

" It was a real consolation to have seen and had so full and friendly a talk with you. I have been thinking of you ever since, and affectionate sympathy moves me irresistibly to pray much for you, and positively to believe that you will, in the end, have grace and courage to do what the Cardinal and your Catholic friends so ardently desire and pray for. With this strong hope in me, ' for nothing is impossible with God,' believe me, dear Father Suffield,

"Your old friend,

" KENELM VAUGHAN."

From his old Dominican friends, friars, and nuns too, he received messages of sympathy and entreaty. " You are nearing that eternity," wrote the Prior of their London home, " about which, in the good old days, you used to preach so earnestly and so eloquently. Most of us owe something of our spiritual life to you, under God, and some of us owe much, and I hope that we are not unmindful of it. If we can be of any service to you, you have only to command us. We all unite in praying that you may have grace and light before ' the night ' comes."

On the 21st a Father was sent from London to seek an interview with him. He received him, but evidently the result was discouraging, for no further effort of the kind was made, if we except a visit paid to the house on the 27th of October by a Roman Catholic lady of rank, who was exceedingly importunate to see him, but he was then far too feeble to carry on even ordinary conversation, and her desire could not be complied with.

Special prayers were meantime offered up for him far and wide; and from the Dominican Convent at Lourdes, a letter was sent to him, expressing the interest taken in his soul by the French Sisters there, and telling of their efforts on his behalf, and their confidence that the Blessed Virgin, who in that neighbourhood was working so many miracles, would assuredly exercise her power over this dead soul, and bring to new life "this poor Father, who has made her known and loved as a mother by thousands."

Another sent him a morsel of cloth, cut from the cassock of the Venerable Curé d'Ars, and wrote :— " I wish I could get you to promise to invoke the great Curé. The great amount of good which you were instrumental in, by spreading devotion to the Blessed Virgin, *must plead grace* for you at the last hour. Oh that you would only make use of it ! The reconciliation would soon be over. Perhaps you naturally feel a certain fear at such a step; but remember how easily this can be overcome."

On the other hand, he had letters from unknown correspondents, earnest Evangelical Protestants, anxious that he should save his soul their way. One sent him a large type " Gospel of John," and emphasised for him its application to himself by inserting the initials (R.R.S.), wherever it seemed as if personal appeal could be made, *e.g.*: Chap. xiv. 7, "If ye (R.R.S.) had known me," &c. Good soul, doubtless the donor, but how did she know that this book, written so long ago, had special application or special authority for any one now living or dying? It was God's word to him or her, not necessarily so, however, to Mr. Suffield or another.

Besides these marks of the esteem and interest with which he was everywhere regarded, he received daily substantial proofs of regard from persons who, differing from him in religion, were admirers of his private character and public work. A carriage was put at his disposal as long as he was able to go out, and fruit and flowers always supplied in abundance.

One who saw him for the last time, on the 21st of October, wrote:—"He was very weak and suffering, but bright and humorous as ever: he told of the visits he had from the two priests named above, made little jokes after his wont, and asked pardon for seeming dull, but said his mouth was so parched and sore that it hurt him to smile. He specially begged that no undue lamentation should be made over him. When I rose to go, fearful of having tired him, he rose up and threw his arms round, and after the old Dominican form of brotherly embrace, we kissed and parted,—till we meet again in God—we and so many dear and good men and women whom we still love and admire, much as they condemn us."

His constant companions during his last illness were the little volumes of Epictetus, Seneca, and Marcus Aurelius, published in the Camelot Series; The Book of Prayers, compiled by the Rev. Crompton Jones, formerly an Unitarian minister, and the Revised Version of the Bible. These remained by his side to the last, when he had ceased to be able to give continued attention to anything else.

On Sunday, Nov. 8th, he had a severe attack of vomiting, afterwards he fell into a state of lethargy, from which he was rarely aroused, and died at 9.50 a.m., on Friday, the 13th inst.

"We are often told that ours is not a religion to die in. He proved that the contrary is the case. His doom was to die by a disease which is incurable, painful, and lingering. For five months he was face to face with death, the only doubt how acute would his sufferings be, and how long they would last.

"He had the most touching letters addressed to him by those who believed that he could not be saved unless he would exchange his opinions for theirs. Kindest messages and loving warnings were sent him by friends anxious to win him back, but he never gave sign of regret, or doubt, or fear. He was brave, patient, hopeful; above all, grateful to the last.

"Not weary of life—far from yearning after a better, for which he trusted God, but professed no knowledge of—he would have rejoiced to be restored, and live and love and work and interest himself again in this dear world: he went the way of death without complaint or repining."

They are the concluding words of an address given at a memorial service, held by his former congregation, at Croydon, on the 25th of November.

"He was to me a very interesting person," writes Mr. Gladstone, and all intelligent people who became intimate with him found him such. It was not merely the singular and varied experiences of his religious life which distinguished him from others; he was, in the true sense of the word, ' an individual,' a man apart; unlike anybody else in mind, manners, features, and dress; it was not that he was odd or eccentric, he was simply himself; and yet he was possessed of a remarkable capacity for understanding the thoughts of others, and he won their confidence even against his will. His personality acted as a spell on those who came under his influence, and it was this very power which made some fear and even suspect him.

He was, perhaps to excess, sensitive to the opinions of others, and cherished expressions of commendation or gratitude with an almost childlike regard. Yet he would never withhold the full statement of his own opinions to gratify a friend or appease an opponent. He spoke what he believed, never seeming to contemplate any other course as possible. If he gave offence by his sincerity, and he did so frequently, both as a Catholic and an Unitarian, he took it as inevitable. A little more policy would have obtained him wider regard, but he united, in a singular degree, the innocence of the dove with the wisdom of the serpent; he was innocent to a fault wherever his own reputation or prospects were concerned; wise enough, when it was a question of the cause he had at heart; a man who understood men, a skilful organiser, a patient and far-seeing contriver.

Throughout all the changes of his life he retained the same simple faith in God and prayer. From the time that he made rubbings of monumental brasses as a young man, to his last days of comparative leisure at Reading, religion was always uppermost in his thoughts, and he regarded everything else from the standpoint it afforded. If "priest" signifies one who represents to the world, in his person and by his calling, the presence and energy of God in the affairs of men, then he remained a priest all his life. The change which came over him was, that he ceased to believe in that Presence as supernaturally revealed in one body of men, and saw and declared it henceforth as truly natural, perpetual, and universal.

CHAPTER XVI.

Funeral and Obituary Notices.

The following account is abridged from *The Reading Observer* of Nov. 21st, 1891 :—

"The remains of the Rev. R. Rodolph Suffield were, in accordance with his own desire, cremated at the Woking Crematorium on Tuesday, previously to which, at mid-day, a memorial service was held at the Unitarian Free Church, Reading, of which he was for several years the minister. There was a numerous and representative congregation. Besides the relatives, there were present Lord Edmond Fitzmaurice, Mr. Geo. May, Mr. G. W. Palmer (representing the Reading Liberal Association), Mr. Walter Palmer (representing the University Extension Association), Mr. Benjamin Batt *(*representing the South Reading Liberal Club), Mr. C. Smith and Dr. Hurry (representing the Reading Literary and Scientific Society), Mrs. C. Smith, Mr. R. Worsley, (representing the Charity Organisation Society), Mr. Owen Ridley (representing the Redlands Liberal Club), Mr. Gleave, Mr. Theodore White (representing the Students' Association), Mr. Colvin, Mr. J. Egginton (representing the Savings' Bank), Bishop-Ackerman (representing the Reading Temperance and General Philanthropic Society, in the unavoidable absence of Mr. W. I. Palmer). Many gentlemen wrote expressing regret that they were unable to be present, including Mr. George Palmer, Mr. W. I. Palmer, the Rev. C. R. Honey, and many friends connected with London Associations.

"At about 11.30 the cortege, comprising an open hearse, and several coaches containing the mourners, with the carriage of Mr. F. P. Barnard, Head Master of Reading School, who was a personal friend, bringing up the rear, left Malvern Villa, Craven-Road, the residence of the deceased, and on reaching the church the coffin was borne in and placed in front of the rostrum. It was literally covered with wreaths of white flowers and other beautiful floral tributes, baskets and vases of flowers being also arranged on and about the rostrum. Wreaths or baskets of flowers were sent by the Literary and Scientific Society, South Reading Liberal Club, Women's Liberal Association, and from numerous friends at Reading and from a distance.

"The service was conducted, in accordance with the deceased's own wish, by the Rev. C. Hargrove, M.A., Minister of the Mill Hill Chapel, of Leeds, an old friend, both as a Dominican Friar and as an Unitarian Minister. The service lasted about an hour, and was simple but impressive, consisting of brief prayer, singing of beautiful and appropriate hymns, reading of selections from the Scriptures, and an address as follows :—

"Friends and fellow mourners,—It has fallen to me to-day to speak the last words over the body of our friend deceased, to bid, in your name and mine, farewell to the form which presently will be restored to the elements of which it is compounded, and the place thereof know him no more for ever. It is my duty, because he asked it of me; it is my privilege, because he was a true man and noble; and it is an honour to be allowed to speak for such; and yet I could have wished it otherwise, that I might take my place among those who in silence mourn him, and pay to his dear memory the tribute of tears and not of words.

" For I have known him long, when he was another man to what you have seen him, and pleading for another faith, and in him I lose more than you do; I lose more than a brother, one who formed the single link between my own present life and my past, and in whom I found the sole partner of cherished memories, now my own alone. For his, too, was, as you all know, a broken life, a life whose years were divided against themselves. For twenty of them he was a Roman Catholic Priest, devoted, zealous, entire in the absoluteness of his submission to that Church and her teaching, full of zeal to win those outside to acknowledge her claims, and those within to conform mind and soul to them. During another and the last twenty, he was an Unitarian Minister, asserting for himself independence of judgment, and exercising his reason in despite of all authority, while the liberty he claimed for himself and used, he sedulously vindicated for others, preaching to all men, 'Think for yourselves! Seek the truth and fear not! Let neither church, nor sect, nor priest, nor minister compel your faith, believe that only of which you are inwardly convinced.' Yes, it was contradictory. Rome cannot and will not reconcile itself with reason, and who advocates one disparages the claims of the other. And yet he was not two men, but one; the Dominican Friar and ascetic was the married minister of free religious thought, and we shall miss the true lesson of a noble life if we leave one or another out of account and think of him only as what he was long ago, or as what he was known by you, his later friends. Yes, it was the same man, he with whom I first became acquainted some thirty years ago as a renowned preacher of saintly life, and he who has been my dearest friend and comrade these many years in the ministry of that Church which all the Churches condemn. And these, if I read him aright, were the distinguishing traits of his character, whether he appeared under the Friar's white robe or in the plain black coat which scarcely distinguished him from men of secular calling :—*Truthfulness* and *Earnestness ;* truthfulness, to profess openly what appeared to him true ; earnestness, to bear witness to the same among men, indifferent whether it was to his own profit or his hurt, whether they would think worse of him for it or the better.

" He was brought up in a curious indifference to the divergent forms of religious belief ; not as if all were equally false and useless, as some lightly say, but rather as if all were good and each had its proper merits. He was Catholic and Protestant at the same time, attending daily prayer or Mass as occasion served, and apparently equally at home at either. But for such a nature it was impossible that this comfortable indecision should long continue. While yet a young man at Cambridge, the question presented itself, 'Do I believe or do I not? To what Church do I belong?' And deciding for the faith of his fathers, he straightway resolved to devote himself to the priesthood. It was a resolve he never went back upon. He ceased indeed to be a Roman Catholic priest; he never ceased from the service of religion as it appeared to him—the service of truth and God. While he admitted and realised the supreme claims of his Church, he consecrated to her use all his faculties and substance. If it was indeed, as he believed and as she taught, the one Church of the living God, the one ark of salvation for dying men, no devotion could be excessive, no zeal on her behalf misplaced. Early in his career he abandoned all he was possessed of, giving it up to the purposes of missionary effort in his diocese, and with unwearied pains gave himself to the work. He had already won distinction far and wide as an effective preacher and as a skilful director of souls, when what seemed a higher and more perfect way opened itself before him. It was self-denial more complete, sacrifice more entire and irrevocable than he had hitherto practised; he joined himself to the Dominicans, who combined the austerities of the monastic life with the active labours of the missionary priesthood. He bowed himself down and entered the noviciate to learn as a novice among boy novices the ways of obedience and humility. He came back to the world in a new garb, but with the same or greater fervour, only to win more upon the hearts of Catholics high and low, who looked up to him as one who combined in his person practical wisdom and heavenly sanctity, whose word won the multitude, and whose counsel was sought by all.

But doubts darkened his path. Was the Pope indeed infallible? The question must needs be faced, for it was being everywhere discussed among Catholics, nor as yet decided. And if the Pope was not, was the Church?—the Bible? These questions followed one upon another, and in vain he sought to silence them by prayer, by fasting, by work, by retirement. The answer came clearer and more decisive as the studies which he began in order to satisfy himself and confirm his faith progressed. No! there was no infallibility; neither in pontiff, nor council, nor in book. And all that he had accepted hitherto with such implicit faith, because the Church taught it, all vanished from before his eyes as the fabric of a vision, beautiful, solemn, unreal. It was a very earthquake, and his life seemed ruined by it. To men on whom religious beliefs sit lightly, it will seem a small matter to change one form for another, but to one to whom his faith had been his life, the experience was awful. His dismay was complete as had been his devotion, and what must he do? One course was easy and tempting—to stay in outward communion with the old Church, interpreting its doctrines and its rites to suit his new beliefs, in daily Mass offering to the Creator of all, sacrifice under the symbols of bread and wine, ackrowledging that all being and life were His; absolving penitent sinners by way of assuring them of God's pity and pardon; and so by a little ingenuity finding true spiritual significance in every old ceremony and superstition. Could he bring himself to this, he might keep yet all that was dear to him, friends and their love and esteem, position and reputation, and—what to a good man is worth all—opportunities of doing good. It was but a little while he dallied with the temptation; it could not be. Impossible to live a lie and think by a lie to serve God. He came out leaving all he valued on earth, came a stranger, almost a pauper among strangers, who yet would have gladly welcomed the priest could he have brought himself to conform to their views. The Church Established had promise of place, influence, honour; but he passed by her invitation, and went to ally himself with the smallest of all the Protestant denominations. It was but a half welcome he could expect, for he knew that many of them had no sympathy with, what seemed to them, his extreme views, and others no trust of a priest, even if he came as a convert. There was within the narrow bounds of the free Churches no scope for distinction, no room for attaining popularity, no positions of power or emolument to hope for; but he found what was more precious than these, that which he seemed to miss in all the other Churches, liberty and religion, full recognition of the right of free thought and reverent acknowledgment of the natural instinct of worship.

So with them he cast in his lot ; and among them he died, to the last thanking God that he had found a home where he might continue his old ministry of religion, under conditions which bound him no wise, but to be true to himself and to those who had chosen him pastor.

" He had his troubles there too, for it is impossible to be truthful and please all the world, to be earnest and not displease those whose own honest convictions are different. Had he been given to self-seeking, or envy, or discontent, he might have been a disappointed man, might have complained of want of appreciation among new friends such as he had been wont to receive of old ; but, intimate as I was with him, I never heard him utter a word of regret or disappointment. Freedom has its drawbacks, and one is, that in the use of it men will disagree one with another, and hinder one the other and the common cause of all ; but you must take the advantages and the difficulties together; and he bore what might have seemed to others humiliations and contradictions, with the most kindly and philosophic spirit. He made his choice and never repented ; consecrated himself anew to the service of God and humanity and freedom, and gave himself to serving on committees with the same zeal he had before shown for guilds, confraternities, and sodalities.

" There were those who accused and suspected him of insincerity—Catholics who thought it impossible that he could in his heart have abandoned a faith once so precious to him—Protestants who doubted whether he was whole-hearted in his opposition to a Church of which he would never allow himself to speak with bitterness or contempt. There were worldly men who called him a fool to give up such good prospects of distinction and advancement;—"He might have been a bishop," they said, and so saying, gave effective answer to his accusers. For what was there but inmost conviction and sincerest loyalty to it, which could have led him to choose the Unitarian ministry for his calling. As a paper of last week, which advocates a form of Unitarian Christianity more conservative than his, rightly says, speaking of Notable Converts :—

'No position, office, or emolument could have biassed them, for such did not exist along the line of an unorthodox faith. It was more likely that harsh treatment and ostracism and loss faced them in their conclusions. And even now, in this more liberal age, we have nothing to offer but a free field for investigation, instruction, and spiritual worship to those who are willing to join our ranks. The only and best recompense any one can have is the consciousness of having sought for the truth of God, which is the pearl of great price. For, after all, a man's life and happiness consist, not in what he has of wealth and honour, but in what he is.'

" No! Truth and Truth only was his mistress. He sought her, he served her with equal devotion as priest and minister; for her sake he gave up what all men value, and what good men count most valuable, and repented not, nor even murmured. And in his new found faith he lived, and in it he died, fully persuaded, and peaceful and satisfied to the last. There were dear kind souls who prayed for him and wrote to him, beseeching of heaven, pleading with him, that he might give up his own convictions and adopt theirs. He heard all they had to say, and appreciated the loving anxiety which old friends showed for his salvation; he was never moved to anger, except when some word hinted a doubt of his sincerity,—but was disturbed in his faith not an instant. He was for months face to face with a painful death, and never quailed. 'Don't think I am unhappy,' he said to those who watched in pain his agony. And he was not unhappy, for faith in God sustained him. "Yours for ever," I wrote to him. His answer was, "Yours for ever *in God*." Yes, in God, he is ours still, for He is God of the living, and "all live unto him." In God are we and they, in God nothing is lost; what has been is and shall be for ever.

"One last look back upon the life ended on earth marred in its strength, and happiness, and repute by its double-alliance, as of a soldier who has fought well and bravely, only now on *this* and afterwards on *that* side of the war of Churches. Alas for the phrase, yet it is but fact, and we differ one from another, and are equally confident of being in the right on whatever side we are. Nay more, we differ from our own selves, and now are as assured that this is true as before we were that it was false.

"And what shall we say then? What did he say? Truth is not to be found, and it is folly to seek it,

Q

and delusion to think you know it ? Not so he; who always condemned the easy attitude of indifference as clearing a free course for error, and superstition, and fanaticism. But, on the contrary, though the mind of man cannot hold truth in its entirety, be true to yourself, and you will be nearer the truth. Be earnest, and you will find what will be sufficient for your need; and recognising your own insufficiency, be tolerant of those who differ the most widely from you—reverently, not scornfully tolerant. Dear friends, his and mine, who condemned him so hotly, who mourned for his fall so bitterly, who prayed for him so earnestly, who now despair of God's mercy to him, because he died believing otherwise than once he did, and now *you* do—may the good God repay into your own bosoms of your zeal and love, and lead us all at last through devious ways to know the true Church, which he never left, which he always served, the Church which is not yours nor ours, but God's,—the company of all who love truth and righteousness, and do God service such as He only asks and accepts of us, in serving as best they know how their brother man.

"And now, a last time, farewell, friend and brother. It is over, the sure faith, the painful doubt, the new hope, dim, but not less firm than that which went before. It is over—the uncertain twilight in which we still live and are so bold. It is past—the pitiful conflict, the sundering of dearest ties, the wild judgments of men who knew not—past the months of pain and shadow of death.

"*We* still argue, and assert, and doubt. *We* must still look forward to death which is over for thee. *We* still only, 'as in a mirror darkly,' can see whether the present or the future.

"God *knows !* and now passed into His Light, it is well with *thee.* 'Let him do as seemeth him good.' Fare thee well, for ever, 'in God.'"

"At the close of the service the coffin was replaced in the hearse, and, followed by the mourners above-named, in carriages, was taken to the S.W.R. Station, and thence conveyed by train to Woking, where, previously to the cremation, the Rev. D. Amos conducted a brief service in the pretty chapel set apart for the purpose."

The urn containing his ashes was brought back to Reading the same day, and deposited in ground of the little chapel which had been his latest charge.

"Feeling and kindly references were made to the late Rev. R. R. Suffield at St. Lawrence's Church, by the Rev. J. M. Guilding (Vicar), and at several other places of worship of various denominations in the town; as also at the Liberal meeting in the New Town Hall, on Monday evening.

"At the University Extension Lecture, held on Monday last, the president, Mr. Walter Palmer, before calling upon the lecturer, alluded to the loss the University Extension Movement had sustained in Reading by the death of the Rev. R. R. Suffield. He was one of the vice-presidents of the Reading University Extension Association, and his last public act was on the occasion of the Annual Meeting in the

Abbey Hall, in May last, when he took part in the formation of the Extension Movement in Reading, on a more permanent basis."

So far the *Reading Observer*.

A Roman Catholic gentleman, who had been his pupil as a boy and remained all his life warmly attached to him, wrote in the pages of *Truth*:—"It is with deep regret I record the death of the Rev. Rodolph Suffield, who, previous to his secession from the Catholic faith, was celebrated throughout the length and breadth of the land as the most brilliant preacher, and most influential ecclesiastic of his time. His 'perversion' or 'conversion' in the year 1870, caused a sensation in religious circles only second to that which attended the late Cardinal Newman, when he some years before transferred his allegiance to the Church of Rome. Well do I remember serving Father Suffield's last Mass in the chapel of Bosworth Hall, and accompanying him on that memorable August journey, when, turning his back on the little Hermitage at Husband Bosworth, and laying aside the robes of his Order, he re-entered the ever-restless world of theological doubt and dispute. As I write there lies before me a massive bundle of letters in which he recounts his subsequent struggles and temptations, and I cannot but indite a few sympathetic lines to the memory of a distinguished, affectionate, and much-loved friend and a most experienced master, to whom I owe the deepest debt of gratitude."

The following notice from *The Catholic Times* of

November 27th, is here added, for two reasons. First, as evidence of the friendly spirit in which numerous Roman Catholics continued to regard him, notwithstanding their reprobation of his 'apostacy.' Secondly, and principally, to repel the insinuation contained in it that he was contemplating or inclining towards a return to their Church. He was particularly sensitive on this point during his life-time, and on one occasion, when rumours were in circulation to the effect that his conversion might be shortly expected, he wrote to the British and Foreign Unitarian Association a formal protest against what he regarded as a calumny, and took pains to have it publicly contradicted in the papers, omitting the words, "and other former colleagues," for he was seen only by the two mentioned; the paragraph is verbally accurate, but the well-meant wish of the writer has led him to make too much of Mr. Suffield's gratitude for the kindly sentiments of his visitors, and to exaggerate his regard for the honesty and goodness of those with whom he had been so long associated. That regard was indeed genuine, but the more intimate became his acquaintance with the larger life of the liberal Protestant Churches, the less was he disposed to exalt the Roman system in any of its forms. Indeed he more than once called down upon himself the severe animadversions of the Roman Catholic press by his strictures on Roman ways and morals.

"Mr. Robert Rodolph Suffield died on the 13th inst., at Malvern Villa, Reading. During his last illness he was visited by Father Kenelm Vaughan, Father Ambrose Smith, O.P., and other former colleagues, and he expressed great gratification at their kindness in desiring to reconcile him to the Church. Unfortunately the end came before this was accomplished, but it is gratifying to know that he who was the chief human instrument in bringing about the secession of several priests, notably that of Mr. Addis, Mr. Whitehead, and Mr. Matthews, should have been consoled in his dying hours by several priests who had *not* lost their faith. In spite of his own unbelief, Mr. Suffield always kept the Dominican picture of Our Lady of the Rosary in his room, and in his public utterances he usually spoke with deference of the Catholic Church, and frequently alluded to the pure and stainless lives of the men with whom he became associated at Ushaw, when he first thought of joining the ranks of the priesthood, and to the happiness of his sacerdotal career previously to his apostacy in 1870. He had some great qualities, but he had also great weaknesses, and it would have been better for the tone and spirit of Ushaw if he had been kept in a humble position during his collegiate career.—R.I.P."

His 'great weakness,' from this point of view, was undoubtedly his marked individuality. He could not, spite of best intentions, bring himself to conformity with the accepted type of Catholic sanctity. His faith, his piety, his devotions, were too much his own, and if this gave him influence and distinction, at the same time it constituted a difficulty and a danger.

Requiescat in Pace.—It was the last kindly word of his earlier friends, whose faith he had championed and abandoned, and whose dearest convictions he had learned to regard as, at the best, beautiful delusions. Another, who came to know him in his last years, and owed to his counsel and teaching a higher faith in Him, "who is able to do exceeding abundantly above all we ask or think" in our kindest moods—in whose Divine Day the 'little systems' which divide us so painfully here are merged and lost,—wrote, expressing what many thought, this Sonnet to his memory.

SONNET TO THE REV. R. RODOLPH SUFFIELD.

DIED NOVEMBER 13TH, 1891.

" God's finger touched him and he slept."—*Tennyson.*

He's gone from us; the gentlest, sweetest soul,
That dwelt in human clay. We knew his worth,
His mind of noblest touch. He trod the earth
Among us. Now he's gained a higher goal,
And breathes an ampler air, beyond earth's strife.
Gracious and gentle, he, tender, refined,
Rare scholarship was his, a cultured mind,
A sympathetic soul, a blameless life.
We mourn for him. Earth's noblest ones are rare
Amid the noises of this dreary earth.
Thou, true of heart, for Truth's sake all didst dare.
He suffered for his conscience; yet no dearth
Of pity had his tender soul; his care
Was helping others. Well *we* knew his worth.

READING.   K. D.

Happy the man, whatever his lot, who could win such loving disinterested tribute from his fellows left behind!

FINIS.

APPENDIX.

FENIANISM,

AND THE ENGLISH PEOPLE.

GENTLEMEN,

I would claim your indulgence, as the subject on which I have to speak is surrounded with many difficulties, difficulties caused at once by prejudice and virtue; by patriotism and by animosity; by fear and by suspicion. The statements I would make this evening are not volunteered by me, but rather forced from me reluctantly by circumstances, and by the urgent request of others. Several Irish working men of intelligence and respectability have, during the last fortnight, requested me to call a public meeting in which they might express their indignant repudiation of the fearful and damnable outrage at Clerkenwell, and of other similar outrages supposed to be in contemplation. They felt at once indignant, wronged, and humbled, under so horrible an imputation; they felt that the English would begin to look upon them, not as the kindly inheritors of the virtues and the sufferings of an ancient people; not as a nation admired even by its enemies for generosity, courage, tenderness, poetry, purity, and chivalry; but as abettors of acts of insane brutality, rendered even more detestable by the coward secrecy of the perpetrator. Their whole nature blushed with indignant shame, that they should be supposed to sympathise with secret assassination, with outrages directed against the feeble, with destruction of private property, with desire to injure edifices of public charity and public utility— in a word, to become the enemies of society, the destroyers of their country, the betrayers of that honour and faith that remained to it, when all else had perished! Gentlemen, I profoundly appreciated the spirit which could make them thus desire to clear themselves from such unjust and cruel aspersions; I

An Address, delivered at a Public Meeting of English and Irish, Protestants and Catholics, in the North of England, [West Hartlepool, Jan.,] 1868.

appreciated the kindly good will testified by the chief employers
of labour in this town, who, disbelieving such accusations, still
desired to have them publicly denied. But I could not bring
myself to permit them to take upon themselves the humiliation
of even an indignant denial. They may have their faults and
their weaknesses, perhaps love may have made me blind to
them, but they are not a nation of cowards and assassins, that
a handful of them need assemble and throw a dishonour upon
their nation by a denial which would impute a certain amount
of guilt. Anyhow, it would have been but the expression of the
voice of a few men, unknown except by the families they support, the employers they faithfully serve, and the neighbours
of all creeds with whom they live at peace. But if there is to
be a denial, let it come from one who pledges his public name
and public position—from one long and intimately interwoven
with so many hundreds of the Irish people in England, in
Ireland, in America, in Scotland, who for eighteen years of
priestly life has shared with them hopes and fears, joys and
sorrows, who has known all their feelings, and heard the most
unguarded expressions, and received the most fearless information, both by word of mouth and by letter, from all parts. Let
one be heard as the representative of so large a multitude whom
he intimately knows, and let me give to those calumnies the
most indignant denial. Never have I known an Irish Catholic
but what would execrate such acts as in attempt have been
imputed to them during the last few weeks. But, gentlemen,
you will say "that such may be true of the great mass of the
Irish people, but there is a foul dastardly society called the
Fenians, and it forms throughout the country a secret league
for the committal of organised acts of brutal destruction and
dastardly assassination. From its secret council issue decrees
of hidden wrongs to be inflicted, and reckless destruction to be
produced." That society, you will say, is in itself numerous
enough to need the suspension of all our liberties, and the
surrounding with armed bands almost every public and private
building of costliness and special importance.

You will say that it is clear that the enormous preponder-
ance of the Irish people approve such foul designs; for, until
the law interfered, they accompanied, in imposing numbers,
those symbolic funerals which you say were to mark their
approval of murder. You say that the Catholic Church herself
is compromised in such actions, because she absolved, at Manchester, three men whom the law condemned, and followed
into eternity with her benediction murderers condemned by
justice to the gallows. Ah! gentlemen, by *justice*. It is a great
word; it has been abused as often as the name of *liberty*. Now,
at first aspect, there is great force in such an argument, especially when it addresses itself either to passion or to fear. For
a moment, I will not say whether I think the Irish people
mistaken or not as to the facts; but they do not believe that
such an organisation, with such foul designs, does exist at all.
They believe that there is a secret society condemned by the
Catholic Church just as the Freemason society; that a person
could not save his soul unless he withdrew from it—inasmuch
as the sacraments are forbidden to its members. They believe
that this is the application of the old law of the Church, which
invariably condemns rash oaths, and forbids its children from
entering any society in which they are bound to follow---as it
were in the dark—into doubtful actions, unknown or irrespon-
sible leaders. They believe that the Fenian Society would
organise risings, invasion, war, the seizure of Government
stores, but they do not believe that it would plan or encourage
assassination or wanton destruction of private property. As
the O'Donoghue said last week, "It is not proved whether the
three men executed at Manchester were Fenians at all. If
they were, they will have withdrawn from the secret society
before receiving the Sacraments." The Irish followed in the
papers the details of these trials, and they do not believe that
the men liberated were either justly or even legally in custody;
they do not believe that those who, in a rapidly-formed com-
bination, resolved to free them, intended to shoot any one.
They believe that poor Brett was shot accidently by a man

firing through the lock to open it, and that he had no more intention of shooting Brett than the two men along with him whom they came to save. They believe that the evidence given was bought and perjured ; that the man who so unfortunately shot Brett is now in America. They no more believe the witnesses who declared that Allen shot Brett, than the larger number of witnesses who swore to the complicity of Maguire, who was not there at all. They therefore regard the three men who were hung as only guilty of the forcible liberation of two men who were not in legal custody, and they lament the untimely death of Brett. They consider the trials to have been a parody of justice. The funeral processions were meant as symbols of love for any who had suffered, even by an error, for them ; and perhaps the funeral march seemed to them to befit a people who had watched around the tomb of their country for eight hundred years, and wearied in hope because to them there was never a resurrection. The dreadful affair at Clerkenwell they regard as an execrable crime, created by an ignorant and base informer, that he might obtain money for exposing an outrage he invented and prompted. Say, if you like, that the Irish are very foolish, and ill-informed, and perverse, to imagine such absurdities as I have just stated. I simply declare that I know it to be in that light that they regard these events ; and, therefore, if they are perverse in their judgment, they are, at least, not brutal or base in their intentions. If you had arrived at the same opinion as to the events, your feelings would accord with theirs. Suppose their judgment be warped by national prejudice,—perhaps others' judgment is also warped by another national prejudice. And now let me mention stern facts, not regarding the views and opinions of the Irish, but regarding events. On this also I have a right to speak ; for I not only know the Irish heart as only a priest and a friend can know it, but I have had a singular access to the knowledge of *facts* about Fenianism from its earliest introduction into these countries. It is said, and very likely with truth, that two or three persons in founding the Fenian society made themselves acquainted with the working of the Carbonari and Freemason societies abroad, and tried to carry out the infamous principles of the former. A secret society is always essentially liable to be dragged into any evil. But as far as I am aware, after considerable and lengthened knowledge of the Fenian society and workings, I should say that Carbonarism has not impregnated it, and that at present the Fenian organisation has been simply political, but accompanied with circumstances bringing it under the censure of the Church. In these countries, their number is really very small. The enormous majority of the Irish people, whilst sympathising in the object, do not approve the means. Even Mitchell himself, though sanguine of the future, " does not approve the calling on the Irish people to contribute at present to secret funds, not feeling assured that at present it would be properly and effectively used, and not thinking it right at present to incur the responsibility of calling on the Irish race at home and abroad to pour into their hands the savings of years." The English Government has reason to fear a nation discontented, and backed by millions in America ; but I do not believe there is any Fenian council plotting outrages against life and property. The Fenians (proper), in this country, are a secret society. I do not know what is the teaching of the American Bishops as to the American organisation. I do not know whether or not they have dropped what would bring it under the censures of the Church. In these countries, certainly, no person who has taken the secret oath can approach the sacraments without renouncing its obligations. Some people fancy themselves to be Fenians and are not. A stranger suspecting the sympathies of another proposes to him the Fenian oath, which is given, and something a week paid, and there is the beginning and end of the affair. It was a mortal sin to take a rash oath. But the man who has taken it will never hurt any one except himself.

Then again, vast numbers are called Fenians merely because they desire Irish Independence. Whenever I use that expression, I mean to be understood to characterise what is within the law—a National Government—like Hungary, or even like our own colonies—all are governed according to their own ideas and not ours. The national sympathy is intense, and under certain circumstances would be at once united and powerful, but Fenianism hangs together very loosely, not to be compared to the Freemason society, except that nationalism is the root of the former, revolution and infidelity of the latter. To return. —What other outrages have been traced to Fenianism, or to any person representing in any degree Irish sympathies? Literally none. There have been rumours circulated from almost every town in England. We have been at the command of every joker, or of every one influenced by malignant intentions against the Irish, or in any way interested in inventing an accusation and creating a panic. Such an attempt was made last week in this town. Fortunately, one of the Liberal papers treated it as a hoax; but newspapers published at a distance described it with an imposing heading as an "Attempted Fenian outrage at West Hartlepool." An English Protestant gentleman who would have spoken this evening, unless business had taken him away, could have told us how, a few months ago, a comical collection of incidents were worked up into Seaton being in the possession of the Fenians, and how there were all the accompaniments giving a colour to the absurdity, everything except the substratum of truth. Every anonymous scribbler who wished to bring odium on the Irish, has had merely to drop in the street or into a letter-box, some outrageous letter threatening vengeance and violence; and the military are called out, and the police armed, and the special constables are sworn in. Some people ask: "Why do not the Irish offer themselves more numerously as special constables?" Because they would think it as rational to be sworn in against the fairies. Whenever outrage is really threatened, depend upon it, they will as ever be loyal to their employer, and brotherly to their English fellow workmen. But what cause has been gained by all these rumours of imaginary outrages? Under a timid and suspicious Government we have been pushed back a

thousand degrees towards despotism. In Ireland liberty has
entirely ceased; and in England the liberal measures are
almost check-mated by panic. The Irish are a clever and
intelligent people. You cannot travel through Ireland and
visit the humblest cabins without discovering a discernment
far superior to anything existing amongst a similar class in
our own country. Do they not easily see that every outrage
committed in their name, or threatened in their name is not
only a crime but a treason against their country? It is not
only wicked but insane. There is not a single act proved which
justifies us in ever suspecting that they would thus act with
the wanton recklessness of escaped lunatics. When Stephens
was liberated; when the Manchester prisoners were liberated,
there was cleverness, secrecy, fidelity, reticence, and success.
There was an object, though criminally rash. There was the
exercise of a clemency which has been betrayed. We gain
nothing by ignoring these facts. The calm declaration of what
is wrong will influence an intelligent, and Catholic, and high-
minded people. But if we treat them as at once ruffians and
insane, we are powerless to serve them; we cannot persuade
them, we can only manacle them; and for every one we
manacle on a false pretence, we create ten thousand sympathis-
ers, who will begin to think such fetters more honourable than
a liberty that degrades itself to calumny. No, gentlemen, the
real danger is not Fenianism. The danger is a nation at once
oppressed and insulted—a nation at the mercy of the most
degraded informers—until at length, their character ruined, they
are driven to desperation by the insidious calumnies of enemies
whom they can never meet. My own suspicion is that the
Clerkenwell outrage is the work of some informer who has
bribed or prompted some stupid wretch to do the deed, that he
might get a greater bribe by his information. The *Star*, to its
honour, has had the courage to point this out. An informer
told the plan, the hour, the mode; why did he not name more?
His information is believed, the prisoners are removed; if they
had remained in the usual yard of exercise they would doubt-

less have been slain. So that a Frenchman who knew something of our politics, naively remarked to me, that it was clearly an Orange scheme for putting to death the Fenian prisoners! At the hour signified, a barrel of gunpowder is wheeled up against the walls, which they were told were to be blown up with gunpowder, police are looking on, detectives are looking on, by order of the authorities persons are actually stationed within the prison walls with firearms, on account of what is going to take place. Of course we are bound to suppose no complicity on the part of either the government or the police: but if an equal apparent amount of complicity could have been adduced against some Irish secret Fenian tribunal, we might have been justified perhaps in speaking of the horrible *Fenian* outrage at Clerkenwell. As it is, we perceive the authorities all prepared, but the Fenians, literally unprepared, no arrangement made for receiving the prisoners if they had escaped death amidst the explosion. Though the witnesses seem to have wonderful powers of observation, and to have seen everything, and be able to swear to everything; yet there is nothing which compromises any discoverable organisation. One way to produce crime is continually to suggest it, unceasingly to impute it, and to make those accused unjustly, suffer as if they had perpetrated it. If an event could have occurred calculated to injure the Irish cause, it was this Clerkenwell affair—it was instantly telegraphed over Europe. It was instantly laid at the door of the Irish and of Fenians. Since the Manchester executions a current of European and American sympathy was surging up on every side. On all sides the impression was arising that the Government had made a mistake. But now fix the calumny on any party, however remotely interwoven with Irish Nationality, and everything was changed. And then every idle rumour was again fixed on the same, and telegraphed over Europe. The disastrous explosion at Newcastle was described by telegrams to America as a horrible Irish Fenian outrage. Truly, two or three base characters can effect an infinity of mischief. We have had experience

of this ourselves as English Catholics. Let any one read in
Macaulay the narrative of Titus Oates, a degraded loathsome
wretch, telling lies at once for lucre and for pleasure ; and yet
the English people, generous, intelligent, and kind, were dragged
on, infatuated, and the noblest and purest characters perished
as criminals on the scaffold, almost without a pitying tear.
When we find an informer declared on oath as unworthy of all
credit, and yet instantly ready to swear to the man prosecuted
as a Fenian ; when we find the terrific ease with which the
witness keeps "remembering" and multiplying—we see the
force of the example recently adduced of the witnesses multiplying, the instant that one link of the chain of evidence was
needed in the trial of Madeline Smith, till the very multitude
and assurance of the witnesses invalidated their testimony.
They had seen too much, and thus had remembered too well.
We call to mind how, many years since in Dublin, a wretched
informer named Delahunt, murdered a boy, that he might lay
the charge on an innocent man, and receive the bribe for the
information. By the mercy of God the wretch was discovered,
and he was hung in the place of his innocent victim. These
bribes for information are terrible engines of fraud and oppression. In 1820, the *Times*, then at the head of the Liberal
Press (how changed now, when it desires to make of Ireland a
Jamaica) attributed the Thistlewood conspiracy to a gentleman
informer named Edwards, and as got up by him to retard
Reform, and such has been since the Whig tradition. I have
myself had a sad example of this system of spies forming con-
spiracies, suggesting and instigating crime, and then, like the
hyena, pouncing upon the prey. Not for one single moment
can any sane man attribute the knowledge or encouragement
of such villainy to any official of the Government—to insinuate this would be a calumny as detestable as the calumny
we repudiate. Again, no man who knows the Irish con-
stabulary and those functionaries who preside over it, those
men of high integrity, unblemished reputation, and self-
sacrificing charity, can ever for a moment insinuate against

them the knowledge of such turpitude. But what can they do? If an information is given, and insisted on, they can only hand it on. Perhaps they might almost say it is more the nation that must investigate it than the courts. For we presume that when the nation is calm, the courts are just. When the nation is panic struck, the hall of justice descends to the popular passions. The nation should be guarded against the true danger—and some at least must have the courage to speak, though the malignant may impute sympathy with the bad. On a certain occasion, a man who had been proved always to have spoken the truth on these matters, who was a Fenian, and had refused renouncing the society according to my advice, came to me afterwards, and said he should withdraw, and then stated that a person had invited him to join in a kind of assassination club, whose members should draw lots to assassinate the Lord-Lieutenant and the judges on the day of passing sentence in Dublin on the State prisoners. Horrified at such a terrific proposal, this man declined, and implored me instantly to communicate the design to the authorities, so that no great crime could be possible. Of course I did so; just giving the information which he enabled me. Afterwards he sought me again, and told me that he was convinced by circumstances which had come to his knowledge, that the man who suggested the horrid crime was himself an informer. He authorised me to mention this, but feared to give any details lest he himself and some others should be compromised. I laid it before the proper authority under the Government, but though every kind and honourable consideration was given, and the statement was believed, it was not sufficiently tangible to act upon.

For the sake of mercy, of justice, of peace, do not let us blind ourselves to this source of danger and of crime. The more we offer rewards, the more we encourage rumours, the more we excite national animosities on either side, and play up to the vulgar cowardice of a panic, the more are we placing our lives and our properties in the power—not of Fenians who

want war and separation—but of wretches who want to excite
to dastard crimes, to arson and to murder, that amidst the
desolation they may inform, may plunder and may destroy.
The Irish clear themselves and apologise? In the name of the
Great God of Justice what have they done? The apology
should come from those who without evidence, beyond the
purchased evidence of spies, have cast on them the foulest
imputations. It is the English who having, through fear,
encouraged a panic created on purpose, should arise, and with
generous indignation defend the honour of an outraged nation.
Have we come to such a pass as this; that whereas the English law heretofore accounted every man innocent till proved
before his countrymen to be guilty; that now every Irishman
is to be accounted guilty till proved by overwhelming testimony to be innocent? If generosity does not prompt us to
this, let prudence at least compel us. The measures we invoke
on the Irish will speedily fall upon ourselves, and destroy our
liberty and independence. We are rushing from imaginary
conflagrations and imaginary assassinations into the real appliances of what we shall end by finding to be a galling despotism.
We are getting an armed police, a fettered press, a system of
universal suspicion, spies and informers of the basest character, prompting the government first to folly and then to
injustice. Surely even revolution itself is better than despotism; amidst the crimes and horrors of a revolution, grand
characters arise and overtop the rest by the force of genius or
of virtue, like the mountain summit soaring above the clouds
and the storm. In the raging of a revolution, the Church may
press to her wounded breast, her children returned to her as
martyrs: but at least she is not tempted to become the spiritual
police salaried by a power that at once patronises, despises, and
crushes her. Beneath despotism nothing flourishes except the
theatre, the army, the police, and the favourites of the Court.
Do not let us permit the Government to expiate the party
crime of giving us a Reform, by frightening us back into the
era of the Tudors and the Stuarts. Besides, will the experi-

ment succeed; suppose we establish amongst us permanently the state of things existing now—destroy the liberty of the press—imprison every one an enemy may choose to suspect—telegraph over Europe and America that the Irish are assassins and insane—pursue by social persecution the very Irish servant girl, and drive her as wicked from the home in which we have ridiculed her—go on packing juries—purchasing witnesses—trying in chains men supposed by the law to be innocent—making Irish homes the residence of detectives, who, (it has been more than said) have informed against the families, the virtue of whose daughters they failed to seduce. If we pay people to write letters to Catholic Bishops and Priests, threatening them with vengeance; so that amidst the general panic, even they begin half to suspect a people who for 1300 years have surrounded them like a wall of fire—If by the appliances of so many artifices we succeed in poisoning the educated mind of the country, till it comes to be a question whether a prison cell is not too good a place for an untried Irishman; where is it all to end? Will such means as these conciliate? You may flatter and coax the priesthood, when, because in obedience to the laws of the Church, they condemn what the Church condemns, and you may seem partly to succeed in making it look as if because some are deceived by repeated assertions, that therefore most would palliate the injustice and calumnies directed against their people. But where, I say, is it all to end? What is to be done with a nation united in a sullen hopelessness of your rule? Can you imprison a nation? Send them afar into penal servitude? They will remember; and they will return: but how? You have seen and know. Let us at length try and enter into the feelings of others. Let us remember that the love of country has been planted in the breast by God, just as much as the love of the family. Domestic fidelity and patriotism go side by side, and kneel before God's altar for His blessing. Do not,—because it is not our case, let us adopt the aggravating tone of an affected spirituality, and pretend that it would be more holy for them to be indifferent to their country :

we do not say to a son, Never mind the cottage of your childhood and your family; there is a stranger who will come and
keep it neater than you, and has got the latest plan, and will
manage your home better for you, for you have odd, random,
dreamy ways; but the stranger can do things properly. Besides, there are too many of you; and the stranger will, all for
your good, tear away half your family, and people with cattle
the plot you so foolishly love. For the stranger can fleece your
cattle; but you, your sentimental feelings, are not worth considering; you shall have more to eat, but you who are at once
poor and perverse, what have you to do with sentiments?
Leave the sentiments of patriotism and of honour to us who
will manage your affairs for you, and you shall be allowed to
live as a helot more comfortably on a land which, if you were a
better Christian, and had more sense, you would not retain as
your own.

It is asked, Are the Irish loyal? Gentlemen, at least they
have not insulted her, as the Orange Lodges agreed to insult
the Prince of Wales, when he went to Canada, as the representative of his Royal Mother. I think they are even more loyal
than the English would be, were the Queen to become a
Catholic, to marry the O'Conor Don, to live in Ireland, and
recreate in Killarney and Connemara, to hold her Parliament
in Dublin, to establish the Catholic Church in England and in
Scotland, to deprive the Protestant Bishops of their seats in
the Peers, of their palaces and cathedrals, and to make their
titles penal; to abolish the English customs, to govern England after Irish ideas, and to make a flying visit to England
about once in a dozen years. Remember James II. and
William III. But visits and graceful courtesies will not suffice
now. The wound has widened—like the gulf at once dividing
and uniting Ireland and the West. You cannot heal the gaping
wound by playing with it, or denying its existence. Unless
something be done, the result can only be the existence of a
nation maddened with the first possession of independence; or
a massacre such as the world has never seen. That something

to be done, may the great mercy of God create the genius to inspire, the courage to accomplish. May the statesman speedily arise who shall dare to say of Irish independence, what the Iron Duke said of Catholic Emancipation. Let some statesman full of loyalty to the Crown, and loyalty to the people, demand Ireland for the Irish; and frankly act upon the admission that they would be rather badly governed by themselves than well by us. Let such a statesman, in a spirit of courageous generosity, grant everything which it is not high treason to ask. If we are to lose Ireland let us rather lose it by generosity than by oppression. But if such a grand legislation should succeed,—and many reasons concur to make it probable —then Ireland, prosperous, loyal, and united, might become the truest guardian of the British monarchy against the up-heaving of the English democracy. The feeling that pervades now every grade of Irish society, is one of intense yearning after national government. But it is not a feeling of personal hatred to the English, or of rancour towards the English Queen: though doubtless they would love her better if she seemed to love them more. They would honour her more if she seemed to honour Ireland more. I will not venture to say what their political sentiments may be; but I am sure of this, that the first Lady of the Land, personally, need not guard herself against the Irish. They will do *her* no wrong, nor her children; she may walk through the length and breadth of Ireland alone, and no hand will be lifted against her, no voice will be raised to insult her. They are a people full of tenderness and of ancient chivalry—and the woman, the widow, the mother, will not be insulted because she is the daughter of Kings. They compassionate her in her sorrows. They are moved by simple details of her domestic joys. They remember sorrowfully her royal grandfather, who, though opposed to us Catholics, was kind, and honest, and pious, according to his ideas; and they remember the sorrows of that royal race—of that old man who, when deprived of reason and deprived of sight, with his grey beard and wan look, and the star of his ancient order on his breast, would be found wandering through the long stately galleries of Windsor, speaking to imaginary Parliaments and holding imaginary councils, and then singing one of Handel's hymns, accompanying it on his violin, and then, bursting into tears, would pray aloud for his wife, his children, his country, and then for himself, that if it were God's will he might be restored to reason. Depend upon it, the Irish feel kindly towards that royal line, though it has not done much for them. But they are a people to whom love is easier than hate; and who, when wronged, speedily relent in the presence of kindness or of suffering. And whatever may be their political and national aspirations as regarding the English Government, depend upon it that to the people in the different localities, the English employer has never men more grateful, honest, industrious and true, than the Irish; and the English working-man never will find a neighbour more kindly, more genial, more trusting, and more generous. Then be generous towards a generous race. You have done noble deeds, you have freed the very African slave, defended him, and made him your equal. Shield your Irish brethren from cruel calumny, and from the merciless designs of the informer, and then be noble, and make the Irish your equals, restore to them their country, for with the loss of their country they lost everything but their faith and their honour.

As an Appendix to this Address may be added the following letter written to the Secretary of the Amnesty Committee for the release of Political Prisoners, and published in the "THE IRISHMAN" of January 30th, 1869:—

I admit that the prisoners have violated the laws of the English Government in the same manner as the Sicilians were even advised to violate the laws of the Imperial Government by Pope Innocent IV., in the Brief which, in the name of the Holy Apostles, he addressed to the Sicilians, wherein he says,

S

" People are astonished that weighed down, as you are, by the opprobrium of servitude, and oppressed in your persons and goods, you should yet have failed to seek, as have other nations, a means of making sure to yourselves the sweets of liberty. Seek then, on your part, with hearts that are watchful, how to make your community flourish in the enjoyment of liberty and peace. May it be soon spread abroad amongst the nations that, as your kingdom is distinguished for its nobleness and for its great fertility, so, by the aid of Divine Providence, it may join again to its other prerogatives the glory of a well-grounded liberty."

I admit that the Irish prisoners, beholding their country disarmed and prostrate, and her children wandering to the West, pilgrims at once of despair and of hope, did imitate actions encouraged by the English Government in the Pontifical States, in Tuscany, in Venice, in Sicily, in Naples, in Spain, in Belgium, in America—that, emulating the ancient example of the Swiss, or the recent example of the Belgians, they deserve whatever censure and whatever punishment attaches to those who, in a time of peace, against a powerful ruler, enter upon an enterprise at once perilous and hopeless —that some of them united with this, circumstances which, unfortunately, brought them under the ban of our ecclesiastical law.

I admit that they, perhaps, hardly foresaw that, whilst failing in their real object, they would become instrumental in obtaining for their countrymen at least promises of a national and conciliatory policy, and that their audacity and their sufferings would reunite the Liberal party under, at least, the profession of justice to Ireland.

I admit that their actions in America and elsewhere have proved to the English Government the impossibility of governing in a time of war a hostile population, and thereby stimulated great minds to try and solve the problem how those who have wronged can conciliate those whom they have oppressed.

I admit the humiliating fact that the greatest of English

statesmen, representatives of the intelligence and of the industry of Britain, owe their present high position to men who in a felon's dress are working along with thieves and garrotters within the gloomy walls of our prisons; amongst whom are some of the gentlest character, of the tenderest susceptibility, of the purest domestic affection. One of these (now it is feared beginning to show the first symptoms of loss of intellect,) I remember seeing standing at the dock in Green Street, amongst men whose very countenances belied that base, cruel, and utterly unfounded calumny which imputed to them projects of assassination, robbery. and brutality. I do not envy the spectator, of whatever party, nation, or creed, who could have so divested himself of whatever is generous in human nature, as to have been able without tears of respectful sympathy to have looked on those men and heard them make replies testifying that all, more or less, resemble that one in whom three strong thoughts seemed supreme—the love of his religion, the love of his country, and the love of his aged mother. Their efforts, impetuous and foiled, have by Gladstone's public declaration created at once necessity and the desire to relieve a country for which they rashly dared.

I can never picture to myself their present forlorn and cruel fate, without a shudder of shame and a thrill of horror.

I was formerly asked to sign a petition that two of them might be saved from execution—if they had been bad men I would have signed it, that they might have had time both to repent and expiate. But even in life, there is a punishment more terrible than death—and to save my country from a more public and notorious dishonour, I could not petition that the blood which they freely proffered should be spared, and thus on the tedious years of an unnoticed life there might be heaped all the degradations and privations of the felon. But I would gladly sign with my heart's blood, if it would avail them, a petition containing everything in their behalf—except an insult, a lie, a repudiation, a dishonour, or a treason—if it could only free them from the company of the base and of the wicked, and if.

even without generously restoring them to the sweets of liberty and the homes they love, they were but to be put in possession of those immunities which every civilised nation should accord to political prisoners unstained with crime and suffering for a cause which even their enemies agree demands amelioration.

I beg you to appropriate this additional little offering of £1 toward the expenses being incurred for them, and to believe me, sir, your faithful servant in Christ,

FR. ROBERT RODOLPH SUFFIELD, O.S.D.

AN ECLECTIC VIEW

OF

ROMAN CATHOLICISM.*

I shall not, I think, be mistaken if I surmise that amongst
the members and guests of the Liberal Social Union a very
large number are Rationalists, who regard all the prevailing
Religious systems as mythological, and who earnestly desire the
promotion of a Religious worship and Religious life, in harmony with the experiences of man, in harmony with advancing
knowledge, in harmony with the facts of Nature's mysterious
growth and unity. Such a Religion as this must of necessity
recognise the immanence of God in Nature ; the religious
nature in man ; the universality of law ; the essential elements
of worship,—adoration, trust, aspiration, not entreaty, urgency,
supplication ; and a moral code based on the experiences of
human nature as representing the Will of God. This I venture
to call Cosmic Religion or Cosmic Theism.

There are many who, utterly disbelieving mythological faiths
and worship, earnestly desire to show to those similarly circumstanced the beauty, completeness and spirituality of a Natural
and Progressive Religion. This might be done widely and
effectually by the dissemination of tracts boldly and distinctly
stating what is denied and why denied, and what are the guid-
ing principles proposed, and the results as yet attainable. I
would submit that there is in this Society talent to compose
such cosmic tractates, and that persons interested in the matter
could, at these monthly gatherings of Liberal Thinkers, discover
coadjutors, and arrange preliminaries to be worked out at other
times and places. Such a movement of religious thought,
whilst advancing with the universal growth, would be also

---

* A paper read before the Liberal Social Union, on the evening of Thurs-
day, May 29, 1884, and published in *The Inquirer* of May 31.

eclectic. Each great teacher becomes incorporated in the ages which follow him. His truths and his errors alike grow ; it is the office of eclectic thought to eliminate the errors, to emphasise the truths. How marvellously are the theories of Plato living amongst us now in the creeds of Orthodoxy in the higher illuminations of Rationalism. Each one in this room could thus point to bye-gone but most real influences, influences of a very mixed character. I can trace throughout my own life the distinct influence of three authors read in boyhood, Thomas A'Kempis, Shelley, Rousseau. As also influences derived from the Gospels, from Emerson and St. Theresa. The names will vary, but each one would be able to point to ancestors of his mental and moral being ; saying, I owe to such what I chiefly prize, and what I chiefly regret. And if this be so true as to single books, how important must be the influence of systems ; and of all systems of spiritual thought, there present themselves to my mind as supreme in suggestive power, the Buddhist and the Roman Catholic. As my object is practical, and connected with convictions and results in which I am intensely interested, will you kindly permit me to forget the great divergence of belief existing in this room, and to speak from my own standpoint, viz., that of *utter disbelief* of all supernatural claims, whether sacred books, sacred human personages, sacred traditions or authoritative churches ; of profound *belief* in a Supreme Divine Thought immanent in the Universe, one with the Universe, eternal with the Universe. A Supreme Thought with whom each human soul can commune, and in that communion find sympathy, rest, peace, joy, support, and spiritual illumination. I am not proving, I am confessing to you my intellectual conviction—a conviction which philosophers like Plato treasured among the Greeks, and which formed the central thought of the Vedic, Buddhist, Hebrew, and Christian Religions in the varying and opposing forms thereof.

Then, speaking from the standpoint of Religious Rationalism, of Cosmic Theism, I ask why should not we, like the Roman Catholic (1), encourage one another to the regular practice of

meditation and contemplation. Rejecting as we do the notion
that asking can change God, we should drop entirely what
amongst Roman Catholics is deemed the most important part
of devotion, viz., supplication. But there remain Adoration,
Contrition, Thanksgiving, Aspiration.

Roman Catholics teach Meditation—often too formal and
artificial in mode—often directing all to Christ, nay, to the
very body of Christ, instead of to God; giving prominence to
the getting temporal and spiritual benefits out of God by
petition, by supplication, unwearied entreaty. All such we
should drop as disbelieved by us; but I have often heard Dr.
Newsham, the late venerable President of Ushaw College, urge
on the students that petition is selfish, that the highest union
with God is obtained by adoration and love. At Roman
Catholic Colleges the older boys meditate daily for half an hour
in the morning; and in the evening, like the disciples of
Pythagoras, examine their conscience. This examination is
often injurious, because it dwells so unceasingly on sins, which
though perhaps avoided, become too familiar to the imagination, losing all look of shame and disgust; but surely the
principle is good and imitable. The Brahminical and Buddhist
hermits practise religious contemplation, though often in a
prejudicial way. It flourishes among the Brahmo Somaj—it
is the essential feature of all Roman Catholic institutions,
whether Monastic, Conventual or Collegiate—it is kept up by
very many men and women in the midst of active life in the
world, and I am convinced that it tends in many ways bene-
ficially. The Rosary, when said by those who use it spiritually,
is a mode of contemplation full of consolation to the unlettered,
the aged, the blind, the sick; it is unfortunately entirely a
contemplation of the bodily presence and actions of Jesus and
of Mary, but the idea is capable of transfer to the most philosophic Theism.

(2) Roman Catholics, like the old philosophers of classical
times, like the Brahmans and the Buddhists, have buildings
and institutions adapted for longer or shorter periods of retreat.

In such, confession to a Priest and submission to a Superior are the prominent features and necessary conditions. But along with these there is much of spiritual beauty, repose, and helpfulness, in these homes of holy thought and gardens of serene contemplation. In the midst of the worry and flurry of life it is soothing and elevating sometimes to escape from its noise and turmoil to the peaceful cloister and the tranquil walk beneath the garden trees where those who are seen, speak not. At St. Laurent Sur Sèvres in La Vendée, I have seen farmers, lawyers, tradesmen, students, and nobles driving up in their various rustic vehicles to spend a fortnight in silence. Silence at meals, silence in the large formal avenues of trees, silence everywhere. And then they dispersed to their homes. Not unfrequently women or men seek a lengthened or even permanent home as in the guest department of conventual institutions. Why should not houses arise, not in servile imitation of these, but embodying just what we need?

Roman Catholics draw an infinite distinction between religious and secular pursuits, plans, and objects. We do not. We consider the pursuits of a young lady teaching in a High school quite as religious as those of a Benedictine Nun. We consider that to seek retirement to pursue a special study is quite as holy as to seek retirement to prepare for a general confession or to kneel for hours before the Blessed Sacrament. Now supposing a young lady does not wish to be singular, to be talked about as eccentric, or exposed perhaps to inconvenient circumstances and annoying observation. She is needing rest of spirit, or she is needing a short time for special quiet study. Her father's home is either not attainable or not adapted. She has not unlimited means. What would suit her is not attainable in an hotel, a boarding-house, or a lodging-house. There might be a suitable place, or a companion whose presence might make an otherwise unsuitable place desirable; but she does not at the moment know of such, and has not time to seek it. Or again a decision has to be made—it is the turning point of life:—Roman Catholics can at once find a peaceful home, where without any oddness, without cares of house-keeping, without exciting speculations that something extra-ordinary is looming, such considerations can be pursued quietly and without observation. Or, one has got morally unhinged: he wishes to break off from bad ways and bad companions, to remould his life. Shall I add, he wishes to place himself out of the way of temptation. We have no aid to give to such a person; the Roman Catholic Church has. Thus I might point to numerous cases wherein brief periods of quiet retirement would be invaluable for study, for mental rest, for reflection, for contrition, for forming plans for the future, for breaking through disastrous surroundings, for spiritual contemplation and holy communion with God.

But occasionally there will be cases where some one desires such peaceful home of retirement for long periods, even for life, in which cases the social element would have to be provided for, and a tone of cheerfulness introduced, which would not be needed or even desired during brief periods for special objects.

All this may be ridiculed, criticised, declared not to be needed. Such persons—and by that I mean most persons—would not go to such houses if they existed; but there are some to whom homes of studious, quiet, uneccentric retirement would be an unspeakable boon. These retreats for study and thought would vary in their characteristics. Some might perhaps assume one or other of two forms, which I will call "College Solitudes" or "College Homes;" the word "college," signifying the collective and studious characteristic; the word "solitude," the college adapted for a brief period of retirement for a special object; the word "home," the college adapted for lengthened periods. I should propose the institution of a few rules to protect the objects of the inmates. There should be a warden, or lady warden, and power to request, nay to enforce, the withdrawal of any unsuitable inmate. Some of these college homes might be adapted for married people. As I have remarked, these colleges would vary in characteristics, though I am assuming the total avoidance of anything opposed to the healthy tone of the Protestant and the

Rationalist; but speaking as a Liberal Protestant and a pronounced Rationalist, it would delight and aid me if at such a college solitude or college home I found a solemn and beautiful church always open for the silent devotion of those sharing my retirement. That church might contain paintings of the great benefactors of mankind, the heroes of goodness and of thought. It might be radiant with flowers, and at certain periods inspired with the solemn strains of the organ; or even chanted Psalms of praise and trust and hope might cheer the silent worshipper. Do not deride and dismiss this as the dream of enthusiasm. Religion in the human heart is as much a fact of science as is the sun in the heavens. As the eternal children of Nature and of God, we hold eternal verities, and of them we are component parts. There is nothing in philosophy opposed to the divinest instincts of the soul. When amongst Roman Catholics any good work is proposed, which is in harmony with the Church, they do not shiver it up with criticism; those who are attracted try it, the rest are silent. There are men and women, there are young people who are Rationalists—truth forbids them to be aught else—but they are as full of reverence as any Roman Catholic saint, and walk in awe through the mystery of human life. It is surely an error ever to damp their higher hopes, to embarrass with that cynical censure

" Which drowns in sneers
Youth's starlight smile, and makes its tears
First like hot gall, then dry for ever."

(3) Amongst Roman Catholics there is nothing vague as to their teaching; they teach what they believe, they teach what they deny. When the Church alters anything, such change is distinctly named in books, tracts, and sermons. The Cosmic Theist, the Religious Rationalist holds a Religion which progresses, which grows with the Universe, which, whilst retaining all the treasures of the past, keeps adding the knowledge and experience of the present. We cannot, therefore, have a petrified creed, but each thoughtful man knows what he believes now, what he rejects now. As in each country there is much

of simultaneous in progress ; so we find a singular agreement amongst independent religious thinkers in each epoch ; an agreement which enables co-operation in the publication of tracts, and books for young and old, adapted to unfold and support our present convictions, and to show why other statements are rejected. If we care for our discovered truth, let us distinctly proclaim it,—and each exposed error is a discovered truth.

(4) Amongst Roman Catholics there is a consistency of action, the worship they deem false they refuse to join in ; they explain distinctly to their young people under what circumstances they can be permitted by courtesy, duty, or necessity to be occasionally present at religious services opposed to their belief. Amongst Rationalists, professing to prize truth as an essential part of righteousness, surely there ought to be clear explanations on this subject to young people, supported by unwavering example. Is it so ? *Ex. gr.* if a person believes that Jesus Christ is God, believes that Heresy is a crime to be placed along with murder and adultery, and that God can by entreaty be induced to confer His favours ; let him say the Litany of the Church of England ; but if these statements are opposed to his convictions, how can an honest man take part in them ? A Roman Catholic would not invoke the intercession of Luther ; why are the children of Rationalists to be so frequently the only ones reared in insincere conformity, to get conscience clauses for others, seldom to use such for themselves.

(5) Roman Catholics continually and successfully encourage the feeling of satisfaction in belonging to a world-wide corporation. Non-Catholics probably cannot realise the fact that such a thought is the source of great joy even to the humblest and most ignorant. The joy consists not in any result obtained, but in the sentiment.

Evangelicals experience the same as to all those who by faith are united to Christ as their head. These sentiments have a great and abiding power, and whatever lifts us along with our

surroundings on to the platform of a wider sympathy, must
be delightful as well as elevating. But surely the Religious
Rationalist has a supreme right to this comprehensive and
elevating sentiment. Those who speak of "our common
Master, Christ," or of "the world-wide society of the Catholic
Church" are sectional, and appeal to sectional leaders and sectional results. There is only One Being in whom *all* live and
move, and exist, in whom *all* Humanity centres, by whom *all*
Humanity is inspired, to whom *all* Humanity and *all* Nature is
united. The Universe palpitating with the diversified unity
of the Universal Life. All forms of existence in communion
with Nature's Eternal Mind. All men everywhere, and always
sons of God. The Unity of all Humanity in God. Cosmic
Theism, whilst requiring each man to be truthful in acting out
the convictions he has arrived at, whilst encouraging men to
unite in little groups and societies to testify to their convictions
and to promote them; yet, declares that Humanity is the true
Catholic Church, and the only Master of Humanity is God.
In that truth there is surely sentiment full of consolation to
the world's most solitary exile, full of beauty to the poet, full
of joy to the young. Why do not Rationalists teach this with
distinctness and enthusiasm, instead of pining after flimsy
imitations of services in which they do not believe?

> " Leave your dry discarded dogmas,
> Faith unreasoning, credence blind,
> All the little narrow circles
> Where you wander self confined;
> Plashing in the mire and puddle
> Of your small sectarian pond,
> Heedless of the mighty ocean
> And the boundless Heaven beyond.
> Nobler themes than these invite you
> If you'd throb as throbs the time,
> And would speak to hearts responsive
> Words more human, more sublime!
> ' God is love—and love Eternal;

All things change—but nothing dies,'
Find *this* gospel and expound it,
In the Bible of the Skies."

(6) But the Roman Catholic system possesses an attraction greater even than its vision of universality, in the supposed presence of Christ as the incarnate God in the Tabernacle over the altar of the humblest chapel; that doctrine is the real centre of the entire existing system. May I be permitted to express it by quoting a stanza from a hymn which I wrote in Roman Catholic days ?—

" I rise from dreams of time
And an angel guides my feet,
To the sacred altar throne
Where Jesu's heart doth beat.
The lone lamp softly burns
And a wondrous silence reigns,
Only with a low still voice
The Holy One complains.
Ever pleading, day and night,
Thou canst not from us part ;
O veiled and wondrous Son,
O love of the Sacred Heart."

It is obvious that such a doctrine must when truly believed inspire emotions full of tenderness and of consolation. Still more obvious is it, that a belief so profoundly false, so utterly superstitious, could not be simulated without crime. Has, then, Eclecticism any thing to observe regarding it? Assuredly: the Cosmic Theist adores the Real Presence, presence not of a man's body, but of Nature's soul. The expression of such adoration can be found in Wordsworth and in all our best poets, as can be seen by those who use Crompton Jones's selected poems of the inner life, Martineau's selected hymns of praise, Francis Newman's epilogue " We Praise Thee in thy Power, O God," as found in his " Hebrew Theism," and embodied in Charles Voysey's " Service of Praise and Thanksgiving."

(7) My last eclectic suggestion regards the Roman Catholic treatment of the dead. Protestantism has failed in this matter, has soparated us from the traditions of mankind. The Greek and the Roman poured out libations in honor of the departed, and in many ways made memory of them. The 800 millions in China, from the Emperor to the humblest, on the great anniversary of the dead, visit, each one the tomb of his father and his mother. "Alone there," says Carlyle, "in silence, with what of worship or of other thought there may be, pauses solemnly each man; the divine skies all silent over him; the divine gravos, and this divinest grave all silent under him; pulsings of his own heart alone audible. Truly, it is a kind of worship! Truly, if a man cannot get some glimpse into the eternities looking through this portal through what other need he try it?" Roman Catholicism in this as in other matters adopted, with modifications, some of the pagan modes of commemorating the dead. Hence prayers for the dead, monthly and annual commemorations of the dead, a keeping up of the memory of the dead mingled with religious solemnities. Unfortunately, more conspicuous than these were the superstitions regarding getting souls out of Purgatory by Masses and Indulgences. In revolt from these injurious superstitions, Protestantism severed the dead from all the lines of religious expression. Hence the solemnities of grief find no utterance which seems to unite us with the departed. Yet surely those aspirations which we deem not unreasonable when offered up for one loved and living, must be as admissable when offered for the soul of the loved one departed. If we believe in the communion of all souls in God, in the Eternity of all forms of Mind and Life, it must surely be well to keep up human love consecrated by reposeful trust in a Divine and Eternal hope—and, as it seems to me, this truthful and beneficent thought is beautifully preserved and sanctified by uniting with piety

> "Gracious service to the living,
> Tranquil memory to the dead."

FAREWELL SERMONS

UNITARIAN FREE CHURCH, READING,

SUNDAY, JUNE 17TH, 1888.

———

MORNING.

———

Reserving until the evening a few remarks of a personal character, let me attempt to summarise to-day what I believe to be the truest, noblest, and most beneficent form of religion.

True religion I take to be at once Cosmic and Spiritual. The "Cosmic" regards the universal, the "Spiritual" regards the individual soul in its relationship to God. Cosmic religion is revealed to us through nature, Spiritual religion is revealed to us through the soul.

The entire object of my ministry has been to secure practical religion to those in whose minds the popular faiths have ceased to be credible. I have not endeavoured to shake the belief of others in the legendary or mythological. If a person has caught the spirit of the age and thus questioned the reliability of an inherited faith, I have been anxious to show to such an one that religion remains after the mythology has disappeared. That, as to morals, natural religion presents warnings and sanctions more clear, uniform and emphatic than what can be derived from opposing texts in imperfect translations of documents of uncertain origin and questionable authority. When this unveracity has been recognised, we offer to the seeker after truth a religious home. If he considers that he has courage to persevere in a course needing thoughtfulness and independence, he will derive moral benefit by joining us. Most frequently, however, persons who derive aid by occasional attendance at our services, continue in a mental position somewhat between "Orthodoxy" and Rationalism. A large and increasing number of persons in the Trinitarian Churches have arrived at the rejection of some of the dogmas most injurious to individual spiritual happiness and to public well-being. These form the liberalising element daily, happily, on the increase within all the Protestant Churches. Then the grave question arises—if the authority of the popular mythology is either weakened or destroyed—if the sacred books of the great religions of the world have been proved to be human, though beautiful, liable to error, though often radiant with truth—if it has been discovered that the Prophet of Nazareth, with his luminous soul, spoke divinely because he spoke so humanly, appealing, not to sacred books or traditions inherited, but to the conscience and the heart of man—the question, I say, arises, what is the foundation of the religion of those who have ceased to acknowledge miraculous books and miraculous men? To solve and illustrate this question has been the object of my ministry ever since my secession from the Roman Catholic Church, in July, 1870. The Roman Catholic Church is an imposing organisation, the inheritor of great traditions. I left the Roman Church in order to join, not what is less universal, but what is more really universal. I left a sect in order to join what embraces that sect and all the sects —the Cosmic whole. The word "Cosmos" means order, arrangement, regularity, discipline, method; but it also means the world, the whole frame of the universe—the totality. Thus "Cosmos" denotes the orderly and providential development and growth of the moral, mental, and physical existences constituting the world we know, and what can be seen around the world.

We find ourselves the inheritors of many lines of thought, of many venerable traditions, of various teachings, aspirations, strivings, of great religions, of great philosophies—all these have combined in forming us, in moulding our tone of thought, and our principles of action. We find ourselves with certain mental and moral faculties, blaming in human conduct some things, approving other things.

Practically no one is moulding his conduct entirely and

exclusively on the Levitical precepts or on the Sermon on the Mount—on the Old Testament or the New. Those who suppose themselves to rest on such authority will find as a matter of fact, that they are in reality only illustrating out of scripture what they have learned from the developed conscience of mankind. We express boldly and openly what so many gentle souls think timidly. They, under the influence of good sense and right feeling, interpret scriptural statements and ecclesiastical formularies, so as to meet the requirements of a conscience better instructed and more enlightened. It is not that each man begins afresh, it is that each man begins as the heir of all the past. And not only from one past; the converging lines come from Palestine, from Chaldæa, from ancient India, ancient Egypt, from Athens and from Rome. These all converge in each English soul—sometimes knowingly to the individual—most frequently not known by him. But however unknown to him, each Christian Englishman is, in his moral and religious life, the possessor of what can be traced to the Schools of Stoics and Platonists, to the saints of Palestine, and to the contemplatives of a remoter East. The most ardent Protestant has within him influences derived from the "Imitation of Christ." The most submissive Roman Catholic is the unconscious possessor of a tone of religious and moral thought derived from the German prophet—so gentle by his fireside, so terrible to his foes—who drank the wine of independence in his Saxon cup and, bending his head, not in humility, but in opposition, dashed on into the battle of ideas. Rome had been resting on her golden couch for 600 years; the clarion voice that roused her is now an unacknowledged inspiration to Rome as well as to Geneva. Luther beheld with unquailing spirit the two authorities wherewith the past was clothed with majesty—the Pope and the Empire. To them he opposed his heart—in itself an indestructible power. To Luther even the Bible was subordinated to the individual conscience—the Bible might perish: the eternal gospel is in the soul and in humanity.

T

Such is the Cosmic Faith, the universal foundation, the universal religion. We find it in Abraham, in the Patriarchs, in the Psalms, in Job, in Proverbs, Ecclesiastes, Isaiah, Micah, in the discourses and parables of Christ, in the Epistles of St. Paul, and of St. James the brother of Jesus. Even when the ecclesiastical deluge covered the Paradise of God, the Cosmic spirit passed over the waters and the billows sparkled here and there with unexpected light. That sentence of Abelard—Priest and Monk---was a ray of light. " Reason is an interior and permanent revelation, the light enlightening every man who cometh into this world. Reason has guided to God all the sages of antiquity. Of their salvation we need not doubt."

To us now, in our stage of moral growth, with our antecedents and surroundings, could a thousand miracles make us more certain than we are, that we must win excellence by noble efforts, must subordinate instinct and passion to reason, to conscience, to the purest sentiments of the heart and soul? That we must bend selfish personal ends before the majesty of justice, goodness, mercy? That what we gain now we gain for ever, that what we lose we lose for ever?

" I slept and dreamed that life was beauty?
" I woke and found that life was duty,
" Was the dream, then, a shadowy lie?
" Toil on, sad heart, courageously,
" And thou shalt find thy dream to be
" A noonday light and truth to Thee."

Ecclesiastical practices rest on ecclesiastical authority, but the truths which profoundedly move the soul and the life are the truths of natural religion, natural morals, the experiences of man, and the facts of nature. We have from science learnt the vastness of the universe, the antiquity of the world, and the gradual growth of its inhabitants; that instead of a fall of man there has been a raising up of man; that Paradise has not been lost but has to be won; that God's mode has been by gradual evolution, not by sudden creation. By the recent science of comparative religion we have learnt that sublime truths are scattered here and there amidst the religions and philosophies of the world. That if the Jews had sacred books, so had the Hindoos, and the Parsees, and the Chinese. That if medieval Christianity presented to us a dramatic judgment day, so did Egypt and Chaldea. That Incarnations, and the Trinity, and the Cross are not of Christian origin. That legends and truths are scattered here and there amongst various religions. That some of the sublimest of the moral precepts of Christianity are to be found in the writings of philosophers and in the sacred books of the Buddhists, of the Brahmins, and of Confucius, ages before the Christian Era. That Baptism and the Lord's Supper owe their origin to the Essenes; and that most ecclesiastical rites can be traced to Paganism. These discoveries distress some, who have been resting their spiritual All on one line of authority. Happy for those dear, gentle souls, when they can perceive that what they really prize rests upon a Cosmic and not a narrow basis. I wish not to unsettle another's faith, for some have not strength to brave the mental conflict; but if the faith is unsettled, and at the present time such unsettlement is widely spread, then it is our joyful privilege to invite the ˈtimid soul out of the narrow groove into the wide temple of the universe —there to learn the best things, known not merely to the clergy of one Church, but to the competent within and without all the Churches. In all the most earnest matters we appeal to human nature—to the consensus of the competent —to the moral sentiment of the thoughtful, the disinterested, and the good. Thus, if we are in doubt about a course of action, an appeal to scriptural texts would be of doubtful benefit. But let a man ask himself, (1) What should I advise to a loved friend who trusted me? (2) What should I wish to have done when life is ebbing away and I look back? (3) If my action regards another, what should I wish, if, sorrowing, I were to go and stand by his tomb? (4) What have I thought as to this in my best and highest moments? When,—

" At twilight's holy, heartfelt hour,
" Man in his better soul has power."

One of our novelists describes a young man who has led
another unto sin, and the next morning he awakes and sees
the sun rising, and hears the birds chirping on the honey-suckle
clustering over his window, and he sees the picture of his
mother on the wall, and the memento of a dear friend who had
loved him in the days of his innocence. He is overwhelmed
with shame and remorse, and would give worlds to undo what
he has done, lamenting those happy mornings when he could
look back on his actions and say " In the integrity of my heart
and the innocency of my hand, I have done this." " My righteousness I hold fast and will not let it go; My heart shall not
reproach me so long as I live." That is Cosmic religion, for it
belongs to the whole of the human race. All the best utterances of the Old and New Testament belong to Cosmic religion,
" He hath showed thee, O man, what is good; and what doth
the Lord require of thee but to do justly, and to love mercy, and
to walk humbly with thy God." Such sentiments inspire Psalm
after Psalm: if we omit some expressions of barbaric vengeance,
the Psalter is the Prayer Book of the Cosmic faith; the Book
of Job is its Poem; Christ is its Prophet; St. Paul and St.
James its Apostles. Often have I invited young people joyfully
to raise their hearts to God by an almost daily use of the
Psalms, and then they would become inspired with the Cosmic
faith, God in All. Wordsworth has carried on the same idea in
the melody of his song. How Cosmic was the Ideal of Christ!
He did not even exclude the corrupt—the dews of heaven
falling on the gardens of the just and the unjust. He presented
to his disciples no creed but love—the love of the sinner, the
love of the fallen, the love of the outcast, the love of nature, the
love of God. Love was to be the only mark of his discipleship.
The disinterested, unselfish, self-sacrificing love, which is the
gift and heritage of the pure in heart, who, through the
medium of human love, gaze trustfully into the love of the
All Holy lover of souls. St. Paul, writing to the Romans,

proclaims distinctly the sufficiency of natural religion for the religious and moral guidance of man. Persons reared in any narrow sectarian training try to judge others by the limitations of their creed; but how few are so bigoted as to be able to do so. The Athanasian creed may have been recited in church, but its anathemas are displaced by the Spirit of Christ as soon as the utterer comes across his 'neighbour'; and we know how wide an interpretation Christ gave to that word. It may be that the neighbour says he believes in One God, but knows nothing about His Trinity; reveres the teaching of Christ, but without declaring him to be the Deity, applying to him the saying of his mother, when she said "Your father (Joseph) and I have sought you sorrowing." All your kindly social intercourse is based on the Cosmic idea—the brotherhood of all men, the universal fatherhood of God. Often have I invited our young people to practice acts of Adoration, Contrition, Thanksgiving, Supplication—A.C.T.S.—to God as the all present, all pervading Soul of the universe, with Whom we unite our soul in spiritual communion. That is the great Cosmic sacrament, limited to no sect, needing no priest.

Cosmic religion is in harmony with science, with progress, with liberty, with human sympathy; it includes all men, nay, all worlds and all forms of future life. I am not to day attempting to prove to you the sublime realities of the Cosmic Theism. Again and again during the years of our gracious intercommunion, have I attempted to illustrate the wonders of the Divine mind, and the grounds we have for loving trust in His Paternal Providence. On what trembling balances of powers, on what delicate and almost imperceptible chemistries does man's tenure of earth and life rest, but behind these gauze-like veils we see the sympathetic compassion of our Heavenly Father, with His adaptations and compensations.

Cosmic Theism can never, if honestly and consistently held, be a persecuting, an arrogant, or a contemptuous faith, for it, by its very nature, embraces all. It rejoices in the beauties and excellencies of all religions—all belong to humanity, and all are under God. But the Cosmic Theist gladly beholds a progress in religious ideas. The gods of the Pagan Mythology entered the Elysian fields amidst the Jubilee of Warriors. The god of the Catholic Mythology entered Jerusalem (which means the City of Peace) amidst the waving of the green branches of the early palm and amidst the joyous chaunt of children. The Cosmic Theist has profound trust in knowledge, for knowledge is the revelation of God. Man has to be emancipated from the bondage of error, to be enlightened so as to stand outside its obscurities. Man has to learn to know himself, to know the world surrounding him, to cast the anchor of Knowledge into the rock of Truth, to emerge from fantasies into realities. The Spirit of Truth does not make its temple into a sepulchre of thoughts which once breathed, and lived, and moved, but now are dead. Her temple is the dwelling place of thoughts that live. The Spirit of Truth admits of no finality. The Spirit of Dogma formularises a proposition, and says it must endure for ever. The Spirit of Truth reverently and gratefully looks backward; She sees the Eternal One in the past, but also in the present and in the future. The lover of truth never stops; he is like the Arab, who, when the morning comes, folds up his tent and advances. To us the Universe is a vast cathedral, and the choral chaunts from souls diverse and countless swell upwards in confused but harmonious symphony, tumbling and blending and rolling overhead among the vast arches and around the clustered pillars—whilst the ground of existence trembles joyfully beneath the footsteps of the invisible God. If in a few earnest hearts we can infuse such thoughts,

" We feed the high traditions of the world,"

" And leave our spirits in our brethren's breasts."

Let us strive to follow the Christ of Nazareth, whose immortal utterance will inspire us—" For this end was I born, and for this cause came I into the world, that I should bear witness unto the Truth."

Cosmic religion is a religion not only of duty and of love and of progress, but it is a religion of beauty. The All-Beautiful

God is its centre, its inspiration, its joy. Let no man impoverish the world of one particle of grace or beauty. True religion will cultivate the beauty and grandeur of the Arts; Painting will blend with Poetry, and Music chaunt immortal harmonies.

Let our Cosmic faith be an over-mastering reality. There is only one great vice, namely—Selfishness. There is only one great virtue, namely—Thoughtful Sympathy—Thoughtful Love. Knowledge is precious, but its preciousness consists in this, that true Knowledge is Mercy. We believe in Immortality; we believe in the Eternity of all life and all actions. But our object now is this present life. Whatever may be the future life, when it arrives we must do our best then. But now our duty is to make to others this present life more excellent, more holy, more happy, more wise, more beautiful. If men are at enmity with God, it is because they are at enmity one with the other. Let us strive to unite men—class to class—nation to nation—family to family—in the holy enthusiasm of Humanity. You, much loved and loving friends, acted on that idea when, eleven years ago, you laid the foundation of this Church. You thought You "would put your creed into your deed, nor speak with double tongue." Believing in God, in nature, in human life and in the 'human soul, you desired to remind yourselves and to remind your friends in Reading, that whatever is best and noblest in the creeds of the Churches is what human life has inspired, and human hearts loved, and human sympathy blessed. You perceive that all nature is, through God's presence, supernatural; that Christ was the offspring of humanity, not its Lord; and that his is the greatness of humanity, not the abasement of God; that prayer is not a petition for interference, but an aspiration of Adoration, Contrition, Thanksgiving and Supplicating aspiration; that immortality is of the nature of things, not by some portent; that the infinite grandeur of God cannot be measured by man's littleness; that Christianity is a grand human fact, not a preternatural exception.

You have been attending these services wherein so imperfectly

I have striven to share your thoughts. You have taught the children on Sunday. You have borne witness to the truth as to your souls it seemed. This little Church is a monument of self-sacrificing zeal. You have realised that God and duty belong to the present—at present God to us is only *here ;* to us the New Jerusalem is not in the clouds, it covers the world, and its limit is our furthest horizon. You embarked in an arduous enterprise. Universal Truths are, at first, only held by a few. You resolved to bear witness to the truth ; to remind all our dear and honoured friends around us, that universal religion embraces all of them. At first they resented the erection of this Church. I am not surprised ; they supposed we were going to cast scorn on the traditions they loved. They found it was not so, and to day I gratefully return my ministry to your hands with the happy conviction that a bond of holy sympathy combines us togother, and combines us together with them.

EVENING.

My very dear friends and fellow workers, to day I resign the ministerial charge which you intrusted to me nine years and a half ago. It has always been my opinion that amongst us a pulpit should not be occupied more than ten years. After allowing for absences and occasional repetitions of a sermon, a ministry of that duration implies 864 discourses, which is equivalent to the composition of 36 printed volumes. A man might, by keeping himself up to the level of the times, publish three volumes and a half each year, on topics of mere general interest, but you do not, by considerable sacrifice, erect a church for the worship of God, and the promotion of Spiritual Religion and holiness of life, in order to obtain on the Sunday, a repetition of the ideas which have occupied our minds in political meetings, or in gatherings for literary, artistic, musical or social objects. If, for the sake of exciting wider interest and receiving larger attendances, this pulpit should be used on Sunday for political or other secular purposes, I should cease to be an attendant, and that would be the case with a considerable proportion of those who have hitherto attended our services with regularity.

But, after composing 85 vols. on religious, spiritual and moral truths, or on topics directly leading up to such, one becomes diffident as to one's power of being able to impart continued interest to the treatment of subjects limited in their range, unless recourse be had to mere sensationalism.

This thought was in my mind when, in my circular of last October, I signified my intention of withdrawing from any permanent ministerial functions, so as to devote myself more fully to private literary pursuits. I said, "short ministries are injurious to congregations, and therefore I had declined attractive offers which might have taken me away at earlier dates. But a change of ministry, kindly and thoughtfully made, after nearly ten years is not without advantage," therefore with less reluctance, yielding to personal considerations and objects, I resolved to terminate the ministerial responsibilities which commenced amongst you on February 9th, 1879. After an absence of three months I propose to return to Reading as a continued resident, always, as heretofore, glad to co-operate in local interests in a town endeared to me by many ties; and as a worshipper in our Church, though without any official connection therewith, supplementing my modest pecuniary resources by literary work and occasional pulpit duties, elsewhere, or in Reading, when for a brief period such might be desired, in consequence of gaps arising between more permanent arrangements. But I should like my name to be removed from the Church Board, so that in the event of future temporary engagements arising between us, it should be clear that I act as supplying your pulpit, and not as the responsible minister. It is my earnest hope that you may speedily obtain a resident minister. A succession of ministers, if regarded as candidates for the pulpit, is apt to produce a critical spirit, and preferences arise of a party character. Whilst always glad to render friendly information, I shall not embarrass my successor or yourselves by advice and criticism. But, in the absence of any regular minister, you will know that whenever I am in Reading I shall be glad, when requested, to render those ministerial services needed sometimes in the course of the week, and which cause expense and inconvenience if sought from London. I allude to baptisms, marriages, and funerals. I have nothing else of a personal kind to say, beyond what I expressed to you in my circular; my grateful sense of your affection, your harmony, your zeal and loving earnestness for the great principles of which our Church stands as the local representative. My thanks too are due, not only to yourselves, for much sympathy and much forbearance, but also to many kind friends, here and elsewhere, outside our regular congregation.

On these matters of personal feeling I will say no more, for I do not wish to impart to the joyful occasion of your anniversary any of those painful emotions which belong to parting. Nine years and a half cannot pass without weaving many bonds of pleasant kindly goodwill. It is not always the case that, as now between ourselves, such a period of time elapses without, as far as I know, a single word or feeling having tarnished our perfect harmony. To the Officers of this Church and to our Honorary Organist I offer my sincere thanks.

Turning now from these more private considerations, let me continue a summary of the Truths I have endeavoured to enforce and illustrate from this tribune.

I have taught Revelation as revealed through Nature and through Man. Therefore I have taught Cosmic religion, namely, that religion is not the possession of any one Church or Sect, but is co-extensive with mind; all minds existing in the Supreme Mind. That an Eternal Universe is inspired by an Eternal Mind. That the universe is an eternal growth, an eternal evolution, and might be an eternal progress. That all intelligences have the power of helping on or retarding that growth. Hence, through the ignorance of some, the faultiness of others, the universal growth is but too frequently retarded. That the moral law is the ever enduring manifestation of the Mind of God, to be discovered by the exercise of thought and experience. That each man has within him a faculty, itself the product of ages, whereby he approves goodness and condemns vice. That what is good and what is vicious, he learns chiefly by its effects on human happiness and human character. Rejecting the Hell and the Heaven of the Pagan, Chaldean and Christian mythologies, I have continually dwelt on the indubitable verity, that each act produces its effect and that effect endures. Hence the absolute certainty of retribution. Each good action, each good word, each good thought, each bad action, each bad word, each bad thought, endures alike and always. I have constantly illustrated that great truth from the sacred books of the Buddhists, from the writings of the Philosophers, from the results of modern investigations, aided by the great thinkers of ancient and modern times; we have together desired goodness, heroism, love, devotedness, purity, self-sacrifice. We have read from the sacred books of the various Faiths of mankind, from the pages of ancient philosophy, from the mystical writings of Christian fathers and medieval saints, as also the luminous thoughts of the moderns. We have recognised all as component parts of the universal temple of religion and of virtue. We have forgotten our little sanctuary, with its eighty or ninety worshippers, in remembrance of the universal family of humanity wherein we take our humble place. Under the Unitarian name we gratefully acknowledge our historic origin and the enlightening influences of the Unitarian Theology. But we also prize the name because it has broadened its significance, and now implies the unity of divine operations, and the spiritual unity of mankind. If, as Unitarians or Religious Rationalists, we thus call ourselves " Liberal " Religionists, it is not because we deem illiberal those friends in the Trinitarian Churches to whom our heart goes forth in the fulness of brotherly love; but because we desire to emphasise what the dictionaries tell us the word "Liberal" signifies:— "free by birth"—"gentle in manners"—"befitting a man free and refined"—"generous"—"open-hearted"—"not narrow or contracted"—"enlarged in spirit"—"Catholic." If, amidst the many imperfections of my ministry, any word has escaped my lips opposed to such sentiments of reverent love to all, I lament it and wish such word blotted out by the tear of the Recording Angel. These sublime, universal truths I have not rested on any Bible, Church, miraculous man, or miraculous statement—I do not deny miracles, but I say they are unproved. I dare not found religious and moral life on what may turn out to be merely a beautiful legend. I have never scoffed at those legends. They are held as realistic by some unspeakably dear to us. But I must speak the truth, even though I step reverently over the grave of my mother—These universal truths I have found in the universal heart of mankind. Religion is Cosmic and Spiritual; Universal and Individual. The Cosmic Faith arises out of the Cosmic whole. In its spiritual aspects, as affecting the relationship between God and each individual heart, it comes to us specially from the chosen souls of humanity. Amongst these, one name stands supreme. Like music over the waters the name of Christ comes to us, bearing the spiritual memories of the eighteen hundred years. In spiritual religion the name of Christ is pre-eminent. He was not God. I know not that He possessed any miraculous office, or any miraculous gifts, but as St. Bernard says, "He drank of the torrent and was inebriated with the waters of Divine Life." He did not reveal anything actually new; but he emphasised great truths, and he caused veiled truths to step forth visibly. The Truths of Spiritual Religion—What are some of these Truths?

1.—Fatherhood of God. That the Divine Soul of the Universe is a paternal Spirit, a loving Spirit, fostering, cherishing all with the breathings of a divine sympathy. Philosophy revealed the Cosmic soul. Sanctity revealed the consoling Spirit of Divine Love.

2.—Hence the sense of filial relationship arose ; and St. Paul, the pupil of Hebrew psalmists and Stoic philosophers, was able, with a realisation deeper than he obtained from them, to say with Jesus of Nazareth, " Our Father who art in Heaven." Man in his often sorrowful pilgrimage needs sympathy. He has thus created to himself human Gods. But Christ presented to them the Supreme Beneficence, circling all with the Ever-lasting Arms.

3.—Hence the conscious communion between our soul and God in Adoration, Contrition, Thanksgiving, Supplication. Often have I invited you and our young people to practice those spiritual acts, recalling them by the word " A.C.T.S." Such would be our Eucharist, our spiritual communion.

4.—Hence a consciousness of sin, more spiritual, more deep, more contrite than when regarded solely as a violation of the Cosmic laws which connect goodness with happiness, vice with misery.

Spiritual Religion causes us to realise that sin separates us from union with God, clouds that sanctity of soul whereby once we beheld the Divine Vision. It has been my effort to prove that the Religious Rationalist, holding a Cosmic Theism in harmony with progress, with liberty, with science, history, and thought, has not thereby separated himself from the traditions of sanctity, and the lineage of the holy ones who have walked with God. That to us, as to them, Spiritual Religion is a reality, and contrition something deeper than the fears of prudence and the remorse of kindness. It injures us, injures others, injures the Cosmic order—but also, it distances the soul from God. We reject the Hell of eternal torment, we admit only as a dramatic type, the legend of the general judgment. We find a judgment nearer and more certain.

Cosmic Religion would not be a complete religion, would not be a spiritual religion, would not be a happy religion, unless it could pour the balm of consolation over the heart bruised by sin. Christ is the ideal hero of the sinner; deprive him of that glory, and you shear him of his locks of beauty, and tear from his shoulders the blood-stained garment of his pacific royalty. Christ, like all holy men, realised the idea of sin, and therefore to raise from sin, to bring back to God, was one of the sacred passions of his soul. He enlists in the science of such ideas, all the pathos of Oriental imagery. The philosophers of India, China, Egypt, Greece, and Rome had not exhausted human possibilities. A voice was heard in the East —in that land of poetic dreams, where the very glory of the night is an unceasing miracle, and where the wrapt soul more easily loses itself in God, and exalts itself in sense of conscious union with Him. The voice said " Ego sum Pastor Bonus," and the walls of the Christian Catacombs have made us familiar with the gracious form of the Good Shepherd, a pilgrim on the desolate moor to gather unto his bosom the lamb wandering and wounded.

And again the voice said " Come unto me, all ye that labour and are heavy laden, and I will give you rest." And how would he give them rest ? By leading them on to God, to the paternal God, to his Father and their Father. And so the Prodigal Son is made by Christ to utter his cry of Spiritual Religion. Crushed, destroyed, desolated by sin, he does not remain in the isolation of remorse, but he says, " I will arise and go unto my Father and I will say to him—Father, I am not worthy to be called Thy son." Christ makes it clear who is his Father, to whom the parable points.

The exaggerations and errors of the popular mythology must not cause us to forget our indebtedness to Christ. We cannot spare the heroes of sanctity from the Cosmic Temple of humanity. It is not folly, but gratitude, which has printed the name of the Nazarene on so many sorrowful hearts. Other teachers either compromised with the sinner or rejected him. Christ took him up and bore him on his shoulders as a trophy of spiritual victory, borne into his gracious pathetic school of thought. Plato bore the olive branch into the groves of the Academy. Christ led into his school little children, suffering men, fallen women ; and in Oriental imagery he would be their

Shepherd. In the East, the shepherd goes before the sheep, and they follow him, because they love him. Christ was a poet, and he appealed to the poetic element seldom quite absent from the human heart. Dry precepts would never have moved to penitence ; but who has ever been insensible to the story of the Prodigal, or of Lazarus and his sisters, or the dramatic pathos of Mary Magdalene's history.

Let us not destroy the poetic beauty of ancient legend by lowering it into a dogma. Let us remember the language and the manners of the East, and we shall understand the symbolic legend of Lazarus—how Christ spoke to the youth not physically dead, but dead in sin, and how, when Christ spoke, the dead arose and answered him. We shall understand how and why the sorrowful and the forsaken cast themselves at his feet, a homage which in our colder habits is replaced by the salutation of respect, the kiss of affection, or the hand of friendship.

Cosmic Religion has to come to us in its spiritual form, if it is to heal the sorrows of the soul. The Prodigal Son and Mary Magdalene belong to us as well as to the days gone by. It is our duty and our privilege to show to the sinner—crushed and forsaken, that there is an alternative without having recourse to legends which the reason can no longer maintain. The story of Mary Magdalene embodies Eternal Truths—the sadness of sin—the heroism of the return – the trust wherewith the good love the wanderer restored to noble endeavours. The dramatic characteristics of the narrative have proved an infinite benefit, as serving to show how trust in a good man can redeem the forlorn. Mary Magdalene was described as the woman who was a sinner notorious throughout the city. We can picture her career, we know it all ; we see her in her early youth, her air of liberty, her vanity, and her worldliness. We see her face, her hair, her dress, her attitude. We see her flaunting in the pride of her majestic beauty. Then we behold her, the grace of virtue perished. The heart hardened, first corrupted, then corrupting. Then she, somehow, comes across the Nazarean Teacher. The voice of Jesus moved her—that voice which had so often spoken to God, spoke benignly to Man. The grace of virtue gave it eloquence—sadness gave it pathos—simplicity gave it power. He was to her such a contrast. She, all for effect, he aiming at nothing. She all propriety before others, all license with the criminal, he careless before others, all tenderness to the criminal. She thinks, I have been loved by the wicked, I should desire to be loved by the good, if anything could save me, his love might save me. He has said "The bruised reed I would not break," and often when he saw the peasants in the field blowing up their fire, he said, as a child might speak in his dreams, "The spark in the smouldering fire I would not quench." Perchance the breath of his pure lips might fan the spark in my heart into a flame of holy purpose—shall I go to him?—and she goes; and as she goes her feet print on the sands of time one of the grandest pages of the Gospel. And she goes more valiant than Judith and Deborah—her heart beats, not with fear, but with love and victory. Her cheek is flushed, not with shame, but with spiritual power. According to the Eastern customs, she prostrates herself before the Teacher, she kisses his feet and bathes them with her golden tresses. She takes from her breast the only ornament she has retained, the vase of costly ointment she pours out upon him the fragrant oil, and then breaks the, vase—she breaks it, that it may never be used for another. She becomes the disciple—nay more than disciple—the friend of Christ. He becomes the frequent guest at her house. She is found at his feet when he is speaking—at his cross when he is dying—at his grave when he is buried. She even fancies she sees him appear, tries to touch him, but cannot. She seems to hear his voice—that voice of pathetic tenderness; she at least could never forget that voice that had restored her to hope, had brought her back to God. Such is Spiritual Religion. Not to stay with Christ, but to go on to God. Not to rest on Christ, or on any Saint, or Church, or Sacrament, or Holy Book, but to go to God, and on Him rest, and in Him hope, and in Him eternally rejoice—as may you ever, sweet friends, now and evermore.

THE DUTY OF THOUGHT.[*]

> "In the multitude of my thoughts within me,
> Thy consolations delight my soul." *Psalm* 94.

WE are accustomed to speak of liberty of thought and of free thought, but we advocate more than liberty of thought, we inculcate the religious duty of thought.

The duty of thought! Thought exercised as the highest gift of God, directed towards the highest objects.

Ecclesiastical rulers would rather we did not think: such a one thought 1800 years ago, or 300 years ago,—*you* need not think, *he* did it for you. Just as well say such a one was good 1800 years ago, you need not be good, he did it for you.

The duty of thought—the duty of free thought is falsely supposed by some to mean the right of thinking whatever we like, true or false, right or wrong, according to our passions or caprice—the goal is truth, not license. It is our duty to strive loyally after all truth within the range of our intelligence. If we desire the end, we use the means, therefore we think.

If Clergymen say to us, "you will find all truth in such a book," we reply, "it is only by thought, by examination, by consequent proof, that we can be satisfied whether such a book is all true." Thought can alone decide whether it be the word of God or the word of man. If any one should say, "such is decided by interior inspiration," we reply, "it is only by the exercise of thought that we can decide whether or not the supposed inspiration is only a self-confident illusion." Such satisfying illusions console the holders of opposing beliefs.

---

[*] This Sermon was not intended for publication, and written to be spoken, not to be read, but it was a favourite with the preacher, one of those he preached in his first year of ministry (Croydon, March 23rd, 1873), and the last he delivered (Sale, May 3rd, 1891). Between these dates he preached it 21 times up and down the country, from Edinburgh to Exeter, from Whitby to Swansea.

U

By judgment, by thought, by inquiry, we can only discover whether what claims to be revelation is so or not. We have inherited intuitions, moral and mental instincts, these have to be tested by thoughtful examination.

The Priest says, "submit to my Infallible Church, accept the Pope as your Infallible Guide." By thought we must investigate and test the Infallible claim. If the exercise of thought causes a man to arrive at the opinion that such a Church is Infallible, the infallible claim only rests upon his private judgment, and can not reasonably be regarded as more certain than the conclusion of his individual thought.

A balance of probability has made him decide that such a book, or church, or man, is infallible, therefore all the statements made by such book, church, or man, have to him a balance of probability in their favour—nothing more—a probability rather *less* conclusive than the authority of his own previous conclusion, because it is a step further off. A weak, or an imaginative mind, may, after that opinion has been arrived at, feel convinced that it is infallibly true. But be convinced that your next door neighbour may, after his investigations, feel quite as certain that you are infallibly wrong.

The Roman Catholic Church, and those opposing sects which imitate it, say, "when once your researches have persuaded you that our sect is the only true one, you must never again doubt, or question your conclusion." Such a course for the most part secures permanence, but at the cost of the higher morality, seeing it is not lawful to abrogate the Divine gift of thought.

If, however, it is truly urged that English people ought not to examine the grounds of their belief, but only to read whatever can be said in its defence, the same principle must be true for Hindoos, Buddhists, Mahomedans, and Pagans. In that case Christian Missionaries are guilty of a great sin in trying to make such people renounce the doctrines of their respective systems. Nay, Christianity commenced its career by the perpetrations of such a sin on a colossal scale. If free thought be wrong, the Apostles were the greatest malefactors, for they encouraged free thought to shake the faith alike of Jew and Gentile.

The Christian Missionary reproaches the Brahmin for not inquiring enough, and reproaches the Christian for inquiring at all. He uses the two-fold weapon of inquiry and authority: inquiry is represented as the duty of the Brahmin if he would escape damnation; inquiry is forbidden to the Christian lest he should incur damnation. The Christian foreigner, with his newer Ecclesiastical Religion, urges authority upon the Brahmin whose religion was flourishing in India before Moses fled from Egypt.

Either all men should inquire into their respective creeds and sacred books, or all submit without inquiry to the sacred books and dogmas of the sect in which they have been reared. Whatever is the right mode must be alike right for Hindoo, Jew, Parsee, Roman Catholic, Anglican, Evangelical.

The moral and religious duty of thought does not signify that sceptical indifference is to take the place of orthodoxy, but that thought is to take the place of unreasoning credulity.

It is most important to establish this principle. We must remember that each moral, social, scientific, and religious progress has been a heresy; in other words it has been thought struggling against authority. Moses was a heretic to the Egyptians; Jesus Christ was a heretic to those who sat in the chair of Moses; Luther was a heretic to the Christianity he scandalised; the science of this age is heretical to those who sit in the chair of Luther. All the abuses condemned by thought have appealed to authority. The Divine right of kings —the abject submission of the oppressed—intolerance—the judicial murder of witches, of heretics, and of all independent thinkers—slavery—the subjection of women—persecution— ecclesiastical despotism—all such inhuman errors have rested on the authority of a Bible, or a Church, falsely deemed infallible.

What we want is reverent thought, not license at once

captious and dishonest. License without thought destroys, but does not build up. License may succeed in uprooting religious beliefs, in insulting religious sentiments, in desecrating the venerable rites of superstition, but without reverent and conscientious thought nothing arises out of the desolated ruins. A foolish worship, half comforting, half terrifying the souls of the credulous, ought not to be replaced by a license loosening moral bonds, encouraging ignoble instincts, and destroying human hope; such hideous alternative need not be, and heretofore has not been.

What untold blessings do we owe to thought! Thought has displayed to our reverent vision, or nobler ideal of religion, a sublimer conception of God, a truer and more beneficent view of nature and of man. How much has thought added to the grace and beauty of life.

History so useful when combined with thought : experience, which is thought guided by the accumulation of events: science, which is the result of thought, investigating,—along such road how wonderfully has the human race advanced.

Unless thought had conquered ecclesiasticism, and triumphed over ecclesiastical dogmas, the decree forbidding interest for money, would be rendering commercial life either impossible or criminal, or as in former times solely in the hands of Jews and non-Christians. The drama would still be accursed—a free literature anathematised (*as it would be again if ecclesiastics became absolute*). Investigations would be stifled ; men treated as children or mental slaves ; persecution renewed, and ecclesiasticism instead of striving for a pacific victory in controversy, would be struggling in unholy warfare to possess the faggots of Smithfield ; to enkindle them in the name of Christ for the torture of their adversaries.

Dogmatic Churches like the men who *obey*, but dread the men who *think*. Thought must ever be in advance of dogmatic Churches, therefore thought must ever be a heresy. Each thought which has emancipated and blessed has first been accursed or prayed against—the thinker prayed for as a heretic

—" from everlasting damnation, good Lord deliver him ; from murder, adultery,—heresy, and schism, good Lord deliver him," · · · · · and there has been expressed against him that union of contempt and condemnation which ought next to drag him to the prison or the stake; but thought comes in, and combining with human sentiments—the terrible dogma retreats into the regions of the unreal. The gentle Curate mildly entones the anathema over pews filled with benevolent people, wherein he is gladly conscious that thought has destroyed at once the venom and the meaning of each denunciation he utters. Whilst in an adjacent Nonconformist Chapel the fervent Minister describes to a sympathising, but (technically speaking) unconverted congregation, the exclusive blessings of the converted, and the intelligent deacon listens with approving complacency, not because he delights in the message of damnation, but because thought has instructed him how to explain it away, so that it shall include no one at all for whom he cares.

Thought has already attained so much in religion, morality, social life, and human progress, that we must be hopeful for the future, so long as it is encouraged, not stifled. But it is of supreme importance that the errors detected by thought should be removed from the creeds of the Churches by the agency of those Liberal Churchmen who have detected the gravity of such errors—without their utter removal, no secure progress in a dogmatic Church is possible. Great spiritual leaders like Dean Stanley, Bishop Colenso, Frederic Robertson, Dr. Jowett, and others, may influence and elevate numerous souls, may remove superstitious fears, and the immoral spirit of persecution and dogmatic ill-will; but unless the false dogma is removed from the Creed and the Liturgy, it will remain as a loathsome seed, capable of being reared into a pestiferous growth by the consistent zeal of any ignorant popular Curate.

How noble, how beneficent, would at this moment, be the great historic Church of England, if it had cherished the spirit of internal reform with which it commenced its Protestant career—if in each age, guided by its most thoughtful, independent, and human men, it had kept remoulding Liturgy, Creeds, and Articles—or, better still, dropping all Creeds and compulsory Articles—remoulded its Liturgy into a less dogmatic form, so that all reverent liberal members could have found therein a religious home, without any dishonest compromise. We are driven into reluctant dissent, because we do not deem it conscientious to prevaricate in religious utterances, to respond or to act as if we believed statements which we have proved to be untrue. But those statements are now under the influence of thought, refuted by so many of the laity of the Church of England, nay, even by an appreciable number of its Clergy, that we marvel why they do not urge on reform as in the early years of our National Protestant Church. Surely this would be better than to keep on attending High Church Clergymen, who are acting out the formularies imposed upon them.

Thought distinguishes God from the material universe. Thought distinguishes man from matter and from the brute. If the entire universe without God were by an innate blind force to crush one individual man, "that man," says Pascal, "would be superior to the universe, and more noble than the universe, for he would, by thought, know what crushed him."

There is the grandeur of extent, and the grandeur of nobility —as to extent, man is nothing compared to the universe—as to nobility, a universe without thought would be as nothing compared with man.

Place Socrates, or Plato, or Christ in presence of a senseless giant. Do you believe that the spiritual philosopher would incline before the giant, and render him homage? Magnify the giant until he reaches the skies and contains space, nay, until he becomes the universe, will these accumulations of matter bridge over the abyss which separates bulk from thought?

The grandeur of thought is seen by the sacrifices it inspires. For the results of thought, the spiritual of heroes mankind have renounced ease, wealth, comfort, applause, renown.

The truly thoughtful man does not suppose himself to have attained to all truth, or to have escaped all error. We revere the men who think honestly, whatever may be the results of their thought; thus, we revere honest thinkers who arrive at conclusions which seem to us incomplete, nay, partly erroneous. Privileged souls—princes in the aristocracy of mind—we incline our heads as they pass before historic memory—we see them braving power and persecution, walking with joy to the stake, or exulting mounting the steps of the scaffold. There is a man, whose name, like music over the waters, still vibrates round the world—martyr of spiritual thought, his outstretched wounded hands still bless whatever is purest and noblest in the world.

We esteem not much the man who prizes wealth, position, power, glory; but we revere the man, who, for the results of thought, has sacrificed wealth, position, power, and repose. If a man survives the criminations through which the integrity of thought passes on to independence; and, if in later years, success and honour crown the toils of his mind, and in the repose of life's decline, he seeks within his memories whatever he deems the most glorious; he will unhesitatingly crown with the homage of his heart, and the approval of his conscience, those hours when in solitude and in sadness, his mind painfully worked out the great problems of thought—when he began to live in the world of great souls and great intelligences, and to wander like a king's son in the Elysian fields of great ideas, amidst the solemn shades of mysteries unsolved.

When men have seen much, have lived much, have done much, they feel incomplete unless they refresh themselves with the sweet toils of thought, and elevate themselves with the labours of the mind. This is the charm of books—having treated with men in social intercourse, they treat with men in the tranquil intercourse of books. The mind finds there a society calm, dignified, elevating. The study of the man of thought is a temple peopled with ideas, like the Pantheon filled with the Gods of the nations. There his mind is free, surrounded by the reminders and the weapons of his liberation, there forgetting the ills of life, he obtains courage to surmount them.

Some only esteem thought by its results, forgetting that it is a divine act to exercise a divine gift. Thought elevates humanity; it also elevates the individual thinker. Thought has a beauty peculiar to itself; there is a beauty in the outward world of colour, motion, life; there is another beauty in the silent world of thought, and in its relationship with the Eternal.

To the thoughtless materialist this world is dead, mechanical, and cold; beneath the inspirations of thought, it lives, it is beautiful, it is ideal, it is luminous with ever unfolding splendour. Our interest in others is our interest in their thoughts. He who concerns himself with men, as he would with minerals and forest trees, knows nothing of *man*. In order to lay deep foundations, and to build up nobler edifices of conviction, thought stoops down, digs up the rotten basement, and clears away the mouldering fabric.

The honest thinker is a reverent but strong reformer; therefore like Christ, he has to bear his cross. One of the greatest trials of life is experienced when discussing inherited credulities, and investigating the truths which have to replace them The heritage of thought is at once a glory and a martyrdom. When men submit to authority without thought the expression of the result is a Creed, and Sunday by Sunday they dangle their manacles. When men are guided by thought, the opinions formed are worthy of honour; animated with enthusiasm opinions become convictions, and incorporate themselves into the life. Our ambition should be, by virtue of our convictions, to rival the credulities of the men of faith; it is a noble but a difficult enterprise. Often opinions remain in the head, without penetrating the soul and possessing the heart. A man without convictions is the sport of every levity; he is frivolous and unhappy unless he has realised that great word of Plato, " the only thing which gives value to life, is the love of wisdom, the eternal beauty."

Noble souls judge by the principles of right ; the skilful by the lesson of experience. Each needs thought ; the union of both solves the problem of life. Then the true Ark of God, which has taken so much thought to build, is launched on the troubled ocean of progress and of hope.

> " The waters are flashing,
>   The white hail is dashing,
>   The lightnings are glancing,
>   The hoar spray is dancing.
>
> " The whirlwind is rolling,
>   The thunder is tolling,
>   The forest is swinging,
>   The minster bells ringing.
>
> " The earth is like ocean,
>   Wreck strewn and in motion ;
>   Bird, beast, man, and worm
>   Have crept out of the storm.
>
> " And fear'st thou ? and fear'st thou ?
>   And see'st thou ? and hear'st thou ?
>   And drive we not free
>   O'er the terrible sea,—
>   I and thou."

V

LAST PRAYERS.[*]

MORNING.

O God, Sovereign and mysterious Spirit, Soul of all things that have life, we would raise our thoughts and aspirations by the contemplation of Thy perfection and Thy goodness. Blessed be Thy name, O God; blessed upon the lips of all mankind; for Thou carest for all, and lovest all. Thou art a Father ever unto those who stray from the home of Thy laws. In Thee the prodigal son finds love that fails not,—a love boundless as the universe. Thou keepest watch over men in their darkest moments, when they think themselves abandoned to despair. Thou carest for us from the moment of our birth to that which witnesseth our dying breath. Thou art ever encircling us with the arms of Thy benign laws, Thy wonderful presence. Blessed it is to think of Thee, to lean on Thee; in Thee to seek repose for the wearied spirit; to mourn before Thee over the selfishness of evil desires, and to meditate holy purposes in the light of Thy divine solicitude. May we never pollute our conscience with the cowardice of an unprincipled compromise or the turpitude of a falsehood. May we never yield for applause the integrity of our soul, or for convenience the integrity of our life. In health, prosperity, and strength may we be modest, considerate, charitable, and earnest. When health, and strength, and power alike fail us, may we be prayerful, trustful, hopeful, gentle, and resigned. When the shadows of life's last day close in around us; when the battle is over, because the energy is gone, let not our souls set in darkness,— may we be cheered by the memory of faults opposed, of virtues exercised, of charities done, of goodness and happiness to others

---

[*] These two Prayers are here inserted as being the last used by him in conducting public worship. Composed or selected as they were for use in the service of God, they reveal to us better than any other utterance, the sincerest and deepest thoughts and desires of his heart.

produced. May we then have confidence in Thee, O God, our Father; may we place our hearts in Thy hands.

O, eternal God, we have often sought Thee in Thy holy places, in the silence of the forest, or by the ocean's ceaseless roar: we have listened to Thy voice in the storm, and felt Thy spirit breathing on us in the twilight of the day's repose. We have heard the still small voice of our conscience, inspired by Thee, whispering its solemn warnings; let us now, in the social union of our charity and our prayer, raise to Thee our united aspiration for goodness, wisdom, courage, tenderness, sincerity, charity.

Thy glorious presence here and everywhere surrounds us; breathe into us Thy peace, Thy repose, Thy heavenly calm. Raise us from illusions and vanities into the temple of holier thoughts.

Be merciful to us, O Father. Judge us not as sons of wisdom and of strength, but as wanderers fallible and frail. The judgment we ask, grant that we, O Father, may extend to others. We wander with our brothers and our sisters over the deserts and gardens of the earth, beset with difficulties, oppressed with toil. We began our journey in weakness, we continue it in inconstancy, we accomplish it in weariness. But Thou, O Father, art our strength, our hope, our joy; in Thee, on Thee, we repose. Amidst the crowd of friends we often feel alone, deserted, solitary. May we remember there is no solitude for the mind in sympathy with Thee, O God. The soul is often darkened and the spirit saddened; may we be cheered in thought of Thy strength and Thy joy. From that strength and joy may we gather the inspiration of trust and of gladness. All things in Thy universe are doubtless in mysterious sympathy with Thee. The stars, the seas, the winds, the mountains, look on Thee, and love Thee, and are by Thee inspired. Thy streams of beautiful light flow gently through all souls. Our minds and hearts are bathed in Thee. May we be borne upwards into the region of purest and holiest aspiration through the starry regions of many reverent thoughts. May our spirit ascend to Thee, and on Thee repose.

May our desires and wishes be purified. May goodness and wisdom fill us and unite us in Thee, whether we meditate alone or now in this house of holy thought; or when we walk through the noise of the busy town ; or hide ourselves amidst the green hills; or saunter by the ocean's musical shore.

Thou art the fountain of beauty, of wisdom, of goodness, of thought, of power. To thee all holiness and purity must tend. We thank Thee, universal Father, all-pervading spirit, and in Thee we desire to live, to work, to repose, to die. Amen.

———

EVENING.

O God, the giver of good, we thank Thee in health and joy, our Maker, and our heavenly Father,—We thank Thee, heavenly Father.

For all the glory of the heavens, for the light of day, for the beauty of the earth and sky, for the rain and for the sunshine,—We thank Thee, heavenly Father.

For the blessed hours of silence, when night follows day; for the sleep of weary eyes and Thy providence around us,—We thank Thee, heavenly Father.

For our neighbours, kindred, and friends; for all the good they have done us, and for a tenfold blessing upon them,—We thank Thee, heavenly Father.

For the benefits of liberty and peace, for books of wisdom and genius, and power to read them,—We thank Thee, heavenly Father.

O God, we thank Thee for all the gifts we have welcomed, for all we have forgotten, and for those which by our unworthiness we have lost.

Give us patience, heavenly Father, when Thou breakest the staff which upholds us, and Thy wisdom takes away what Thy goodness gave; when Thou makest the wife a widow and the child fatherless,—Thy will be done, heavenly Father.

When Thou showest man the evil of his ways and bringest

sorrow upon his soul for others, though the wrong word is not yet unspoken, nor the deed of guilt yet undone,—Have mercy on us, heavenly Father; bring us back to Thee, O heavenly Father.

In all time of sorrow, and in the hour of remorse; when we learn the virtue which we believed not, and when our wickedness finds us out,—Be merciful unto us, most merciful Father.

By Thy knowledge of our weakness and Thy love to man make our repentance healthful, and our shame wholesome; and bring us back to Thy holy will,—Bring us back, we pray Thee, heavenly Father.

When we turn from evil and do good; when we forgive those who have wronged us as we ask Thy forgiveness; when we offer ourselves before Thee as guilty, but pray to be made fit for Thy service,—Take us again for Thy children, heavenly Father.

Lead us from our youth upward, and order all our lives; when we are of full age, guide; and in the time of drooping, sustain us,—These things we ask, heavenly Father.

Thou that knowest whence we came, we trust to Thee whither we shall go; teach us only Thy will on earth, and Thy will be done with us hereafter. In Thy hands we leave ourselves, heavenly Father. Thy will be done for ever, O merciful Father. Amen.

POSTSCRIPT.

*Copy of a letter addressed to the Executive Committee
of the British and Foreign Unitarian Association.*

"READING, *June 24th, 1891.*

" DEAR MR. IERSON,

" Having occasion to write to the Committee, I
feel impelled to write also something personal.

" I learn from my local doctor, Mr. May, and the
London Specialist, Mr. Allingham, that my life is in
all probability merely a question of months, as I am
dying of cancer in the bowels.

" Roman Catholics are already, as I was informed
yesterday, again starting reports of my return to the
Roman Catholic Faith.

" I do not want the testimony of the last 21 years
of my life to be thus destroyed.

" I left the Roman Catholic Church in July, 1870,
sorrowfully, because, to my regret, I could no longer
believe it.

" Never once for one minute have I regretted that
step. I now, as heretofore, look upon that act of
secession as the most virtuous act of my life.

" I found amongst Unitarians the religious home
and religious sympathies I anticipated. I am grateful
to them for countless acts of kindness, of friendship, of confidence—let me also add—of forbearance.
During my earlier years amongst Unitarians, I did
not realise that very many deemed it right and true
to render to Christ a supremacy of authority to which
I did not see my way, and therefore I often pained

many by the marked omission of liturgical expressions dear to their inherited sympathies.

"I do not think I was sufficiently alive to that fact during the events accompanying the Theodore Parker controversy.

"If I gave pain, I am sorry, but I was not influenced by any unkind motives.

"I look back to these 21 years as the happiest of my life. Indeed I approach death able to say that each year has been happier than the last. This is doubtless partly due to the fact that 20 of those years have been of married life, not marred by one single incident of disagreement or of pain—one unbroken harmony of a perfect and increasing affection.

"But my wife was and is a thorough Unitarian, and I attribute to her Unitarian tone of mind what has tended to modify the over-strained sentimentalism and romance of my Roman Catholic training.

"I am more than ever convinced that no blessing more precious can be bestowed on the young than to train them in the Christian Theism of the most independent and most reverent tone of Unitarian thought.

"I will ask you to convey this to our valued friends, so that after my death the members of the Committee will be able to say that I lived and died happy in my Unitarian convictions.

"With much gratitude to so many kind friends,

"Always very truly,

"R. RODOLPH SUFFIELD."

www.ingramcontent.com/pod-product-compliance
Lightning Source LLC
Chambersburg PA
CBHW020940030726
47496CB00005B/1286